> **"In my vision, I saw that the real Kevin had been killed the day after you got married. The demon killed him then and took his place."**

Constance's words sent a shiver down Rachel's spine. It would explain so much—but no, it wasn't possible. It couldn't be true. She had a life with Kevin. Not always a happy one, but a life. And how could she have lived with a monster for five years and not noticed? It was just too far-fetched. They had a relationship. They had a house. And they had a child.

The world skidded to a stop as she glanced at Cassidy. They had a *child*.

"Are you saying that Cassidy is a-a . . ." Rachel stuttered.

"You guessed it," Father Daniels said, nodding.

"Da! Mon!" Cassidy blurted, pumping both tiny fists in the air. He burped then, and a tiny tendril of smoke came out, like he was exhaling a cigarette.

Rachel, thinking she'd imagined it, leaned in closer.

"Watch out!" shouted Father Daniels suddenly, as he yanked her hard backward. "Kid's gonna blow!"

Critics adore the "snappy" (*Boston Herald*) novels of Cara Lockwood!

"A lot of funny scenes. . . . A fun, light summer read."

—Book Reporter

"Sure to strike a chord with many readers. . . . Fun, entertaining, and enjoyable."

—Curled Up With a Good Book

PINK SLIP PARTY

"Readers will be delighted by the character-driven zaniness. . . . Snappy repartee and hot sex scenes keep the story moving along nicely."

—*Boston Herald*

"The perfect bath read."

—*Daily News* (New York)

"An amusing chick lit tale. . . . [A] comical contemporary caper."

—All Readers

"Hilarious. . . . I definitely recommend *Pink Slip Party* if you need a good laugh and you know you do if you've received one of those pink slips yourself."

—Mostly Fiction

"If you're looking for a perfect beach read, this adorable, romantic novel is it."

—*YM* magazine

DIXIELAND SUSHI

"A warm and friendly writing style."

—*Library Journal*

"A hilarious relationship novel. . . . Readers who enjoy chick lit will savor *Dixieland Sushi* because, like its main character, it offers a different take on the standard fare."

—Curled Up With a Good Book

Can't Teach an Old Demon New Tricks

CARA LOCKWOOD

POCKET **STAR** BOOKS

New York   London   Toronto   Sydney

Pocket Star Books
A Division of Simon & Schuster, Inc.
1230 Avenue of the Americas
New York, NY 10020

This book is a work of fiction. Names, characters, places, and incidents either are products of the author's imagination or are used fictitiously. Any resemblance to actual events or locales or persons, living or dead, is entirely coincidental.

First Pocket Star Books paperback edition April 2010

POCKET STAR BOOKS and colophon are registered trademarks of Simon & Schuster, Inc.

For information about special discounts for bulk purchases, please contact Simon & Schuster Special Sales at 1-866-506-1949 or business@simonandschuster.com.

The Simon & Schuster Speakers Bureau can bring authors to your live event. For more information or to book an event contact the Simon & Schuster Speakers Bureau at 866-248-3049 or visit our website at www.simonspeakers.com.

Art and design by Alan Dingman

Manufactured in the United States of America

10 9 8 7 6 5 4 3 2 1

ISBN 978-1-4165-5097-6
ISBN 978-1-4391-6674-1 (ebook)

For my angelic daughters

Acknowledgments

Thanks to my family, who give me wings: my daughters, my husband, Daren, my mom, dad, and my brother Matt. As always, gratitude goes to my multitalented agent, Deidre Knight, and my great editors Lauren McKenna and Megan McKeever. Many thanks to my web guru, Christina Swartz, and a great big thank-you to my fearless demon-slaying marketing team: Elizabeth Kinsella, Shannon Whitehead, Kate Kinsella, Kate Miller, Jane Ricordati, Linda Newman, and Carroll Jordan. A special thanks to Carol K. Mack and Dinah Mack, authors of *A Field Guide to Demons, Fairies, Fallen Angels and Other Subversive Spirits*, and to Rosemary Guiley, who wrote *The Encyclopedia of Angels*.

One

"Would you watch your wings? They're in my face," said Gabriel Too (not *the* Gabriel, archangel, but Gabriel, lower-ranking, non-archangel; thus the "too").

"Sorry," apologized Frank the New. "I'm not used to them." Frank the New scrunched his shoulders and folded in his wings so they flapped less conspicuously as they glided toward Earth.

"It takes a while to get used to," agreed Gabriel Too, giving the new recruit a soft pat on the shoulder. "And make sure not to lose the halo. They're always slipping off. They never fit right. They should come in half sizes but they don't."

"Thanks for the advice," said Frank the New as he adjusted his halo, which happened to be tilting a little too far to the right.

"Hang on," Gabriel Too said, holding up his hand and signaling to Frank the New that he ought to stop. "You always look both ways before crossing the jet stream." The two paused as a 777 jet cruised by. "Okay, it's safe to go."

"Thanks for the heads-up," Frank the New said as he kicked his feet out of the long hem of his robe. Frank was slight in build and was much shorter than Gabriel. His white billowing robe swam on him and his ears were a little oversized, a combination that made him look a little like Dopey the Dwarf. His small stature, however, didn't change the fact that if there was a fight at hand, he was going to run in, fists up. He had more courage than he did size.

"So when do we vanquish some demons?" Frank the New asked, rubbing his hands together in anticipation. He spoke in a clipped British accent, not unlike Anthony Hopkins. "I am very ready to trounce some evil."

"Whoa, whoa, *whoa* there, Double-oh-seven," Gabriel Too said, holding up his hand. "Not so fast. I know you are a little tough guy, but we're just watchers. We watch."

"I'm sorry, but I am not a sidelines kind of fellow." He rolled up one of his blousy sleeves and sighed. "How are you supposed to fight evil in these robes?" he asked, sliding out a hand in a fake punch, only to have it covered by the cuff of his billowing white sleeve. He shook his hand loose and then grabbed the golden harp he'd slung under one arm. "And what's this for? Where's my flaming sword?"

"You don't get one. You don't fight evil. You just watch it."

Frank the New grimaced. "I'll have you know that I didn't stop the Antichrist by sitting around and watching." Frank the New was talking about a few months back when he was still an angel in training, and managed, with the help of a reluctant psychic, Constance Plyd, to stop the devil from impregnating a vapid pop princess, thereby preventing the conception of a half demon who would've brought the end of the world. He also happened to do all this while in the body of a French bulldog, which he thought should've earned him extra points.

"You aren't in the Wrath division, or even Messengers, who occasionally get to dust it up. We are *Watchers*. We watch. Period."

"Well, then, the Big Guy made a mistake. I'm not a watcher. I'm a doer." Frank the New finished rolling up his sleeves and started popping his knuckles.

"The Big Guy doesn't make mistakes," Gabriel Too said. "Not even dinosaurs or the platypus. Which, by the way, is a sore subject with the Big Guy. Don't mention the platypus."

"I wasn't planning on it." As the two angels floated down from the sky, the earth came into view below, showing a truck stop and a highway, framed on both sides by long slopes of grass where cattle were grazing.

"Hey, this place looks familiar," Frank the New said, nodding to the cows.

"It should," Gabriel Too said, leading the pair across Route 9 and over to a small grassy subdivision. "This is Dogwood County—the place you saved from the Antichrist—am I right?"

Frank the New nodded.

Dogwood County, population 17,891, sat smack dab in the middle of east Texas and was famous for award-winning chicken-fried steak, the largest pecan pie ever baked (weighing in at thirty-five thousand pounds), and ground zero for the epic battle of good versus evil. Not that most of the Dogwood residents knew their quaint country home happened to be the place where angels and demons fought it out for the souls of all mankind. Only a select few knew about Dogwood's importance in the scheme of things, and God and the Devil hoped to keep it that way. They were waging a covert war that neither wanted on the front page of the *Dogwood County Times*.

The street below came into view, home to about five houses spread out over a little hilly patch and separated by the occasional grazing cow. Gabriel Too stopped above the house belonging to Rachel Farnsworth. Rachel was sound asleep in her bedroom, one foot sticking out of the covers and her arm thrown over her eyes. Her son, Cassidy, had awakened in his crib in the next room, and was eyeing a small wooden train engine on the floor. Both angels could see through the roof, one of their many convenient angel powers, along with the ability to be invisible and hear the voice of God without shattering into a million pieces.

"So what do we do now?" Frank the New asked

as the two settled onto a large branch of a nearby oak tree.

"We watch and report."

"But, correct me if I'm wrong, God already knows what's going to happen. He doesn't need our little reports."

"Yes, God is omniscient. Or omnipotent? I always mix those up." Gabriele Too looked thoughtful. "Anyway, whatever it is, the short answer is, yes, God already knows everything, but he has to give us something to do."

"So it's a test, then?"

"Probably. Most everything is. God likes pop quizzes." The two angels watched as Cassidy tried to stick his arm out of his crib to reach the little wooden train engine. After trying, and failing, to reach it, he stood on sure legs and started climbing up the crib's side, his dark brown curls bouncing as he went. In seconds he'd jumped off the edge and landed in a pile of stuffed animals in the corner of his room. He pulled himself up to standing and then waddled over to the train, picking it up with a look of triumph in his bright brown eyes.

"This is a waste of time." Frank the New sunk his chin into one hand. "I didn't almost die defeating the Devil so I could be on babysitting duty."

"He's not, technically, a baby."

"Toddler-sitting, then."

"No, no, no, I mean he's not technically human. He's half demon. But he's definitely a toddler."

"Demon? How come I couldn't smell him out,

then?" Frank the New took a whiff of the air but didn't smell the telltale sign of burnt popcorn—the trail most demons left behind.

"He's pretty good at camouflage. Must be one of his powers."

Frank the New smashed one fist into his palm. "Well, then, old sport, what are we waiting for? Let's send the demon tyke back to hell." He made as if he were going to march down there and swoop up the child.

"Hold on, buddy," Gabriel chided, grabbing Frank the New by the arm. "There is no vanquishing. There is no fighting. There isn't even any cussing. We don't lay a finger on that boy. We watch him. That's it. *Do you understand?*"

Frank the New crossed his arms across his chest and sighed. "Fine."

"We're supposed to sit here and wait and see if her husband shows up, and if he does, we're supposed to report back to Peter. It's the dad who's the full-blooded demon, and he's gone MIA. Everybody is looking for him, too. Heaven *and* hell."

"Why is he so important?"

Gabriel Too shrugged. "Dunno. Peter didn't tell us. We don't have the right kind of clearance."

"So we can't zap this kid?"

"Nope."

"Not even with holy water?"

"Not even with holy water."

"What if he runs out of the house and eats one of the neighbors?"

Gabriel Too looked down and saw that Cassidy had made his way to the kitchen and was opening cabinet doors. His mother, who was still sleeping, hadn't heard his escape.

"We can't intervene," Gabriel Too explained. "You don't know the h-e-double-l we'd catch if we stuck our noses where they don't belong. We just watch and take notes." Gabriel Too waved around his legal notepad. "That's our job."

Below them, Cassidy was bouncing around the kitchen, half-leaping, half-flying from one counter to the next.

"I can't believe I got a desk job," said Frank the New with a sigh as he took the notepad.

Two

Rachel Farnsworth was used to minor disasters. She was a mother.

What she wasn't used to was quiet.

It was the peace and quiet that broke Rachel's slumber the morning of her son Cassidy's one-year birthday. Her house was never peaceful or quiet.

She glanced at the clock and realized with a shock it was already eight fifteen. Cassidy never slept this late, usually being up at six in the morning, having by then ripped up the bedding in his crib, dismantled the Winnie-the-Pooh mobile, and tried to climb over the rails at least three or four times, all while shrugging half out of his diaper and his pajamas. It was only then, usually, that he'd give a bloodcurdling scream loud enough to wake the neighbors, a sound as endearing as an ambulance siren that Rachel had come to think of as her own personal alarm clock. Her husband, Kevin, naturally slept through it, because he slept through everything. She glanced to Kevin's side of the bed and found it empty. He must've gone to work already.

Rachel threw off her covers and raced to Cassidy's room, only to come skidding to a stop halfway through the door. Cassidy's crib was empty. Rachel's heart stopped. Her first thought was that he'd been kidnapped by some horrible child predator, like the ones she'd always see on TV being caught soliciting sex from twelve-year-old virgins. She shook the thought from her head and told herself not to panic. That's when she came to her senses and realized he must've jumped out of his crib, because there was a trail of rumpled clothes and toys along the floor. Rachel comforted herself with the knowledge that a predator wouldn't have bothered to stack up his alphabet blocks on his way out, so Cassidy must've sprung himself. The little Houdini had done it again.

"Cass?" she called, trying not to sound mad, in case he might be about to stick his head in the oven. "Where are you?"

Cassidy could be anywhere. There wasn't a restraint made by man he couldn't get out of. Clothes, diapers, high chairs, even car seats were no match for the grubby, quick hands of Cassidy Henry Farnsworth. Even at the tender age of one, he'd mastered all but the most complex of latches. Last week he even managed to open their front door and sprint out, naked as a jaybird, much to the dismay of half the neighborhood. Rachel knew what the other moms said about her. That she was careless. That she didn't pay attention. But, honestly, Cassidy was simply too quick and too smart for his own good. Just last week he'd unlatched his car seat. A flash of corduroy overalls in her rearview had clued her into the fact that he was happily hopping up and down on a sack of groceries in the backseat. That little surprise had nearly made her veer into on-coming traffic.

Plus, he always seemed quicker than he ought to be, and smarter, too. She didn't know of other babies who took their first steps at five months, for instance. The other moms never believed her, but Rachel swore he could do things he just shouldn't be able to do.

"Ma-ma!" came a muffled shout from some-where in the vicinity of the kitchen. This was fol-lowed by a clatter that sent Rachel sprinting. She stopped at the threshold of her kitchen and her mouth fell open.

It looked like a hurricane had blown through. Cassidy had hit the pantry and raided the snack cabinet, somehow dismantling the so-called child-proof lock on it. The floor was covered with spilled Goldfish, a rumpled bag of Doritos, and a half dozen apple-juice boxes including one that was ac-tually open and spilling out across her kitchen tile.

How on earth she'd slept through *this* little di-saster, she had no idea.

"Cassidy Henry FARNSWORTH!" she cried, hands on hips, as she stared at the floor in dismay.

"Da! Mon!" he blurted in an almost gleeful tone. "Da! Mon! Da! Mon! Da! Mon!"

She had no idea what he was saying, but she followed the sounds. But no matter where she looked, she couldn't find him.

"Cass? Cass!" He was here somewhere. She could hear him.

"Da-da-da-DA!" he babbled. "Mon! Mon! Mon! Mon!"

Rachel realized, with a sinking feeling in her stomach, that the sound *wasn't* coming from the floor. Or anywhere near the floor, which was where her little one-year-old usually spent most of his time. It was coming from much, much higher.

And that's when a little cheddar-flavored Goldfish fell on her head from above like a little snowflake from Pepperidge Farm.

She looked up, dread in her throat, and saw Cassidy, naked as the day he was born, do a little jump that made the dark curls on his head bounce. He was balancing precariously on the top of her refrigerator, grubby hands full of cheddar-flavored fish crackers.

"DA! MON!" he cheered.

Rachel's whole body went cold. She flung up her arms, praying he stayed away from the edge long enough to get him down without a free fall. She didn't have time to wonder how he got there. She just wanted to get him down in one piece.

"Come to Mama," she commanded, hoping to keep the panic out of her voice. "Come now."

"No!" Cass shouted gleefully. Standing up on the refrigerator, he raised his arms like he was preparing to do a swan dive onto her tile floor. Rachel grabbed one of his chunky legs and then the other, and soon she had him cradled safely in her arms.

"No climbing. *NO*," she said. "Why do you have to scare Mama like that?" Her heart rate was slowly returning to normal, her panic draining away. Now she had the time to wonder just how Cassidy managed to climb up on top of the counter *and* reach the top of the refrigerator. No matter how she studied the scene of the crime, she couldn't figure it out. It was like he had sprouted wings and flown there. She wondered, briefly, if there was an explanation she was missing. If she hadn't birthed Cassidy herself after twenty-eight hours of labor, she just might have thought he fell from space in a meteor like Superman. The boy simply did things Rachel couldn't explain.

Cassidy wiggled in her arms, and she was reminded again her one and only son was without a single stitch of clothing, which was a particularly dangerous state of affairs, given the likelihood he'd take this opportunity to baptize her robe. He liked to let things fly when it would do the most damage, usually right after Rachel had changed clothes. She marched him straight to his room and clapped a diaper on him, and then went back into the kitchen and grabbed her mobile phone. She speed-dialed Kevin. This was always her first reaction when Cassidy got himself into trouble. Somehow, when he was bad, Rachel always thought it was Kevin's fault, even if he wasn't in a two-mile radius at the time. Fact was, Rachel knew it had to be *his* genes at work. Her mother had always told her she'd been the perfect child. She was sure that she'd never danced naked on top of the refrigerator at age one.

Kevin's mobile phone rang once and then went straight to voice mail. He had it turned off. But why? Rachel tried again. Yep, it was definitely turned off. She called the store, the one her dad had willed to them, and Vanessa picked up. She was their adolescent part-time help.

"Hi, Vanessa. Is Kevin there?"

"Nope," Vanessa said, and Rachel could hear her smacking gum. Vanessa was borderline rude to Rachel on a regular basis, and it grated. But Kevin didn't want to fire her because she lived with her grandma and had no money and was a good kid, blah, blah, blah. Rachel suspected that Vanessa didn't like her very much. That she might even have a crush on Kevin, although she always dismissed the thought as soon as it popped into her head. Kevin was old enough to be her father and he had a pot belly. She couldn't imagine a teenager being seriously interested in him. Still, at that moment, the fact that she had to deal with Vanessa's attitude made her all the madder at her husband.

Where *was* he? If he wasn't at work, then there was no excuse for him not being here to help deal with his devil child. Cassidy squirmed on her hip, so she set him down.

"Have you seen him at all? Did he even call?" She stooped down to start cleaning up the mess. Near her, Cassidy grabbed a stray Goldfish off the floor and popped it in his mouth. With bigger problems on her mind, Rachel let him eat it.

"Nope," Vanessa said and paused. "And nope."

For a second Rachel wondered if Vanessa was lying and covering for Kevin. Then she figured otherwise. Vanessa sounded too surly. If Kevin had been there, or even asked her to lie, she would've been giddy about having his added trust.

"If you see him, you tell him to call me *right away*," Rachel said and hung up before she could hear Vanessa's indifferent reply. She walked closer to the window and glanced down their little street. It was particularly pretty this time of year with all the dogwoods in bloom. Soon, it would be Dogwood Festival time, a big deal around Dogwood County. Normally they put it on in September, but this year they'd moved it up to March, hoping to draw larger crowds. The county judge in Dogwood had made tourism his number one priority, which is why the county saw itself as a back-drop for a major movie a few months back, a movie that they didn't finish filming because its star, Corey Bennett, mysteriously dropped out of the project and moved to a remote cabin in the Fiji Islands a week after filming began, refusing to do any interviews. There had been some rumors that Dogwood County had driven Bennett plum crazy.

He wouldn't have been the first. Rachel had always liked her hometown, but it wasn't for everybody. You had to like being in a small place, far from shopping malls and night clubs, where the most exciting thing on a Friday night was the high school football game. What it lacked in basic amenities, Dogwood made up for in tall tales. Dogwood was supposedly the most haunted place in Texas (being the subject of three episodes of *Ghost Hunters*), and the most religious, with a church on every corner and more reverends per capita than any other county in Texas. All the churches somehow managed to thrive, which meant either that some people around here went to two or three different churches every Sunday or the people who did go were very generous with their donations. But Rachel had a soft spot for Dogwood and the crazy stories that came along with it. Like the one about Dogwood's founding father, a radical preacher named Jeremiah Hicks. He was the one who planted the dogwood trees across the county. He thought they could repel evil. Of course, he also spent all his days ranting about a war with demons, so Rachel wasn't sure how much of what he said you could believe. Still, she liked the dogwoods, a special species of the tree that bloomed twice a year—once in the fall and once in the spring.

Of course, Cassidy seemed to be allergic to the county's namesake, as every time he stepped outside, he'd start sneezing. He wasn't the only one. Kevin practically had to hold his nose when he walked outdoors, claiming he actually got physically ill from breathing in dogwood trees. It was weird, since his dogwood allergy only seemed to pop up in the last couple of years. Back when they first met, while still in high school, Kevin used to love festival time—and dogwoods. But then again, a lot changed after they'd gotten married.

He'd become a different person since they'd met in high school, back when he was a lean, mean football player heading to state for the Crockett High Cougars. That was before half the defensive line of Houston Central turned his right knee into Play-Doh and the college scouts stopped coming to his games. After that he just seemed so defeated. But he tried to make a go of it. For at least the first five years, he really tried to make things work. But then he went to a small business convention in Phoenix and came back a changed man. Rachel didn't know what happened on that long weekend. It was like he'd been abducted by aliens, if Rachel believed in that sort of thing, which she didn't. He was just a different person. He'd gone there a semi–health nut and came back a smoker who sat on the couch and drank beer. It was like he'd just given up on his life.

For a while, she suspected maybe he'd had an affair, but she never found any proof, and he seemed satisfied to stay with her. Rachel remembered a time, before the conference, when Kevin would leave little notes for her around the house. Just tiny Post-its normally saved for grocery lists and take-out numbers, and he'd write little hearts on them, or just a quick *xo*—his way of a virtual hug and kiss. Sometimes she'd find some on her bathroom mirror in the morning that just said "Do nothing. You're perfect." She was surprised how much she missed these little shows of affection. She hadn't had a Post-it note from Kevin in years.

He had been the one who had wanted at least four kids and had always tried to convince her to start a family. Rachel had been the one putting off that first pregnancy. When she finally felt ready, two years ago, Kevin didn't seem very excited about the prospect. She nearly had to convince him it was a good idea. She thought maybe he was just having cold feet, but now she wasn't so sure. Rachel thought Cassidy might help change things. She knew, deep down, it was dumb to think so, but she thought if they started a family, things would be different. But they only seemed to get worse.

Rachel kept telling herself it was just a phase and that he would get over it. But time ticked by, and nothing seemed to change. Still, she held out hope that one day she'd see the old Kevin again.

At this point, though, she'd settle for seeing *any* Kevin. It wasn't like him to just disappear. He would forget her birthday and their anniversary on a regular basis, but he used to always have the good sense to at least answer his phone and take the tongue-lashing he deserved. They hadn't had a fight recently, so there wasn't any reason for him to be sulking. Rachel wondered briefly if something serious had happened to him. Just as quickly, the thought left her head. Somehow she just knew that Kevin had done this on purpose.

"Your daddy better remember to pick up your birthday cake," Rachel told Cassidy, who was staring intently at something on the kitchen floor. That's when Rachel started to smell smoke.

She turned around and saw that somehow, the package of Goldfish near Cassidy's foot had caught fire.

"Oh, my God!" Rachel shouted, lunging for the bag and stomping out the small flame with one worn slipper.

Cassidy, completely unfazed by his brush with a fiery death, simply clapped his hands together and squealed, delighted. Rachel swept him up in her arms and did a frantic check of him, looking for any signs of third-degree burns. He was completely unharmed, and giggling to boot. But of course he was. No matter what kind of pickle the little guy got himself into, he managed to never actually get hurt. It was the one thing Rachel was grateful for. He took the worst tumbles and yet never seemed to bruise.

Next, she did a meticulous sweep of the kitchen floor. There were no matches, no lighter, nothing that would explain how the bag had caught fire. It had simply spontaneously combusted.

"What on earth . . ." Rachel, puzzled, started to feel like something was really, *really* wrong as she looked at her half-charred pink slipper. Cassidy was staring up at her with a big smile on his face.

Her mobile rang, blaring the Dixie Chicks. She pushed aside her unease about Cassidy and flipped the phone open. It was her best friend, Constance.

"Do you need any pre-birthday-party prep help?" Constance asked, her voice high-pitched and chipper.

She'd been ridiculously happy since she'd hooked up with one of the Garrett brothers. In Dogwood, they had a reputation for mowing through women, but apparently, Constance had managed to reform one of them.

"Did you have sex this morning?" Rachel demanded. She still wasn't used to Constance being so cheery. It was a little unnerving. "Wait—don't tell me."

"Can't a friend just offer another friend help?" Constance said. Her voice sounded far too relaxed. She'd definitely had sex. At least one of them had. Rachel tried to think back to the last time Kevin had even attempted to do the deed. She couldn't actually remember. It had been that long. Rachel used to mind, but then she just kind of got used to the drought. It wasn't as if she felt very sexy these days. She was always finding mashed graham crackers in her hair or mac and cheese on her clothes, courtesy of Cassidy.

"Sorry, sweetie, I'm just ticked at Kevin and taking it out on you," Rachel said, feeling suddenly contrite. She shouldn't begrudge Constance happiness. It was a long time coming. She'd been married to the county's laughingstock—Jimmy Plyd—before he got himself murdered by a drifter last fall. It had been a rough year for Constance, and the fact that she'd managed to come through it—and half the county's suspicions she might have done her husband in—healthier and happier than she'd ever been was a near miracle. Rachel shouldn't rain on her parade. She deserved a good man. And so far, despite his reputation, Nathan Garrett seemed to be just that. And if Constance had been a little distant—a little busier than usual—in the last few months, Rachel shouldn't blame her for that, either. The fact that the once-so-close friends who had never gone a day without speaking would sometimes now go weeks was a fact that Rachel knew she was as much to blame for as Constance. Most days she had her hands full with Cassidy and would look up and realize a whole day had flown by.

"Kevin is missing, and Cassidy is . . ." She glanced down at her baby boy, now pulling himself to standing using her legs, and sighed. How do you describe his impossible feats of the morning? ". . . well, he's just being Cassidy."

"Say no more," Constance said. "I'll be over in ten minutes."

Fifteen minutes later Rachel had thrown on some clothes, whipped her dark hair up into a ponytail, and cleaned up most of the mess in the kitchen. Cassidy was content playing with his wooden blocks in the corner when Constance arrived. The scene was so happily domestic that Rachel couldn't believe just a few minutes before she'd been stomping out a Goldfish fire. Honestly, these were the things even her best friend just wouldn't believe.

Constance, her honey-wheat hair neatly blown dry, came prepared, her arms full of glass trays topped with white plastic lids. Constance owned the

Magnolia Café, the best restaurant in town. She had
volunteered to bring over the party food. As Rachel
stubbornly didn't cook anything that wasn't already
prepackaged or frozen (her mother taught her that
learning to cook would only insure she spent the
best part of the party in the kitchen), she was glad to
have a friend who did. She liked to eat; she just didn't
like all the work that went into getting there.

Seeing the Pyrex trays, Rachel actually felt a
little lighter. At least Cassidy's party would have
food. Good food.

"Constance, I love you," she said, and almost got
teary.

"Yeah, I know," Constance said and grinned,
wrinkling her freckled nose. "Now let's put these
in the fridge and I'll help with decorations."

By quarter to twelve the balloons were in place,
the party favors were out, and Cassidy even had
pants on. It was a good start. Rachel had called
Kevin at least a dozen more times on his cell phone,
leaving increasingly irate messages. He had been
the one who was supposed to pick up the cake, and
the party started in fifteen minutes.

Constance was playing with Cassidy, who was
giggling and tossing blocks across the kitchen floor.
Constance stood to fetch one, and when she turned
back around, she gave Cassidy a bit of a funny look.

"What's wrong?" Rachel asked, immediately
worried her son had done something crazy.

"What?" Constance asked, her attention snapping back to Rachel. "Oh, well, uh, nothing."

"You had a look like something was wrong. Did he spill something?"

"No, no." Constance shook her head. "Nothing's wrong. Really. Just spaced out for a second." Constance gave her friend a weak smile, and then twirled a bit of her honey-colored hair around one finger; Rachel recognized this telltale sign that her best friend since fifth grade was lying to her. But about what? Maybe she'd seen Cassidy pick his nose. Lord knows, the boy had done worse things. Still, it was strange Constance just didn't 'fess up. But Rachel didn't have time to dwell, because just then the doorbell rang, signaling the arrival of the first guest.

Rachel swung open the door, and her mother swept in. She was wearing her uniform of long jean skirt and crisp white blouse, her salt-and-pepper hair shorn close to her ears, her trademark silver talisman necklace, matching earrings, and oversized silver bangles. She was carrying a white cake box and a big sprawling arrangement of dogwood blooms.

"I would've been by earlier but I was stuck at the bakery," she said, giving Rachel a quick peck on the cheek. "I've got the cake and candles," she sing-songed to Cassidy, who clapped his hands and cried, "'ake!" She set down the cake and the dogwood blooms. Cassidy took one look at the flowers and wrinkled his nose in distaste. Then he sneezed.

"But Kevin was supposed to get the cake," Rachel said, confused.

"I know; he called me," Gladys said, smiling as she handed the cake to Constance. "Constance!

Have you lost weight? Or is it just that Garrett boy keeping you busy?"

"Mrs. Keller!" Constance exclaimed, turning tomato red.

"That Garrett boy," Rachel said, sending Constance a smile.

"Um-hmmm, thought so," Gladys said.

"So, wait, back to the cake. When did you talk to Kevin?" Rachel grabbed Cassidy as he raced toward the front door, which was still slightly ajar.

"This morning," Gladys said. "He said he was stuck at the shop."

"He did, did he?" The back of Rachel's neck grew hot. She was now officially furious. First her husband up and disappears on her and then he lies to her mother? Well, that was about one screwup too many.

"What did that son-in-law of mine do now?" Gladys said, tapping her foot. There was no keeping anything from Gladys. She could sense a Kevin mistake a hundred miles away, just like a shark sensing a floundering fish.

"A disappearing act," Rachel said.

"I knew something was up," Gladys said, nodding. "That boy never asks *me* for any favors."

It's true that Gladys and Kevin didn't get along. For the first few years of Rachel and Kevin's marriage, everything was fine, but Gladys and Kevin had a falling-out two years ago after he had had too much to drink at Gladys's one Thanksgiving and insulted her pumpkin pie. Rachel had demanded he apologize and he did, but the two never really buried the hatchet. Truth be known, Gladys would be more than happy to bury it in his back. The argument was just a symbol of the tension that had been growing for years. The pie was almost beside the point. Gladys didn't like how Kevin treated her daughter.

Gladys had made it clear she thought Rachel could do better. Rachel spent most of her time trying to convince her mom that Kevin was a lot better than he seemed, but lately she found the argument harder and harder to make.

"You know I keep telling you that he doesn't treat you right," Gladys said, with hands on hips and that knowing look of an overprotective mother.

"I know, I *know*," Rachel said, starting to really believe it this time. She was tired of defending Kevin, especially when he didn't deserve it. Her mother was right.

More guests arrived, and Rachel found herself expecting Kevin to turn up in the middle of the throng. He probably was waiting to slink back home at the height of the party so she couldn't actually kill him in front of all those witnesses. Well, she had news for him. Their basement was darn near soundproof, and she planned to use it.

But as more people arrived, Kevin didn't. The party hats circulated, the food was set out, and still no Kevin. Two hours in, and the kids at the party were getting restless. They wanted cake, and so did Cassidy, who was inching ever closer to naptime, which meant he was about to have a serious meltdown at any moment. And that would not look good in pictures.

Rachel waited as long as she could, hoping that Kevin would show up at the last minute and trying to ignore the knowing looks sent her way from her mother, who would gleefully reference this little gaffe of Kevin's for the next decade. Eventually Rachel decided to bring out the cake. Just because her husband was AWOL didn't mean that Cassidy should suffer.

The single candle on his cake lit, Rachel carried it out, setting it on the kitchen table just out of arm's reach of Cassidy's high chair. Everyone sang, and as the last notes of "Happy Birthday to You" rang out, Rachel leaned over and said, "Okay, honey, make a wish and blow!"

Fully expecting Cassidy to blow a raspberry and not actually extinguish his candle, Rachel sat poised, ready to do it for him. Cassidy gave her an uncertain look.

"Go ahead, honey, it's okay," she said, trying to look encouraging. She puffed out her cheeks, just like they'd practiced a zillion times in the last week.

He looked back at the cake and the tiny flame. Rachel decided she was giving him three more seconds, and then she was going to blow out the candle for him.

But then Cassidy puffed up his cheeks and exhaled.

And right before everyone's eyes, the entire cake went up in flame.

Three

A few miles away, J.D. Lamont was hoping for a great big fire, one that would consume his little bar and give him a great big insurance check for his trouble. J.D. often daydreamed of disasters—natural and man-made—that would wipe his bar off the map. This came after three decades of being the sole owner and bartender of Branson's—Dogwood County's most famous hole in the wall—where there were no menus, only whiskey and two kinds of beer, neither one light.

J.D. wiped off a couple of glasses behind the bar and daydreamed of a Category Five twister that would set down in his parking lot and break up the bar like matchsticks. Then he'd be done with the headache that had hung on him for what seemed like forever. Every night it was a new group of angry drunks, but the same old fight, and the same broken tables.

Branson's was a magnet for ne'er-do-wells, and

while Dogwood might only have a few, Branson's was close enough to the Interstate to pick up any hothead within a two-hundred-mile radius. For some reason, despite the lack of a big highway sign, thirsty guys in search of a fight always seemed to find their way to his door. It had been that way for the thirty years he'd owned the place, and the sixty years before that when Branson's served bathtub gin during Prohibition. Most of the other bars around town managed to find some respectability since then, but not Branson's. Somehow, with its sticky tables and sawdust-covered floors, it kept the seedy feel of disrepute. The drinks were awful, but cheap. Some even suspected J.D. still made bathtub gin, but he didn't. He actually ordered it in bulk from China, at the cheapest price and highest proof. He always thought that one of these days he'd start watering down the well, but a perverse sense of pride kept him from it. Branson's was not a place where you went to find watered-down booze.

If J.D. were a superstitious man, he'd say that the building just had bad juju, or whatever you'd say for a bad luck streak that just kept coming. For his part, J.D. was tired of the smell of stale smoke and desperation that seemed to cling to the bar stools. He sometimes thought that Branson's was the devil's way of balancing out all those churches in town. He should've known something was wrong when Carl, the bar's previous owner, had sold it to him for five hundred dollars and the keys to J.D.'s pickup truck and laughed all the way out to the parking lot. J.D. had thought he'd gotten a steal then from a man who was too drunk to know the difference, but now, after nearly a lifetime behind the bar with only debt to show for it, he was beginning to think it was Carl who had taken him for a ride.

J.D. kept holding out hope that one day a customer would just level the place so he could cash in on the insurance. He had every kind of insurance sold for just that possibility. Last year, after one of his drunken patrons kicked a pipe so hard it came loose in the men's restroom and flooded half the bar, he even got flood insurance, despite the fact that the closest body of water was a tiny stream thirty miles away. J.D. was nothing if not prepared. He guessed you might call him an optimist. But none of his customers ever managed to rise to the level of total destruction. They just managed to cheat him out of his thousand-dollar deductible once a month. But one of these days, if nobody else did, he was going to torch the place himself and then open up a little cocktail stand on the beach in St. Thomas. One of these days, he swore, he'd do it.

Today, however, was probably not the day. It was J.D.'s fifty-ninth birthday, and he was hoping to get through it without seeing law enforcement— for once. He had just fixed five chairs and two tables from the last brawl that broke out in his place three days before. There were so many fights there that buying new furniture hardly seemed like a good investment. Cleaning it didn't do much good, either, J.D. thought, as he watched Duncan, one of

the regulars, slump over the bar and spill the very
last of his beer chaser down his bar stool. He was
passed out, and it was just two in the afternoon.

J.D. couldn't rely on Duncan to take down his
bar. He didn't hold out hope for the skinheads shooting pool in the back, either. They would probably just
break his pool table, the eejits. The skinheads came
off the Interstate ten minutes ago and had already
downed a bottle of 99 proof straight from China between the four of them. Two of them had swastika
tattoos on their biceps, and one of them sported a
bright red Mohawk. J.D. didn't like the look of them
and he didn't care for their politics, either. That is, if
you could call stupidity political. Why did the punks
always come around on his birthday? J.D. thought,
and then he mused for the thousandth time that he
was too old to be running a bar.

"Happy Birthday, J.D.," croaked Lizzy in her
pack-a-day smoking voice. She was the only female
customer and his only waitress. She drank more
than she served, but J.D. wasn't complaining. Lizzy
was like the bar's mascot. Rough around the edges,
but beneath the worn exterior, a heart of gold. Or,
on second thought, J.D. mused, maybe just a heart.
Gold might be pushing it.

"Want to buy me out of the bar?" J.D. asked as
he usually did every Wednesday.

"Hell, no, honey. What do I look like? A fool?"
Lizzy cackled, running a hand through her over-
dyed hair, which today was a bright mustard yellow. Her bangs were doing battle with a teal green

scrunchie and, so far, the hair was winning. "I'm playing the Powerball lotto today. Gonna win me some millions."

The door swung open then, bright sunlight cutting through the smoke of the place, and J.D. held his breath, hoping there weren't more swastika tattoos coming through the door. Instead, in walked a tall, dark stranger, who wore a plain black T-shirt and Levi's. He had a ring of tattoos around his arm in what looked like Latin or something else unfamiliar, but no swastikas that J.D. could see.

J.D. put the man's age around thirty. The stranger was a big guy. Strong, too. He could do some damage to the bar if he put his mind to it. J.D. thought right off that the man might have a temper. He could sense that in people—especially since he'd seen his share of basket cases. And this guy—wearing a scowl on his face like it lived there—looked like somebody with anger-management problems.

The man took a quick glance around the place and then walked straight toward Lizzy and J.D. He flipped a picture from his back pocket and said, "You seen this man?"

J.D. suddenly got a whiff of something that smelled like cinnamon. He wondered if Lizzy was wearing new perfume, then shelved the thought. Lizzy only ever smelled like Marlboro Lights, no matter how much perfume she sprayed on. Nicotine seeped out through her pores. The smell was coming from the stranger. He'd never known a tough guy to smell like cinnamon. Odd.

"You sure do smell good, stranger," Lizzy said, leaning over his arm and almost spilling out of her shirt. Lizzy was clearly entranced. She didn't show her cleavage to just anybody, unless it was the first of the month and rent was due. It was the fifteenth, so she had nothing to hustle for.

"You seen him?" the man asked again.

"You a cop?" J.D. asked, wary.

"Nope," the stranger said and shook his head once. He didn't say what he was, and J.D. didn't ask again.

J.D. glanced down at the photo and saw it was Kevin Farnsworth. He had been in the bar a few times. J.D. knew him more from the hardware store where he went to buy the plywood to nail his tables back together.

J.D. wasn't one to give up information—of any kind. You don't stay in one piece as a bartender at a place like Branson's if word got out you had a loose tongue. And yet, glancing in this stranger's stark blue eyes, J.D. found himself spilling the beans without even meaning to. His mouth opened, and instead of saying "Don't know him" as he usually would, he said, "Yeah, I know him. He's Kevin Farnsworth. Works at the hardware store in the square. Lives with his wife, Rachel, on Crockett Lane 'bout five miles down the road."

Lizzy sent J.D. a look of surprise, but no one was more surprised than J.D. himself. He wasn't usually so chatty, but there was something about the man that was compelling. If he wasn't a cop, he should be.

"Thanks, J.D.," the stranger said, and Lizzy perked up even more.

"He didn't tell you his name, stranger," Lizzy said. But then he turned his blue eyes on Lizzy and she went all soft again. "What did you say your name was, sugar?" she cooed.

"Sam," the man said, just as the swastika tattoos in the corner broke out into a loud bit of laughter.

"Hey, you dumb hick," the Mohawk skinhead shouted to J.D. as he smashed an empty bottle on the ground. "What the hell do we have to do to get another round over here?"

J.D. weighed the possibility of kicking them out of his bar versus sending them more booze and possibly being able to pay his Visa bill this month.

When Sam glanced over at them, the skinhead with the Mohawk sneered, "What are you looking at, boy?"

"They bothering you?" Sam asked J.D., still looking at the Mohawk man.

"Everyone bothers me," J.D. said. "I'd ignore them, if I were you."

"It's okay," Sam said with an eerie kind of calm. "I got this."

He strode over to the crew by the pool tables, calm as you please, and J.D. thought, not for the first time, that Branson's was the kind of bar where good sense came to die.

"You're gonna need some new furniture," Lizzy predicted, then sighed. "I hope they don't hit his face. It's a good-looking face," she added, as Sam walked straight up to the group and nodded as they challenged him to a game of pool. Cash was put out on the table, and J.D. reached under his bar to feel for the shotgun he kept there. He hoped he wouldn't have to use it, but he would if they looked like they were going to break more than cues. Those pool tables were expensive. Besides, he kind of liked that Sam fella and hated to see him get hurt, even if he was asking for it.

Sam took a cue stick and walked to the end of the table. He leaned over and then struck the cue ball seemingly without even looking, and the rest of the balls on the table miraculously fell into each of the corner pockets.

"What the hell?" the red Mohawk man said, clutching at his pool cue and gaping at the empty table. "How did you do that?"

Sam said nothing, just glared. The look said enough, it seemed, because another skinhead stepped up, pulled out a rumpled hundred, and said, "Double or nothing."

Sam nodded, racked up the balls, and hit them the same as before. J.D. even swore the balls went in the same holes, the eight ball last in the far corner pocket. Each skinhead took a turn, each one losing the same way, until one of them got the bright idea not to let the stranger go first. Like J.D. thought, they weren't the sharpest shivs in the prison yard. Of course, whether Sam went first or second didn't seem to matter. The balls all sank into their holes the minute he picked up his cue stick. This went on for a few minutes, until the boys had lost everything they had. Sam went to pick up the cash. None of the skinheads looked happy about it. The big one with the Mohawk snarled, "Cheat!" and balled his hands into fists and got ready to charge.

Here it comes, J.D. thought, mentally tallying up what it would cost to replace his pool cues, as Lizzy picked up the cordless phone, preparing to call for the county ambulance. Mohawk rushed Sam, pool cue swinging, but Sam easily caught it in one hand and then plucked it out of the skinhead's fingers like he was taking a sippy cup from a toddler.

J.D. had seen some interesting bar fights in his time (including one where a guy used his shoe to knock out another guy), but he had never seen a man with such quick reflexes. Or so strong.

The Mohawk man blinked twice as if he couldn't believe it, then squared himself and swung at Sam with a meaty fist. Sam dodged the punch easily. The Mohawk man charged again, but Sam stepped quickly to one side, grabbing the man by the back of the shirt and tossing him into the back wall with such velocity that the pool cues lined up in a rack came crashing down on the man's head. The man, woozy, tried to stand up, but fell back down.

J.D. wasn't quite sure what was more shocking—that Sam had tossed that two-hundred-pound bully like he'd been a bag of Fritos, or the fact that he'd managed to knock out the guy without breaking any tables.

The other three skinheads were equally shocked,

and having seen their biggest and strongest taken down in seconds, all quickly backed away and ran for the door, leaving their comrade dazed on the floor.

Dumb and *cowardly*, J.D. thought. Though he wasn't surprised.

Sam dusted off his hands and then picked up the cash the foursome had left behind. He walked directly back to the bar and slapped down what looked to be ten hundred-dollar bills.

"For your deductible," Sam said.

"How did you know about that?" mused J.D. out loud, thinking that the surprises just kept coming.

"You some kind of angel, sugar?" asked Lizzy, full-on in love with the man now.

Sam gave a bitter kind of laugh. "Lost my wings a long time ago," he said, then turned to J.D. "You see Kevin, do me a favor and don't tell him I'm looking for him."

Money aside, having just seen Sam take out a skinhead without breaking a sweat, J.D. had no intention of getting on his bad side. "You got it, stranger," J.D. said.

"Just call me Sam," he said, then walked straight out J.D.'s front door.

"Well, happy birthday to me," J.D. said after Sam had left, as he fanned out the hundred-dollar bills on the bar.

Four

After the cake had gone up like a six-month-old Christmas tree, Rachel's mothering instincts kicked in, and she grabbed Cassidy and pulled him up and out of his high chair, even as Gladys tossed the pitcher of sweet tea she was holding onto the cake. Gasps went up from the crowd. In seconds, Constance had grabbed a stack of tea towels, and she and another guest leapt on the remaining bits of fire and smothered them out completely. The fire out and the cake a melted, mashed mess, awash in sweet tea, the crowd around the table started to chatter.

"How on earth . . ."

"Was it one of those trick candles?"

"I never saw such a thing."

"That candle must've been made in China. I'd bet money on it."

"Maybe there's been a recall."

And on and on. And Rachel listened, dumbfounded, as a roomful of grown-ups convinced themselves that a combusting cake could be so easily explained. She clutched Cassidy tighter to her chest, even though he didn't seem the least bit upset. He squirmed in her arms, eager to get down and pick up the soggy, burnt pieces of cake on the ground. She held him tighter, frantically going over every inch of him, looking for signs of a burn. There wasn't a single scratch, not even a little red mark. As usual, Cassidy was boo-boo proof.

Something in her stomach told Rachel it wasn't a candle from China, or a manufacturer's error. This was the second time today Cassidy had set something on fire without matches or a lighter. She had a sneaking suspicion he'd done it himself somehow.

She remembered an old movie she'd seen: *Firestarter*. Could her Cassidy, with his sweet brown curls and bright brown eyes, be like Drew Barrymore? Could he start fires with his mind? She blinked away the thought. That was just ridiculous. Those things didn't happen in real life. Or did they?

Constance was the only one at the party who didn't try to explain away the candle. She, in fact, looked quite reserved, staring at Cassidy for a long while after as if she might be a tad bit scared of him. But then Rachel brushed the thought away. Surely she'd been seeing things. Constance was Cassidy's godmother. She wouldn't be afraid of him. When Constance left shortly thereafter without hugging

Cassidy and with a mumbled excuse to Rachel, she found it odd, but she was too preoccupied to dwell on it. The rest of the guests eventually followed, each one promising to write the candle company on Rachel's behalf, and one telling her she ought to call Oprah. On her way out, her mother stooped to hug her and said, "I'm so sorry about the candles. But they were the ones Kevin said to buy" in a tone that implied she meant it was all his fault.

Cassidy had gone down for his nap shortly after the ruckus died down, and was now sleeping peacefully in his crib, his hand wrapped around his favorite stuffed animal, a one-eyed elephant he called Boo. Rachel watched him sleep for a beat or two. Normally this was the time when her heart grew all warm and fuzzy because he looked so angelic while he slept. This time, however, she couldn't get past the worry knotting her stomach. She felt certain that something was wrong with her little boy. These things just didn't happen. Maybe he had some kind of genetic disorder, like the kind she was always reading about in those profiles in the back of *People* magazine. But instead of being born blind, or without a femur, he was born with the ability to set things on fire. Maybe there was a scientific explanation. Maybe it was some kind of disease.

She walked out of her son's room and went to the cordless phone in the kitchen. She thought about calling her mom, who was probably home by now, but Gladys was staunchly in the "he'll grow out of it" camp, and Rachel didn't feel like being reassured at the moment. She wanted answers. Rachel had Cassidy's pediatrician, Dr. Matthews' number memorized pretty much since her son had learned to roll over and managed to tumble out of his bassinet at four weeks old. She dialed the number and listened to it ring.

"Hello, Dr. Matthews' office," came the familiar voice of Rhonda, Dr. Matthews' secretary.

Rachel cringed a little. She was hoping Rhonda was sick today. Rhonda thought Rachel was just another nervous mother.

"Hi, Rhonda. It's Rachel, I was wondering . . ." Rachel didn't get to finish her sentence.

"More trouble with Cassidy?" asked Rhonda, who couldn't quite keep the judgment out of her voice. Rhonda had three grown children and suspected Rachel was just one of those frantic mothers who couldn't cope with anything. Rachel was always rushing Cassidy into the office claiming he'd fallen or hurt himself, but there was rarely, if ever, a mark on him. By doctors' standards, Cassidy was the healthiest boy in the county—never had an ear infection or even so much as the sniffles.

"Do you have any extra appointments today?" Rachel asked. "We're due for his first-year checkup on Friday, but I thought maybe we could come in early because today we had a little mishap."

"Mishap?" Rhonda didn't even sound surprised.

"His birthday cake caught on fire."

There was silence on the other end of the line for several long moments.

"I'm sorry, honey, but did you say *fire*?"

"That's right."

Rachel could almost feel Rhonda shaking her head in judgment.

"Does he have any burns?"

"Well, no, not that I can see, but I'd like Dr. Matthews to take a look at him anyway."

"You know he's probably fine." Rachel could almost feel Rhonda rolling her eyes on the other end of the line.

"Yes, yes, but I just have a few questions." Rachel's voice was starting to sound a little more urgent. Rhonda let out a long sigh on the other end of the phone, as if silently asking some higher power for patience.

"All right, then. You can come in at three."

"Thanks," Rachel said, but Rhonda had already hung up.

In Dr. Matthews' waiting room, Rhonda waved and smiled at Cassidy, who grinned a gap-toothed grin at her. When she glanced up at Rachel, she gave her a tight, barely polite smile as she asked her to sign in. Rachel just nodded back and tried not to let it bother her. She knew there *was* something wrong with her son. He just wasn't like other boys.

They waited for what seemed like forever before being called back into one of three patient exam rooms. During this time Rachel imagined just how she would punish Kevin once he finally resurfaced. She decided the silent treatment wouldn't be enough. He'd have to do a lot to make up for missing his son's first birthday *and* near brush with death. Painting the house might do it. Or finishing that bathroom as he was always promising. Or both. Plus sleeping on the couch indefinitely for the next five years.

Cassidy was on his best behavior, waving and smiling at the nurse, his dark curly hair and cuter-than-possible dimples making him look like he ought to be in a commercial for baby food or diapers.

Dr. Matthews bustled in the door a few minutes later. He was around the age of seventy-five and had at one time been Rachel's own doctor. He was the county's only pediatrician and while he might be a little out of date, you certainly couldn't beat his experience. Rachel sometimes worried he might have lost a step or two, but she wasn't about to have to drive an hour to Dallas for a new doctor. Cassidy was way too accident-prone for such a distance between him and medical attention. The fact that he rarely had a mark on him didn't ease Rachel's mind any. One of these days he was going to hurt himself, and when he did, Rachel wanted to be close to a doctor.

"So how's the baby today?" Dr. Matthews asked, his thinning white hair curling under his ears, his hand a little shaky with the stethoscope he used to listen to Cassidy's heart.

"He's fine, but this morning, I caught him on top of the refrigerator, and—"

"A climber, eh? That's how I was as a boy."

"Yes, but Dr. Matthews, how did he *get* up there? It just doesn't seem possible that he could do it on his own. There wasn't a ladder, and the cabinets are too high for him to reach."

"Oh, I wouldn't worry." Dr. Matthews sat on a little stool on wheels so he could be eye level with Cassidy to look in his ears.

"And then he set his cake on fire, and it wasn't the first time. I swear he'd set a package of Gold-fish on fire."

"With matches?" Dr. Matthews suddenly sounded alarmed as he looked up at her sharply.

"No, nothing like that," she said. "Is it possible— I mean for him to—"

"A-bugga-bugga-boo," Dr. Matthews cooed at Cassidy, giving his belly a little poke. Cassidy giggled like the Pillsbury Doughboy and smiled broadly. Dr. Matthews put away his ear-examining device and reached for a pocket penlight and looked into Cassidy's eyes.

Rachel pressed on. "It's going to sound really weird, but Doctor, I think there might really be something wrong. He's just not *normal.*"

"Oh, pooh, no such thing as normal." Dr. Matthews pocketed his little light and wheeled back to the counter, grabbed a tongue depressor, and then scooted back to stick it in the boy's mouth. Rachel watched as Cassidy sat patiently through the exam, and she wondered why he was being so good. Normally, you couldn't even get a new diaper on him without him screaming bloody murder, and yet, here he was, sitting for the doctor as if he were the most patient, helpful baby ever.

"Are you a troublemaker, little one?" Dr. Matthews asked Cassidy, who just clapped his hands together and giggled. "Or is your mother just exaggerating?"

Rachel felt her face burn. Dr. Matthews was treating her like she was a hysterical housewife.

"But, Doc, I really think maybe you ought to run some tests."

"Like what kind of tests?"

"I don't know. Genetic tests? Maybe there's something he has. I don't know. Some disorder. He's just too advanced for his age."

"Most mothers don't complain about that," Dr. Matthews pointed out.

"But he walked at five months!"

"Some babies are just like that." Dr. Matthews wasn't the least fazed. "Rachel, you sure you're doing okay? We talked last time about postpartum depression."

"I don't think it's postpartum anything," Rachel said, bristling. She was getting nowhere. He was treating her like a woman with a mental problem— as usual.

"Maybe just stress, then. Some people don't handle parenting as easily as others."

Rachel realized it had been a mistake to come. Part of her knew it would be, and yet another part was relieved that Dr. Matthews was so calm about her son's antics. Maybe they weren't that outland-ish. Maybe Rachel was overreacting. He was the one with the medical degree, after all, even if he did get it sometime around the Korean War.

"I don't think there's anything wrong with Cassidy," Dr. Matthews continued, wheeling backward on his stool and putting his hands on his knees. "He's just a little more active than some boys. You just need to keep a closer eye on him. Keep the matches and candles way out of his reach."

Rachel let out a long sigh and nodded. This is where the visits always ended up. With a small lec-ture about her parenting skills. And part of her be-lieved it was her fault, somehow. She'd never been a mom before. She was making this all up as she went along. Maybe she did need to pay more atten-tion. Maybe things were getting by her. Maybe she was blowing things out of proportion.

"Now it's time for shots," Dr. Matthews said, wheeling over and grabbing a tray with needles. While most babies would start to cry at the sight of needles, Cassidy didn't seem the least upset. In fact, he rarely even sniffled when he got a shot. Other mothers told Rachel she should count herself lucky, but Rachel worried that something more was wrong. Who didn't cry at getting their first shots?

"Hold still, little one," Dr. Matthews directed, as he poked a needle into the boy's left thigh. Cas-sidy didn't even flinch. His eyes were wide and dry as he looked on. "That's odd," the doctor said, re-tracting the needle and then trying again.

"What is it?"

"The needle isn't going in," Dr. Matthews said as he poked again, this time harder. After a third try, he dropped the needle into the trash. "Must be defective," he mumbled. He tried two more needles, but neither one broke the boy's skin.

"Must be the whole batch," Dr. Matthews said, scratching his head. "Have to ask Rhonda to call the med supply place."

"Don't you think that's a little weird?" Rachel asked, pointing to the tray. "I mean, this is what I'm talking about. What if it's not the needle?"

"What if Cassidy has superskin?" Dr. Matthews finished, and then gave a gruff little laugh. "Next thing you'll tell me he has a red cape and can fly."

"I hardly think that's what I was saying," Rachel said, voice angry. "I just think we ought to—"

"Bring him back in a week or two," Dr. Matthews added, cutting her off. He snapped off his plastic gloves. "We should have new needles in by then. You lucked out, little man. No shots today!"

Cassidy clapped his hands and giggled. Rachel sighed, giving up.

She slapped his clothes on and in a few minutes they were back outside, with Rachel vowing she would find a new doctor, just like she did after every visit with Dr. Matthews. *He can't see what's in front of his face*, she thought. Of course, no one in Dogwood seemed to be able to, either.

First, her neighbors didn't see anything wrong with an exploding birthday cake at Cassidy's party, and then the doctor decided a whole box of needles was defective just because Cassidy couldn't have his shots. She wondered if not being able to see the obvious was a problem with everyone in Dogwood.

At her white minivan, she lifted Cassidy into his car seat, but he had no intention of going peacefully, his patience with acting like the Perfect Little Boy having run out. Rachel's mobile phone rang. She grabbed it and flipped it open.

"Hello?"

"Hi," said Constance. "Sorry about running out on you earlier. Um, have you heard from Kevin yet?" There was a note of worry in her voice.

"No," Rachel said and breathed out a frustrated breath as she finally managed to get the kicking Cassidy into his seat. She closed the back door on him just as he let out a loud wail. "And I'm just coming from Dr. Matthews' office."

"How's Cassidy?"

"Oh, fine. But I'm not sure Dr. Matthews would know if he wasn't."

"So, I, um, wanted to talk to you about Cassidy."

"Yeah?" Rachel asked, as she slipped into the front seat and turned the car ignition. Cassidy was in full-on tantrum mode, trying to wiggle out of his seat. Rachel could barely hear Constance.

"Maybe I should come over? This isn't going to be easy to explain."

"What? Constance, I can't really hear you. Cassidy is throwing a full-on fit."

"It's just, I don't know how to . . . well, it's sort of

complicated, really. . . . And you'll think I'm totally crazy, but . . ."

Cassidy managed to get hold of his stuffed Curious George and lobbed it into the front seat. It hit the back of Rachel's head. She whipped around and gave Cassidy a warning look.

"No throwing," she cautioned. "Now, sit back. We're going to go home and get a snack. Don't you want a snack?"

Cassidy thought about this a second. "'nack," he repeated and nodded.

Constance was still talking, but Rachel hadn't heard a word. "Why don't you just come by later?" Rachel asked her.

Back at her house, she let Cassidy free of his car seat, and the boy sprinted to the kitchen and the awaiting promise of a snack. The only thing he loved more than getting into trouble was eating.

Once inside, Rachel dispensed the nonburned Goldfish quickly, and then grabbed the phone from the counter and dialed her husband's cell phone for the hundredth time. Again, straight to voice mail. Now she was beginning to worry. It was a dark, slick feeling at the pit of her stomach. And the fact that Kevin made her worry just made her all the madder at him.

She jammed the end call button on her cordless handset, thinking how less satisfying it was than slamming down a receiver in its cradle. Maybe this and other technological advances were why people were so stressed. If you can't take out your rage on a phone, then no wonder high blood pressure was on the rise. *The world was a healthier place when you could slam down the phone*, she thought. Rachel was thinking about whether spiking the cordless receiver and potentially breaking it would make her feel better when the phone in her hand rang. She noticed that the caller ID screen wasn't working—still. Kevin had promised to fix it or buy a new phone for the last four months. Clearly he'd done neither.

She instantly clicked the green call button.

"Kevin, you had better be in a ditch somewhere, I swear to God," she said into the receiver.

"Um, excuse me?" came a woman's voice, someone Rachel didn't recognize.

"Oh, I'm sorry. I thought you were my husband."

"I see," said the terse voice of the woman. "Well, I'm not. I'm with America's Best Mortgages, and I'm afraid you are three months behind on your mortgage. I'm calling to inform you that if you are in default on your mortgage, we are going to start foreclosure procedures."

"Foreclosure? There must be some mistake."

"I'm speaking to Rachel Farnsworth, correct? Of 124 Crockett Lane?"

"That's right."

"There's no mistake. I've talked to your husband, Kevin, many times now and he's promised a payment that hasn't been made. As well as two home equity loans . . ."

Rachel felt the room start to spin.

"Home equity loans?" she echoed. "What are you talking about?"

"He refinanced twice, and took out two home equity loans last year. Both of those are now in default."

Rachel slumped into a nearby kitchen chair. This was the first she'd ever heard of this. How had Kevin possibly done this behind her back? There must be some mistake. It just couldn't be true.

"I'm afraid without a full payment on what's owed, we're going to have to evict you by Friday," the woman was saying.

"What? No, I didn't know," Rachel said, heart thumping in her chest as she frantically worked to figure out how she would get out a mortgage payment today.

"I explained all this to your husband."

"Yes, but he isn't here and he never told me. . . ."

"I'm sorry, ma'am, but either you pay the balance in full by Thursday or you'll need to be out of the house by noon Friday."

She went on to talk in some kind of legalese that Rachel hardly even heard about their mortgage interest and back payments and about three other attempts that had been made to reach them, and something about the bank repossessing the property. Rachel listened to all of it numbly, not sure she was processing any of it.

Then the woman clicked off, and Rachel put down the phone with shaky fingers. She went to the study that Kevin used to store all their papers and stopped in front of his giant rolltop desk that he kept locked, ostensibly to keep Cassidy out of the bills. Rachel slid open the unlocked drawers, but she didn't see the key. She figured Kevin must've taken it with him. She searched for something she could use to pry the top loose. Her eyes lighted on the burgundy curtains hanging over the window. She jumped up on a chair and grabbed the curtain rod, letting the curtains slide to the floor. She took a deep breath and then jammed the narrow rod into the seal and put all her weight on it. The lock popped open with a crack of splintering wood. She rolled up the cover and immediately piles of pink and blue envelopes slid out onto the floor. Her feet were covered in an avalanche of past-due bills. The mortgage wasn't the only thing Kevin had let slide. The electric bill, the water bill, and gas—all were neatly folded into frightening pink envelopes with threatening notices about shutting off service.

Rachel sat down in the chair, a feeling of icy dread settling in her stomach. She glanced up at the computer screen sitting on the desk. She brought up a new Web page for her bank, and typed in her account log-on with numb fingers. Rachel sought out the account balance, and the icicle in her stomach dropped straight through her—she felt like she was on a roller coaster in a free fall.

Kevin had drained their checking account. Frantically, she looked up her other accounts online—her IRA and even Cassidy's small college fund. She found them empty.

Kevin's disappearance was no accident. He'd run away. And taken all their money with him.

She knew in that instant that Kevin wasn't planning on coming back.

Rage boiled up in her throat, burning the fear away.

Wherever Kevin was, she was going to find him. And when she did, he was going to wish he'd never been born.

Five

The demon formerly known as Kevin Farnsworth waited at the departure terminal at the Dallas airport outside a Starbucks stand. He wore sunglasses and a new jacket and kept glancing over his shoulder every two minutes, while he tried to nonchalantly look about him for a suitable new host. He tapped his foot nervously as he sipped his latte, wishing he'd changed bodies at the truck stop near Route 9 instead of waiting until he got all the way to the airport. But, the fact was, he simply hadn't found a body he wanted to inhabit. They were either too fat, too short, or too ugly, and he had his standards. He was a Sloth demon named Pan, and he wasn't about to go to all the trouble of actually killing somebody for their body unless their body was actually worth killing for. He didn't have the energy or the patience for a fixer-upper.

Pan glanced at the man with the huge beer belly who tottered to the Starbucks counter and shook his head. Nope. Behind him was a woman who had enough Botox in her face to poison a small nation. No way. Next to her was a little boy with freckles. No kids. He wasn't about to spend the next ten years scraping his broccoli into a potted plant. Behind the boy stood a pregnant woman. Definitely not.

True, he was lazy and didn't want to have to switch bodies again because he picked the wrong one. But it was also true that he didn't actually like to kill people. It was his embarrassing little secret. Demons were supposed to relish murder, but Kevin just . . . didn't. It was like squishing a bug. He was just squeamish, especially when he heard that splurting sound of the soul leaving the body. It was something he'd rather avoid. Honestly, he'd much rather just hang around and watch TV. He didn't even really like leaving his couch. Sure, it was the Sloth in him, but even most other Sloths tried to get other people to do their killing for them. Pan didn't even like to do that.

But he had to find a new body, and soon. There were too many people who knew what he looked like as Kevin Farnsworth. Sam, for starters, and he was the worst of the bounty hunters. He couldn't be bought off, or easily duped, and he was stubborn. He was one of the most feared bounty hunters of all time, and that included a very large, fire-breathing Wrath demon named Deanz who was known for killing half his bounties rather than bothering to turn them in for his reward. All the best hunters would be after him now, since Kevin had broken

Satan's top five most wanted. How he'd become so important in the scheme of things, he had no idea. He'd been flying under the radar for centuries, and now suddenly everybody was after him.

He'd been AWOL from Satan's army for at least a millennium with hardly anybody caring. He'd left the Sloth regiment, becoming bored with tempting the souls of the clinically depressed and having struggled with extended bouts of depression himself. Unlike other demons, Sloth demons often found themselves questioning the whole purpose of Satan's Grand Plan, and wondering if it really all mattered in the scheme of things. Sloths had a tendency to be depressed, nihilistic, and perpetually lazy. AWOL Sloths rarely were of any interest to anybody. They were hardly helpful to Satan when they were in his army, since few of them could drag themselves out of bed long enough to do his bidding. Sloths had a notoriously bad work ethic.

No one should care about Pan, and yet suddenly everyone did. The only explanation he could think of was the fact that he was one of the few beings in the universe who happened to know where Azazel—one of God's most powerful fallen angels—had been imprisoned for eternity. That's the only thing that made Pan special, as far as he knew.

It had been about a hundred years ago, and Pan had been looking for a nice place to hibernate. It had been at night, and Pan hadn't been paying attention to where he was going, and he'd fallen down quite a large hole. More like a cliff, really, and when he landed down below with a hard thud, he found himself staring at God's Judgment Seal. He'd had his share of Latin and Aramaic, and he could read the warning. It said WHOSOEVER COMES THROUGH THIS DOOR SHALL BE JUDGED. AZAZEL, BANISHED SON OF GOD, LIES HERE FOR ALL ETERNITY. That was Godspeak for this was the tomb of a fallen angel named Azazel.

Pan had heard about Azazel. He'd been one of the most powerful fallen angels since Lucifer. Azazel had turned his earth assignment into an opportunity to romance half the women in Rome. He'd had designs on siring a half-breed mutant army that would rise up against heaven and hell. Neither God nor Satan liked Azazel very much. He had been placed in a very remote tomb, and here, Pan had stumbled onto it.

He hadn't thought much about it until later, when he'd crawled out of the hole and gone to see his cousin, an Envy demon named Larry, and managed to let slip he knew where the tomb was. That very night Pan had awakened to find a knife at his throat and Larry demanding to know the location. Pan had only just managed to escape by teleporting out of there in a puff of brimstone, and he'd been on the run ever since. He decided after that it was too dangerous to stay with family, and he'd spent most of his time sleeping in remote caves.

About fifty years ago he awoke to find most remote caves flattened and populated with condos, and that in the years he'd been sleeping, he had somehow made Satan's most-wanted list. Pan figured that Larry had blabbed to anyone who would listen that his cousin knew about Azazel's tomb, and now—bam!—he was being hunted by every tracker from here to purgatory.

A Greed demon might have found a way to bargain the information he knew and make money off of somebody. Like Pan's half brother, Sean, a car salesman in Chicago who always, without fail, managed to make people buy above list price. If Sean were in Pan's shoes, he could no doubt work the situation to his advantage. Pan could've called him for help, but after nearly being sliced and diced by Larry, he'd had enough help from family, thank you.

So that left Pan pretty much on his own. He figured out quickly that hiding in plain sight was sometimes better than hiding out in caves, and he started taking over people's lives. Before this one, he'd lived a couple of lives, including a traveling salesman who never sold anything and a woman who lived alone with thirty cats, but Kevin Farnsworth was by far his favorite.

He'd snagged Kevin in a convention center bathroom after he'd given a speech to a group of small business owners. He'd taken Kevin Farnsworth because he'd been strong and fit and confident and seemed content. That meant he had a happy life somewhere that Pan could slip into and maybe find a little bit of happiness himself. That's all he really wanted, anyway.

In the last five years, he'd tried so hard to *be*

Kevin Farnsworth that he'd nearly forgotten he was a demon at all. Rachel was no ordinary woman, and he'd fallen a little for her blunt way of talking and her sharp brown eyes. Of course, deep down, Pan knew Rachel suspected something was wrong. That he wasn't the man she'd fallen in love with. But he had managed to make things work so far. He should've said something to her before Cassidy was born, but he'd been too deeply in denial himself by that point, too deep into Kevin Farnsworth's life to want to admit the truth: he wasn't Kevin Farnsworth. He was a Sloth demon named Pan who without a human form looked a little like a cross between used Silly Putty and a slug.

He'd gotten so comfortable in Kevin's life. He'd even started to care for Cassidy. The little guy had a lot of spunk. And while Rachel might nag him a bit now and again, part of him was satisfied—even comfortable—being her husband. It helped that Rachel was pretty easy on the eyes. She was a cut above your average housewife, a fact he took pride in, even though he had nothing to do with it. He felt a small pang of guilt when he thought about Rachel. Yet another thing a demon shouldn't feel—guilt—but there it was. He'd grown to be quite fond of her in the last five years since he'd taken over her husband's body.

But now he'd never see her or his little tyke again, and worse, he'd gone and drained the little guy's college fund. It was a move that most demons would feel pretty good about, but he just wasn't that kind of demon.

He sucked down the last of his latte. If he didn't find a new body, and soon, he was going to miss his flight. Of course, there just might be someone better once he reached his final destination: Brazil. A lot of models came from there. He might be able to take over one of their bodies. That is, if he got there in one piece.

A dark-haired woman moved past his line of vision then. She was wearing sunglasses, too, but he could tell she was pretty. Her long dark hair hung down her back, and she was wearing a short black minidress and heels.

Pan glanced at the woman again and decided that maybe inhabiting a pretty girl's body might be just what he needed. They always got more without having to do much. Even better, the woman turned down a relatively bustle-free corridor, heading for a remote bathroom at the end of the hall.

Pan dumped his cup into the trash and followed her, sweat breaking out on his forehead. He walked quickly, glancing only one time behind him to see if there were witnesses before ducking into the bathroom, praying he didn't run into a gaggle of other women. Inside, the bathroom was empty except for the one stall inhabited by the lady in black. Kevin took a deep breath, mentally steeling himself for the distasteful work of killing her, and reached for the door. Next thing he knew, the door had swung open, smacking him in the nose and sending him flying backward into the sinks. The automatic water came on, spraying the back of his pants, as his hands went up to hold his stinging nose, which was now bleeding profusely down the front of his shirt.

"Whab da hell?" he moaned, cradling his bleeding nose as he watched the woman in black, fully dressed, come walking out of the stall. She plucked off her sunglasses and tucked them casually in her purse. Her eyes glinted red, and Pan knew he'd been fooled. She was a demon—a powerful one, given the speed at which she'd sent him into the sinks. No doubt, she was one of the devil's trackers. He scanned the room quickly for exits. There was only one and he wouldn't be able to make it to it in time. He was trapped. There was no place to run.

"Stop worrying," she said, as if she could read his mind. "I'm not after the bounty."

"You aren't?"

"No," she said, shaking her head slowly as she took two steps closer to him, pressing him even farther against the sink.

"If you want information, you will be sorry you have it. If I tell you where Azazel is, then everybody will be after you."

"Relax. I happen to already know where Azazel is buried."

This was not something Pan was expecting. As far as he knew, he was the only demon alive who knew that little bit of information. The only others who were supposed to know were two Judgment angels and God himself.

"How do you—"

The woman flashed him a cold smile. "I happened to be one of the earthbound women who loved him. That was before Satan was kind enough to give me these." Her eyes glowed a fire-engine red as she licked her lips. "I was judged with Azazel. I saw him buried. It was part of my punishment."

"So if you're not after the bounty, and you don't want information, what *do* you want?"

She put one red fingernail on his chin. "You're going to help me catch one of the bounty hunters— a Fallen named Samsapiel."

"Sam?" Pan sputtered. "The fallen Wrath angel? The world's most successful bounty hunter? *That* Sam?"

The woman nodded. "That Sam."

Pan thought about all the times Sam had nearly caught him. It had been Sam who'd sniffed him out in his last two lives, and then again in this one. He was good. Too good. He'd smell a trap from a thousand miles away.

"No way. Too dangerous. Wish I could help, but—"

Before the words had left his mouth, the woman had reached behind him and was drawing her fingernail down the mirror behind his head, making a nearly unbearable screeching sound. Pan got the whiff of burning plastic and glass and glanced over in time to see her nail making a long, dark mark down the center of the mirror.

"What I meant was, yes, certainly, I'll help," Pan amended quickly. The mirror hissed and popped as small drops of acid fell from the black mark to the sink, burning a hole in the white ceramic. Poison. Only the really strong demons had poison. Pan swallowed hard.

"I thought you'd see things my way," the woman said, glancing at herself in the part of the mirror that was still intact. She whipped out some lip gloss from her bag and applied it carefully to her bottom lip. She glanced over at Pan's bloodied nose and frowned.

"Go on, clean yourself up. We're going to Dogwood County's Mega-Mart."

"Are you *insane*? That place is crawling with demons. Everyone there will fight for the right to turn me in for that bounty."

"I'll handle them," she said with confidence. "Anyway, I need to put you someplace high profile, so Sam will come for you, and you can convince him to help me."

"Sam doesn't help anybody."

"He'll help me," she said.

"Just who are you?" Pan asked, amazed at her brash confidence in the face of what had to be the worst plan he had ever heard.

"I'm Casiphia," she said. "And soon, everyone will know my name."

Six

Sam double-parked his motorcycle outside Farnsworth's hardware store and glanced up. He was so close to Kevin Farnsworth now he could smell it. Once he bagged him, Sam could happily claim to have the most top-five captures of any bounty hunter, ever in the history of time. No escaped demon was safe when Sam was around, and that's how Sam liked it.

He'd spent the better part of a thousand years getting demons on the run and turning them into the devil for an apt reward—his angel powers, fully restored, minus, of course, the wings. If he stopped the bounties, he would lose his power and become human, with all the pitfalls of sickness and age.

Fallen angels didn't become human overnight, but they did eventually. Most simply skipped to the chase, pledged their souls to Satan, and joined his army, where they usually got a permanent boost in their powers and a promotion to boot. But Sam didn't have a taste for the devil's army. He wasn't about to pledge allegiance to anyone, least of all Satan. But he wasn't ready to grow old and die, either, so he'd been walking the fine line between doing the devil's work and staying a free agent.

Sam told himself that the demons he caught and returned to Satan did less damage within his army or in hell than loose on their own. In the ongoing war between heaven and hell, there were ground rules. A freelance demon played by no rules whatsoever, and that was dangerous. And, half the time, the really nasty demons Satan just destroyed anyway, since he didn't like anyone who might compete with his own power. It was one of the reasons Satan's army was never really a match for God's. Satan kept executing all his strongest soldiers.

Besides, Sam did good deeds now and again. Truth was, he did more good fallen than he ever had as a Wrath angel. Back then, when God told him to kill a demon or level an entire town, he would do it without asking why. Without even wanting to know why. God said it must be so, and he was a Wrath angel just following orders. He would tell himself what the other Wrathers did: that they deserved it. That the demons or the people had it coming. That God knew best, and their deaths were all for the greater good.

If truth be known, most of the angels in the Wrath regiment felt they were better than humans. They were altogether superior in strength, stamina, and speed, and should they keep their wings, they would live forever. Humans, by comparison, were weak and fragile, destined to spend a very short time on earth before their bodies returned to dust.

If he were honest with himself, Sam would admit he felt the same from time to time. But his prejudices were shaken to the core that fateful morning when God sent him to Sodom. He and his platoon were ordered to rain fire on the town, and they did. Normally, he could separate himself from missions, but this one bothered him more than most. The town wasn't full of demons. Or sinful soldiers. This one had whole families, including women and small children. They had died in a fire blast so horrific that most of them were simply incinerated on contact.

He was supposed to make sure there were no survivors. He'd picked through the rubble, finding mostly death. And, yet, amazingly, he had discovered a woman and her baby still alive, half-buried under a charred roof and badly hurt. The mother, with severe burns on her legs, sat holding a small baby boy close to her chest as the boy slipped in and out of consciousness.

She had glanced up, squinting against the glare of sunlight as she pushed her dark hair from her face. Seeing his bright white wings and the golden armor he wore across his chest, she had let out a sob of relief and said, "You are here to save us."

She had missed the flaming sword in his hand, of course. The one he was supposed to use to strike down the sinful. But no matter how he tried, he couldn't imagine what sin a baby and his mother could've committed that would be so terrible as to merit a fiery death sentence from him.

In the time it took him to pause, his commander had appeared near his shoulder.

"You must do this, Samsapiel," Ethan, the leader of his platoon, had said.

"But why?"

"There is no why." Ethan, Sam well knew, didn't believe in the why of anything. He only believed in the how—as in the how he would get promoted. "You do this or I will. We have our orders."

"The baby . . ." Sam's voice drifted.

"Is dying anyway," Ethan said. "No way to save him."

Ethan was right, of course. The boy was mortally wounded.

Sam turned to the mother and raised his sword, but as the relief on the woman's face turned to dawning dread, he knew he could not kill her.

"I won't do this," he had said, dropping his sword to his side.

"He'll have your wings."

He knew Ethan was right. This was God's will, and betraying it meant treason of the highest kind. And, in that instance, Sam decided that any God who would order him to kill a dying baby and his mother was no God he wanted to follow.

"If he wants me to do this, then he can take them. I don't want them anymore." And Sam put down the flaming sword, and he simply walked away. He didn't make it far enough to escape the sound of the screams that followed him, the screams of the mother who was likely killed by Ethan's own hand.

After that, the Judgment angels found him quickly enough. They took his wings with quick, surgical precision, and left him near death. He thought he would die from the pain that was so blinding he could hardly move for three days. But, somehow, he'd survived. The bleeding had stopped, the pain receded enough for him to contemplate moving, and eventually he stood and then walked. He wandered aimlessly for days on legs not used to the full and constant weight of his body. He had to stop many times to rest, and every morning he woke with his muscles screaming murder and his feet aching and raw. He wrapped them in bandages he tore from his robe and kept going.

He considered curling up somewhere and letting himself die so that he could pass through this life and into another in purgatory, or wherever God chose to put him.

Then, quite by accident, he'd stumbled upon an AWOL Gluttony demon who had trapped a man and his family in a cave and was trying to eat them. Sam mustered his strength and dispatched the demon back to hell. He saved the family and managed a small reward from the devil in the process. The devil gave him strength, healed the blisters on his feet, and offered him a high-ranking post in his cabinet. Sam had declined. The devil, not one to give up, suggested Sam become a full-time tracker, a freelancer, and Sam had agreed, knowing full well that the devil planned for Sam to become addicted to the power Satan would give him.

Since then, he'd turned in demon after demon, saved a few people in the process, and managed, so far, to resist Satan's offer of immortality and eternal servitude. Sam wasn't sure, however, how long he'd be able to manage to stay neutral. Doing too many deals with the devil was never a good idea. Eventually he got you. One way or another.

At the moment Sam felt a little weaker than usual. It had been too long since he'd claimed his last bounty, in part because Kevin had proved slippery and more wily than Sam expected. Hiding in plain sight was a bold move, and not one that most demons could pull off without slipping up now and again. AWOL demons tended to kill people at will, and they couldn't stop the urge, even if they were undercover. But Kevin had shown remarkable self-restraint. He blended in very well among people and was hard to spot, since for all practical purposes he acted like an actual person. He didn't murder his neighbors and eat them for dinner, like a Gluttony demon, or set up Ponzi schemes like Greed demons.

Now Sam was closer than ever to finally getting Kevin, and he didn't plan on losing him again. Sam looked at the hardware store and shook his head. There wasn't a low that Sloth demons wouldn't sink to, but the fact that this one actually had to work for a living went against his grain, Sam was sure.

Sam pushed open the hardware store door, and the bell attached to it dinged. He scanned the aisles, his extrasensitive ears and eyes picking up the fact that there was only one person in the store: the girl behind the counter. She had white earbuds in her ears and gum in her mouth. Seeing him, she popped the earbuds out, her mouth slightly parted. He could sense her curiosity, and something more. He could hear her heart start to pound a little faster. She was attracted to him, like most people were. He had about him a strong animal magnetism.

"I'm looking for Kevin Farnsworth," Sam said. He smiled a little to encourage her, as his eyes flicked down to her name tag, which read VANESSA. "You know where he is?"

"Um, no, like, I haven't seen him, but could, uh, I help you with something?" Vanessa asked, batting her eyes at him. She was barely older than a child.

"You sure?" Sam asked again, as he willed her to help him. He knew she would. It was the look Sam was giving her. Few people could resist it. They naturally were compelled to help.

She was a pretty girl, and he could tell she was used to being the one who took control of the flirting, despite the fact she wasn't even out of her teen years yet. He could hear the girl's heart speed up even more, and her eyes grew wider. She was now caught by his gaze.

"His wife was looking for him, too," the girl said eagerly, "but I haven't seen him. Wish I had, so I could tell you where he was. Yesterday was the last I saw him. Late afternoon at closing when he dropped me off at my house before he went home. He lives on Crockett Lane; you could check it out, if you want. His wife has been calling here *all* day. She likes to check up on him. She's been crazy jealous of me, ever since I started working here, and especially when she was pregnant—"

Sam put up a hand, surprised. "You're saying Kevin's wife had a baby?"

"Last year," Vanessa said, leaning farther over the counter. "And boy, has she let herself go . . ." Vanessa kept talking but Sam didn't hear most of what she said. He was too busy wondering what kind of woman had a demon's child.

Maybe she'd sold her soul to her demon husband. Some women did. Others were just oblivious. Sam guessed she was power hungry. Maybe she was hoping for immortality. A lot of people did a lot of dumb things when they were offered eternal life. He wondered what Kevin had promised her. Whatever it was, she wasn't going to get it. Not that Sam felt sorry for her. *You make your bed*, he thought, *you lie in it*.

Vanessa was going on about how unattractive she thought Rachel was. She was pushing this so hard that Sam was beginning to think they weren't facts so much as wishful thinking. It sounded to him like Vanessa was the one who was jealous, not the other way around.

Realizing the girl knew nothing more, Sam waved a hand. "Thanks, Vanessa," he said.

When he turned to go, she reached out a hand and touched his arm. "Wait, are you going so soon? I mean, you could stay. There aren't many customers and, I mean, if you want to . . ."

Vanessa might just be on the brink of offering him something untoward, and Sam was in no mood for it. He had long since tired of the possibility of having practically any woman he wanted at any time. You would think it would be a power he'd relish, but the fact was, he wouldn't mind someone to stand up to him now and again. Having women turn into willing zombies was just a turnoff. For once, he'd like one to give him a little bit of trouble. Just for kicks.

"Sorry," he said, shaking the girl's hand loose. A look of surprise and hurt crossed her face. She wasn't used to rejection, he could tell. But it wasn't his problem.

He turned his back on her and walked down the aisle displaying sprinklers and lawn care tools. He was nearly to the door, when someone pushed through it. His head snapped up, and his eyes narrowed. It wasn't just any person. It was Marcus, a thousand-year-old Sloth demon who'd crossed his path once before. He'd run into him back when he was tracking down a Pride demon who moonlighted as the Zodiac Killer.

Upon seeing Marcus, every muscle in Sam's back tensed. The last time they'd met, they'd fought, and Sam had won—barely.

"Sam—old friend, relax! Relax," Marcus said

and smiled, showing yellowed teeth. Sam guessed it was because the Sloth demon didn't bother to brush. Or probably shower, either. They were notoriously lazy about everything, including personal hygiene. Sam could see Marcus's true form below his human disguise. He was bloblike, and green, like some kind of nuclear ooze. Too lazy even to form a proper shape. It was probably more effort than he liked to maintain his form as a human.

Sam just nodded and frowned. "What do you want, Marcus?"

"What? No 'glad to see you again'? That hurts. I thought we were friends."

"I don't count any demons among my friends," Sam said, voice low.

"But, my fallen friend, it's only a matter of time before you defect to our side. Surely you know that. Isn't the defection rate like ninety-nine percent?"

Sam's eyes flicked to the exit. Marcus had two more demons with him who were waiting outside, smoking cigarettes. Sam could probably take them, but not easily and not without causing a scene.

"How's your strength these days, anyway?" Marcus asked, a sly twinkle in his eye. "Word is you've had a dry spell."

"I'm fine," Sam growled.

"Tsk, tsk," Marcus said, shaking his head. "I don't believe you. You're so proud. Always have been. I think you'd make a fine addition to the Pride regiment."

"And you'd get full credit with Satan for turning me," Sam said. "And get a promotion, no doubt."

"Exactly," Marcus said.

"Well, you're going to have to work a lot harder than that. I'm not interested."

"You know us Sloth demons don't work hard," Marcus said and made a face as if the very sound of the word "work" was distasteful.

"Which is why I'm surprised to find you here," Sam said. "I thought you gave up the bounty business. Too much effort, you said."

Marcus shrugged. "We got a tip. Besides, bounties are just a side business. I run the Mega-Mart."

Mega-Mart was one of several demon training grounds, like the DMV, tow-truck companies, and state-run prisons.

Sam wondered who had tipped off Marcus about Kevin's whereabouts.

"So, our little demon has been hiding here," Marcus added, picking up a small gardening hoe and then dropping it again. "Seems so boring." His eyes flicked back to Vanessa, who was watching the two men with interest. She was too far away, however, to hear what they were saying. The cell phone in Marcus's front pocket buzzed. He picked it up and flipped it open.

"Bill—I hear you. You at Kevin's house? Good. Let me know what you find." Marcus paused, listening. "No, you can't burn down the house. Because you just can't." Marcus flipped the phone shut and shrugged. "Demon trainees," he said. "They are always so eager."

Sam realized he was one step behind Marcus and that the demon had been stalling, keeping him here on purpose while his thugs surrounded Kevin Farnsworth's house. He might be too late. They could have him already. Instantly, he leapt forward, rushing out of the store before Marcus or his trainees could react. He counted on a slightly slower reaction—given they were Sloth demons—and wasn't disappointed. He was on his motorcycle before they had taken three steps. Sam turned the ignition on his motorcycle and sped down the road, hoping he wasn't too late.

Seven

Rachel had just made Cassidy some mac and cheese for dinner, when the front doorbell rang. She wiped her hands on a kitchen towel and headed to the front, swinging open the door without bothering to look through the peephole, figuring Constance would be standing on her porch. But it wasn't Constance. Instead, there were two men she'd never met before, one of them giving her a strained smile, and the other frowning.

Right off, Rachel didn't like the look of them. For one thing, she didn't know them, and she knew almost every living person in Dogwood County. Just being strangers was enough of a problem, but there was something else she didn't like. They were both wearing jeans and golf shirts, and she put their age somewhere in the thirties. She couldn't put her finger on it, exactly, but she definitely didn't like them.

"Mrs. Farnsworth?"

Rachel nodded, keeping the screen door closed. "We're looking for your husband. Is he at home?"

"He's on his way home," Rachel lied.

"Mind if we come in and wait for him?"

"Who did you say you were?" Rachel put her hands on her hips and tightened her grip on the door, ready to shut it.

"We're, uh, business associates," the one with the strained smile said. He stretched his fake smile a little wider. His partner, still silent and sullen, just stared.

Rachel heard a loud plunking sound from behind her, and then Cassidy sing-songed "Uh-oh!" No doubt he was throwing silverware and half his dinner on the floor while her back was turned. Rachel stared at the men on her porch, wondering if they were with the Mob. She'd seen her share of TV shows. Had her husband made some bad bets? Did he owe these people money?

Then her eyes happened to catch the blue name tag on the strained smiling guy. It had the Mega-Mart logo on it, and below that BILL. Rachel blanched. Mega-Mart—or as she called it "that Evil Store"—was currently trying to run her small family-owned hardware store out of business.

"You from Mega-Mart? What the hell are you doing here?" Rachel's voice turned sour as she realized she was staring at representatives of her arch-enemy.

"We need to see Kevin. We have business with him."

"Just what business is that?" Rachel put her hands on her hips. "Any business you have with my husband, you have with me."

"I'm afraid we can only talk to your husband."

"Then you're out of luck, *Bill*," Rachel said, stressing the man's name as she started to shut the door. The man with the frown swung open the screen door and blocked the front with his foot, almost faster than he should've been able to. Rachel shoved the door hard against his foot, but it didn't budge.

"Listen, mister, if you want your foot back in one piece, you'll move it *right now*." Rachel's temper flared. She'd grown up with three older brothers, and she wasn't about to back down from a guy named Bill who worked at the Mega-Mart.

"I'm afraid we're going to have to wait for Kevin."

Rachel heard a clatter behind her and turned to check on Cassidy, when her attention was drawn to her patio and the big sliding glass door, where two more men were standing near Kevin's gas grill. One was short and squat and the other was tall and thin, and both were wearing the telltale Mega-Mart blue vests.

"What the hell is going on here?" Rachel demanded.

"Our associates," Bill said as his partner pushed the door fully open, sending Rachel back a step.

"Just what do you think you're doing?" Rachel asked, as the two men walked straight into her house. She knew Mega-Mart was evil, but she didn't think they sent out people to shake down the local storeowners. Suddenly, she felt very outnumbered. She needed to call for help. And fast.

She saw her cordless phone on the kitchen counter. She went for it.

But Bill was there in a flash.

"I'll take that," he said, plucking the phone from her hand.

"You need to leave my house *right now*," Rachel said. She glanced down at the kitchen drawer where she'd stashed her husband's cell phone. If she could get that without them seeing, she could call for help.

"Why don't you make yourself useful and get us some tea?" Bill asked, nodding toward the refrigerator.

"Why don't you just go to hell?" Rachel replied, folding her arms and frowning at him.

Bill just laughed as his sidekick stalked to her back door and opened it, letting in the two guys wearing Mega-Mart vests. She had to admit, the Mega-Mart uniforms made them look a lot less tough than they would have otherwise. Besides, Rachel thought she could take the tall, thin one. He was probably no more than a hundred and twenty pounds soaking wet. The men began rifling through her living room, as if they thought they might find Kevin hiding out in a DVD case or under a ceramic drink coaster.

Rachel's thoughts were going a million miles a minute. Where was Cassidy? Her eyes flicked to his high chair, but it was empty. She glanced right and left, but there was no trace of him other than a trail of yellow mac-and-cheese stains on her tile floor. Rachel took a second to marvel at how the little Houdini had escaped—again. He'd managed to unlatch the safety belt *and* crawled down from the thing in about thirty seconds. In this case, she was glad. She hoped he was hiding somewhere and that he would stay put. At this point she didn't even care if it was on top of the refrigerator as long as these men didn't see him.

Rachel told herself to be calm as the men started throwing pillows in every direction. Mega-Mart was a national chain. Surely they wouldn't really hurt her. Then again, that Evil Store did recently open a shop on an ancient Hawaiian burial ground. They didn't, as far as Rachel could tell, have scruples.

Remembering suddenly that she had stashed Kevin's cell phone in the far kitchen drawer, she inched toward it and discreetly slid it open, using her own body as a shield. She dipped behind her back, covertly swiped her husband's mobile phone, and plunked it in her pocket. Out of the corner of her eye, she saw Cassidy headed toward the hall-way bathroom.

Since the men were busy ransacking her living room, Rachel hurried down the hall, jumped into her hallway bathroom, and locked the door. Inside, as she suspected, was her Cassidy. His face was covered with dried mac and cheese, and he was currently in the process of unraveling an entire roll of bathroom tissue into the toilet. He gave her a huge, gap-toothed grin. She scooped him up and popped him into the empty bathtub, where he happily started playing with a few of his toys. Rachel was pulling the shower curtain mostly closed when someone knocked loudly at the door.

"Mrs. Farnsworth, we're going to have to ask you to come out," said the voice on the other side.

Rachel didn't answer, just grabbed the cell phone and dialed her neighbor, Jenner. He was the closest thing to help—what with the county sheriff at least a twenty-minute drive away. Jenner was a retired marine colonel, and he kept loads of guns at his house. Maybe, if she was lucky, he was out on his porch and had seen the men at her house. He was often letting her know if strange cars had been by. He had a lot of free time on his hands and hadn't quite gotten out of the habit of doing military surveillance.

Jenner's answering machine clicked on after the second ring. Rachel cursed her luck.

"Jenner? If you're there, pick up. It's me, Rachel Farnsworth. There's trouble over here—"

Just then she heard a loud crack as the bathroom door flew open. The man standing outside had ripped it off its hinges in one quick go, without even breaking a sweat. Rachel let out a surprised shriek, because in real life men didn't just go around peeling away locked doors like the skin of an onion. That was the stuff of action movies and comic books. He reached down and grabbed the phone from her hand.

"Hey! That's mine!" she cried helplessly, even as he stooped down and put a firm grip on her wrist and yanked her to her feet, hard. "No!" she shouted, struggling against his iron grip as he pulled her out of the bathroom. Cassidy was amazingly quiet in the tub, and Rachel hoped he stayed that way. She tugged with all her weight, but the man was too strong; he got her easily into the living room, where Bill had taken a seat on a nearby armchair. The other two were peering under her sofa cushions, as if Kevin might turn up with the loose change.

"Where's Kevin?" Bill asked. "You said he'd be home. When?"

"I don't know. Soon," Rachel answered, hoping to talk her way out of this. Her eyes flicked to the front door, and she wondered if she could make it there if she ran. But the ridiculously strong guy—the guy with the frown—was standing behind her, hand on her shoulder. He wasn't going to let her go anywhere. Not to mention, she wasn't about to leave Cassidy in the house alone with these thugs. She prayed he stayed put in his hiding place. "He disappeared. I don't know where he is."

"Maybe she'll talk if we find her baby," the tall, thin guy suggested, nodding toward the mac-and-cheese-covered high chair.

"He's not here," Rachel said flatly. "He's at my mother's."

There was a clatter in the bathroom—the sound of Cassidy dropping one of his toy trucks.

"Go see what that is," Bill said, nodding to the thin guy.

"No!" cried Rachel, a bit too forcefully as she thrashed to get free. Before she could, the front door crashed open, having been kicked in from the outside, and Rachel held her breath, hoping to see Jenner stalk through the door, armed to the teeth. Instead, in stepped a man she'd never seen before. He was tall, lean, and had a head of dark wavy hair. His eyes were a stark blue, and he had broad shoulders and arms full of muscle.

"Let her go," the stranger said, voice low.

Rachel watched Frowning Man. He didn't move. Bill, however, looked at the man in the black T-shirt and smiled.

"Sam! What a nice surprise. Boys? See to our guest," he added, nodding to the two men sitting on Rachel's love seat. Reluctantly, the two men put down their sofa cushions.

Everything else happened in a blur. Suddenly the man they called Sam had whipped the thin Mega-Mart guy straight out behind him through the open front door and into Rachel's mailbox, head first. Then Sam grabbed the short and squat one and tossed him quite easily through her glass sliding back door, shattering it into big sharp pieces. The short and squat guy, arms bleeding from the glass, rolled into her backyard, groaning. The third one stepped in front of Rachel, hoping to take a piece of Sam, but he was stopped with two quick punches—one to his face, the other to his stomach—which made him double over, gasping for air.

"Enough, enough!" said Bill, standing. "Amateurs," he muttered under his breath. He stood then, and Rachel could've sworn she saw his hands glow red. The next thing she knew, a stream of fire shot across her living room as if from a flame thrower. Sam dodged it easily, but Rachel, unable to believe what she was seeing, stood frozen to the spot as the flames rushed toward her with a whoosh. Then Sam pushed her hard and she landed safely with a soft plunk on her sofa.

Sam tackled Bill then, and in seconds the two were in a struggle that broke the vase on her mantel, a glass serving bowl on her coffee table, and one end table. Rachel kept fluctuating from gladness that this strange man was saving her to complete horror at the fact that he was saving her at the expense of most of her living room furniture.

Eventually Bill managed to get free and scramble out the front door. He and his three Mega-Mart goons ran for their parked car out front, got in, and drove away. Sam let them.

Rachel stared after them and then back at Sam, who stood and nudged a bit of broken glass off his leg.

"You mind telling me what the hell is going on here?" Rachel asked, her heart thumping, her fingers tingling from shock. "How the hell did he do that? With his hands?"

Sam didn't seem to care that the man had flame-thrower hands, nor was he even surprised. For the first time, this dark-haired man gave her his full attention. The minute his eyes landed on her, they seemed to stare straight through her.

"What? No thank-you?" he asked, mildly surprised, as if he wasn't used to ungrateful damsels in distress.

"I'll thank you after you fix my patio," Rachel said, nodding toward the shards of glass in her living room. A small part of her brain was telling her to *shut up*, but she couldn't quite manage it. It wasn't in her nature to be timid, even when circumstances called for it. Actually, she thought, especially when circumstances called for it.

"Where's Kevin?" the man said, not acknowledging her back talk, or her living room. Her eyes traveled to his bicep, where there was a ring of tattoos in a language she didn't know.

"You here for Kevin, too? Get in line." This stranger may have saved her life, and he might just be handsome—in a grumpy kind of way—and strong in the broad-shouldered, flat-stomached way Kevin used to be back in high school when he played championship football, but Rachel wasn't going to be intimidated.

Sam didn't seem to be in the mood to answer, because he turned his back on her and began kicking shards of glass across her floor as if looking for clues underneath them. A loud clatter came from the bathroom as Cassidy tried, without success, to free himself from the bathtub but ended up dumping out the nearby basket of bath toys instead.

Sam's attention was drawn straight to the bathroom.

"It's just my son," Rachel said quickly. Sam went to investigate, and Rachel was right on his heels. He whipped into the open bathroom door and stopped when he saw Cassidy, near tears, trying to hoist himself out of the bathtub amid rubber duckies and plastic trucks. Rachel zoomed in and scooped up the toddler, giving him a fierce hug.

Sam's face twisted a little, like he was reliving a bad memory.

"Not a kid person?" Rachel asked, but Sam ignored her as he turned away and began picking his way over the debris of her living room. He came upon Kevin's cell phone, which lay switched off in the middle of her area rug.

Rachel got a strong smell of something sweet and spicy, like cinnamon. She wondered why her living room smelled like cinnamon after it had been nearly destroyed by thugs. Had her mother stashed a scented candle somewhere?

Rachel turned her attention back to Sam. Suddenly she got a flash of inspiration.

"Are you FBI?"

Sam gave a small little laugh. "Hardly," he said, staring at the phone. "Kevin's?"

She didn't know how he knew, but she nodded. He flipped it open and started thumbing through Kevin's last calls.

"What's Kevin into? Is it gambling? The Mob? What?" Rachel asked.

Sam said nothing, just pocketed the phone.

"Hey, that's my husband's."

"Not anymore," Sam said curtly as he continued to pick through debris, making his way to the other side of the room.

Rachel suddenly spied her cordless phone near the foot of the couch. She took two quick steps and had it in her hands. She got a dial tone and punched 9, but suddenly Sam crossed the room and ripped the phone from her hands. She hadn't even seen him coming; one second he'd been on the other side of the room, and the next he was standing so close to her she could smell him.

And he was the one who smelled like the cinnamon candle.

It must have been cologne, but it was like nothing she'd ever smelled before. She wasn't sure what was stranger—the fact that he smelled so good or that he crossed the room in a flash. She tried to reason it out, but she couldn't. The smell filled her head, her thoughts suddenly became cloudy, and she couldn't concentrate on any one thought for very long.

"We're not going to do that," Sam said as he held the phone away from her. His voice felt like it was all around her, almost like a command inside her own head. For a second she felt herself agreeing with him. Then Cassidy let out a little squeal, and suddenly she came to her senses.

"Give me back my phone," she said flatly, holding out her hand. Sam looked surprised, as if he wasn't expecting her to defy him. As if he was used to women rolling over wherever he went. They probably did.

Sam recovered and tried again. "Tell me where Kevin is."

"Tell me how you got over here so fast," Rachel shot back.

Sam studied her for a second or two, as if he wasn't sure what to make of her.

"I'm going to ask you one more time," Sam said with deliberate slowness. "Where is Kevin?"

"I told you, I don't know," Rachel said, meeting his stark blue gaze. She wasn't afraid of him. And she wasn't going to fall at his feet, either, if that's what he was expecting.

Sam stepped closer.

"You are going to tell me about Kevin," Sam said. "You have a deal with him?" They were toe to toe.

"Well, he is my husband."

"A marriage of convenience," Sam nearly snarled. "He gets his, and you get what? Him?" Sam glanced at Cassidy, who pulled himself up and made a low growling sound.

"I don't know what you're talking about." He was so close now that she had to crane her neck to meet his eyes.

"I'm talking about women like you," Sam said, looming over her. His eyes were so big that she felt like she was going to fall right into them and never get out.

"What about women like me?"

"Women get what they want by sleeping with whoever will get it for them." His voice was a gravelly whisper.

Rachel sucked in a breath to tell him to get the hell out of her house, when he suddenly bent forward and kissed her. It was so out of the blue that she didn't do anything for a second; she was so shocked. His smell was so strong that she couldn't think; she couldn't even move. His lips were soft, and he smelled like cinnamon and something else, like her best and favorite memory, like the promise of everything good about love. And for a second she was convinced she would do absolutely anything he wanted. Then Cassidy let out an angry shriek in her ear, and suddenly the spell was broken and she was back to herself, holding her boy and standing in the shards of her patio door with a strange man taking liberties.

That's when she pulled back and slapped him straight across the face. She'd hit him hard, but he had barely even flinched, surprise and then amusement dancing across his face.

Rachel was flushed with anger and she was breathing hard, and he thought this was all some big joke.

"That doesn't happen very often," Sam said, a smile on his lips, his blue eyes bright, as he gave his cheek a rueful rub. She was guessing he meant that most women didn't mind being assaulted in their living rooms. By the tall, dark look of him, she was sure that was the case. He could probably kiss the life out of just about any woman in Dogwood without complaint. But Rachel wasn't just any woman.

He looked thoughtful. "Maybe I should try again."

Rachel raised her hand to slap him again, but this time he caught it and held it.

"Let me go," she ground out.

"If I do, you'll just try to hit me again," Sam said, the smile spreading across his face. He seemed almost happy at the thought. "Why don't you just tell me where Kevin is instead?"

"I told you. I don't know." Rachel pulled hard on her wrist but Sam wasn't about to let go. Cassidy struggled in her arms, lurching forward with his mouth open wide as if he were going to bite Sam's arm.

"You're telling the truth," Sam said, amazement in his voice, as he loosened his grip a little. It was as if he were discerning by touch her truthfulness.

"Of course I am," Rachel snapped. "Now let go." She tugged at her arm, but he didn't release it.

"Do you even know who Kevin is?"

"He's a dead man if I ever get ahold of him, that's who he is," Rachel spat. "Now let me *go*."

Sam dropped Rachel's wrist. "You don't know about any of this." The look on his face said someone could knock him over with a feather. Then he threw back his head and laughed, a big, booming laugh. The laugh drained away, and he studied her again, as if he were trying to solve a puzzle.

"I was wrong about you," he said. "And I'm not usually wrong about people."

"Well, I'm happy to prove you wrong, but I'd appreciate it if you would get the hell out of my house."

"You're kicking me out?" Sam's grin was back, bigger than before.

"The sooner the better," Rachel said, hugging Cassidy closer and glaring at the door.

He shook his head as if he couldn't believe it, then moved slowly toward the front door. Before he got there, he stopped and turned.

"Kevin is not who you think he is," Sam said. "He's not the Kevin Farnsworth you met in high school."

"What are you talking about?" Rachel asked, wondering how on earth this man knew she met her husband in high school.

As if hearing something she couldn't, he raised his head, listening.

"You'll have company soon," he said, and then glanced in the direction of the outside-facing bathroom wall. "Your neighbor, I think. You'll be safe for now, but I wouldn't spend the night here, if I were you, in case there are more of them looking for Kevin."

"More of them? What do you mean 'them'? Hey—wait a minute." Rachel trailed after Sam, who was nearly out the door. Sam stopped then, and turned.

"If you see Kevin again, which I doubt, leave a message for me at Branson's."

"The biker bar? I didn't get your whole name. I don't even know who you are."

"Sam is the only name you need to know," he said and headed for the front door. She heard a motorcycle roar to life, and then, just like that, the man was gone.

Seconds later, she heard someone scrambling in through her shattered back door.

"Rachel!" shouted a familiar voice from her backyard. "Rachel, you okay?" Jenner, her neighbor, climbed into her living room carrying a Beretta in one hand and a shotgun in the other. "I just now got your message, and I came on over."

"No, Jenner, it's okay," Rachel said. "The men are gone."

The sound of sirens came to her from down the street.

"That's the police. I called 'em," Jenner said. "You sure you and Cassidy are okay?"

Rachel glanced down at Cassidy, who clutched at her arm and gave out a little whine.

"We're fine," Rachel said, then thought about the man with the bright blue eyes and the cocky smile, and added, "I think."

Eight

Nathan Garrett, Dogwood County's sheriff, arrived about ten minutes later. He was Constance's boyfriend, but he was more famous in town for being one of three notorious Garrett brothers responsible for relieving the greater Crockett County female population of their virginity in the early nineties. Time had been kind to Sheriff Garrett, and he was nearly as good looking as he had been back in high school, when Rachel had been a freshman and he'd been a senior driving around town in his red Mustang. He'd fallen for her best friend Constance last fall, when he'd come back into town, and now here he was, pencil in hand, ready to take down her statement.

"You're going to think I'm crazy," Rachel began as she pulled Cassidy into her lap and held him there. He was unusually quiet and sat still.

Nathan gave her a crooked grin. "I doubt that," he said. "You'd be surprised what comes through the sheriff's office. Why don't you try me?"

Rachel could see why her best friend was so taken with Nate. He wasn't Crockett County's most eligible bachelor for nothing. He fixed her with warm brown eyes and Rachel decided she might as well try to tell him the truth.

She still couldn't believe what she'd seen—a man rip a door off its hinges and another spray fire from his hands. It all sounded so far-fetched, but Nathan took down the notes calmly, not fazed in the least.

"You going to be okay if I go?" Jenner asked after she'd finished recapping the story. He was still holding his shotgun.

"I'll stay with her," Nathan said.

"Thanks," Rachel said.

"I'll be keeping watch, just in case." Jenner held up the binoculars he had around his chest. For once Rachel didn't mind his snooping.

"Thanks, Jenner."

Two minutes after Jenner left, Rachel heard a car braking hard outside her house. She jumped a little, until she looked out the door and saw Constance's gold Camry.

"I'm too late! Am I too late?" she shouted, running up to the front door. Rachel, still a bit in a daze, didn't have the wherewithal to ask how Constance knew she'd missed something. Constance came running in, breathless, and saw Rachel and Cassidy sitting on the couch.

"Everything's fine," Nathan said, putting away his notepad.

Constance looked at him, then at Rachel, and sagged in relief. "Oh, thank God," she said, putting her hand on her chest. "I thought I might be too late."

Behind her, Dogwood County's only Catholic priest, Father Daniels, strolled in.

"Father Daniels?" asked Rachel, confused. She knew him from his various trips into the hardware store. He was a regular customer and usually spent most of his money buying bullets. Apparently he was an avid hunter. He was also built far less like a priest and more like a burly old marine. He wore his telltale white collar but also usually chomped on a cigar butt and had his white hair shorn close to his head in a flattop.

"Rachel, you need to talk to him," Constance said, nodding toward Father Daniels.

Rachel was puzzled. "I'm not Catholic," she said. "Meaning no disrespect, Father."

"None taken," Father Daniels said.

"And I don't think I'm traumatized enough to need counseling," Rachel said, meaning her run-in with the Mega-Mart men, or whatever they were.

"Don't be so sure about that," Father Daniels said. "The day is young."

Rachel thought again about the man with fire in his hands and shuddered. Maybe she did need to talk to someone.

Cassidy looked at Father Daniels and let out a little high-pitched whine.

"That's right, I've got my eye on you, kiddo,"

Father Daniels said, peering at the toddler and pointing at both his eyes and then pointing back at the boy. "No funny stuff."

"I should've said something earlier," Constance said. "I should've said something."

"What are you talking about?" Rachel asked, wondering what on earth her best friend knew but wasn't telling her.

"You didn't know this was going to happen," Nathan said.

"Yes, but I *should* have known. I should've seen it."

"You know that's not how it works," Father Daniels said.

"Would you please tell me just what the hell you're talking about?" Rachel declared, standing, unable to take it anymore. Everyone seemed to know what was going on except her, and she hated to be the last to know anything.

"Hell!" Cassidy repeated, struggling against Rachel's firm grip.

"No funny business, you!" Father Daniels commanded, and Cassidy suddenly got quiet.

Constance turned to Rachel. "You're not going to believe me."

"She just had a run-in with a pack of demons. I think she'll listen," Father Daniels barked. "Just tell her already."

"Demons?" Rachel echoed, confused. She focused on Constance, waiting for her to explain.

Constance let out a long sigh. "Okay. Well, the thing is, I have the Sight."

"What do you mean the Sight? The Sight of what?"

"I mean visions. They involve demons and angels. Sometimes, even, the devil."

Rachel just stared blankly at her friend. "You have visions of the devil?" She glanced quickly over at Nathan, who was solemn-faced and serious. He was taking this seriously, and not acting like he was going to lock her friend up in a mental institution.

"Before you go calling the psych ward," Father Daniels interrupted, fixing Rachel with a no-nonsense stare, "know that this whole liberal, 'the Bible is figurative' stuff is for the birds. There *is* a devil, and he does have minions, and they work at Mega-Mart."

"I was getting to that part," Constance said, frowning at Father Daniels.

"What? You're pussyfooting around. You've got to get *right to the point.*" Father Daniels smacked one fist into his open palm. "What's with all this explaining and talking, anyway—I say we just get some guns and go to the store and blow them all back to hell."

Rachel's mouth had slipped into slack-jawed surprise. She realized she was gaping and tried to get hold of herself. She knew Father Daniels was a little rough around the edges, but she had never heard him talk about blowing people to hell. It was a little shocking.

"Father, I'm *handling* this," Constance said, and turned back to Rachel. Rachel met her eyes, hoping for some kind of explanation. Any kind of explanation that made sense.

"I know this sounds crazy. I didn't believe it for myself, but it's true. Remember Jimmy?" Constance asked Rachel, referring to her husband, who was murdered last fall. "He was killed by a demon. Because they were trying to get to me. Because I have the Sight."

Rachel looked at her best friend since preschool as if she'd just grown horns and a tail. "You're saying you're a psychic. Like your *mother*?" Constance's mother, Abigail, had been claiming to have visions since the girls were about five. She insisted Elvis was alive and selling antique guns at a shop in Albuquerque. For most of their lives, Rachel and Constance had agreed her mother was likely just doing it for attention, nothing more. Now, suddenly, Constance was buying into ESP?

"She does have the Sight, but it's limited. I can see much more." Constance was as serious as Rachel had ever seen her. And Rachel had known Constance since she was in diapers. The girl couldn't tell a lie without playing with her hair, a telltale sign she was fibbing. She was more honest than George Washington and his cherry tree. She didn't play practical jokes, either. What she was saying, she believed.

"Dogwood County is a battleground of sorts," Father Daniels said, piping up again. "For good and evil."

Rachel let this sink in. She should be shocked, or

at the very least skeptical, but suddenly it all seemed to make sense. Dogwood always had its share of oddball stories, and just plain oddballs. Adding demons and angels to the mix seemed to make perfect sense. Then she thought about the Mega-Mart man who managed to throw fire from his hands.

"So the men from Mega-Mart . . ." Rachel said, connecting the dots.

"Are demons," Father Daniels said.

Rachel just shook her head slowly and whistled. "I *knew* that store was evil."

"Even more evil than you know," Father Daniels agreed.

Father Daniels picked up a photograph on her mantel showing Rachel, Kevin, and Cassidy last Christmas. He studied it, then put it back down.

"Okay, say that, just for kicks, I believe that the Mega-Mart guys are demons working for Satan," Rachel said. "Why are they after me?"

"They're not," Constance said. "They're after Kevin. I saw it in a vision just this afternoon. I called as soon as I saw it, but I should've come earlier. I didn't know you were in danger. I thought I had time."

"What about Kevin? Do you know where he is? Is he hurt?"

"He's not hurt."

Rachel's shoulders sagged in relief.

"But . . ." Constance swallowed. "But, Rachel, he's not who you think he is. He's not Kevin Farnsworth from high school."

"You can say that again," Father Daniels said.

"What do you mean he's not Kevin?" Rachel snapped. She was getting tired of hearing this. What did it mean? "I've been married to him for ten years. I think I should know who I'm married to."

"Rachel," Constance said, putting her hand on top of her friend's. "I think your husband is a demon, too."

"We *know* he is," Father Daniels corrected.

Rachel blinked twice. "Well, I know he's a first-rate jerk, but I've never heard him be called a demon before."

"Rachel," Constance said, face deadly serious. "I'm not kidding around. I saw him in a vision. He's not *human*."

Rachel faltered a little, unsure, since her friend seemed so certain. "You have to be wrong," she said, finally. "He's not a monster."

"He's taken human form," Constance said. "A lot of them do that. He's been hiding here, in Kevin's life, for the last five years. He's been hiding because there are others looking for him. Like the ones who came to your house today. He's a Sloth demon."

"He's not slothful," Rachel cried. "He has clinical depression."

"All Sloth demons do," Father Daniels said.

"That's ridiculous," Rachel said, but her confidence was fading. And Kevin certainly wasn't there to defend himself.

"In my vision, I saw that the real Kevin had been killed five years ago, the day he was at that conference. That's where Pan found him. The demon who took his place."

Rachel went stock-still. Five years ago. The conference. The time when everything about Kevin changed. So he hadn't had an affair. He'd been taken over by someone else. It would explain so much—such as how Kevin seemed like another person right after that. How he withdrew into himself, and became lifeless and distant. Rachel allowed herself to start to believe for a fraction of a second.

Maybe there was something otherworldy about Kevin. A dozen memories hit her all at once. Like that time the barbecue pit went up in flames last summer when he was standing right in front of it and Kevin didn't get even so much as his eyebrows singed. He'd said he'd been lucky then. But maybe it was more than luck.

But, no. It wasn't possible. It couldn't be true. She had a life with Kevin. Not always a happy one, but a life. And how could she have lived with a monster for five years and not noticed? It was just too far-fetched. They had a relationship. They had a house. And they had a child.

The world skidded to a stop as she glanced at Cassidy. They had a *child*.

"Are you saying that Cassidy is a-a . . ." Rachel stuttered.

"You guessed it," Father Daniels said, nodding.

"Da! Mon!" Cassidy blurted, pumping both tiny fists in the air. He burped then, and a tiny tendril of smoke came out, like he was exhaling a cigarette.

Rachel, thinking she'd imagined it, leaned in closer.

"Watch out!" shouted Father Daniels suddenly, as he yanked her hard backward. "Kid's gonna blow!"

That's when Cassidy burped again, but this time a flame shot out, like he was a fire eater at a traveling carnival. It shot five feet straight across her kitchen, nearly licking her curtains and singeing one of her red-cherry-print tea towels.

Nine

"She's taking the news really well," Gabriel Too said, watching as Rachel whipped her baby boy into her arms and sprinted him to the bathroom where she doused him with cold water from the shower. He and Frank the New were sitting on the very top of an oak tree across the street from Rachel's house.

"Are you serious?" Frank the New said. "Are we watching the same woman? She's clearly having a freak-out."

"Well, I would, too, if I saw my toddler spit fire. Oh, dear. I hope she's not going to drown him," Gabriel Too said. "I've seen it before. Like in Salem."

"She's not drowning him," Frank the New said, rolling his eyes. "She's worried he's hurt himself. She's trying to figure out if he's burned."

"Demons don't burn."

"She doesn't know that. And anyway, when was the last time you were on Earth duty? People are more enlightened now. They don't drown demons."

"Well, technically, they can't drown."

"You and the technicalities," Frank the New said, as the two watched Rachel frantically wrap her son in wet towels and put him in the bathtub. Constance, who had been trying to help, was hovering near the bathroom door trying to tell Rachel that her son was fine. Father Daniels was shouting that in no way was it possible for him to actually be burned. Nathan was standing helplessly by the door, watching the commotion and asking if he ought to call the fire department.

"Now do you believe we ought to help? They clearly need some guidance down there," Frank the New said, nodding toward the chaos. "Rachel will need help if she's going to find Kevin."

"Not our problem," Gabriel Too said.

Frank the New glanced back at Rachel, who was now putting Cassidy into a clean T-shirt. "Told you she wasn't going to drown him."

"Yes, well, I guess times change."

"I still say we should've kicked those Mega-Mart demons out ourselves," Frank the New said.

"We're just supposed to watch, and besides, Sam did a fine job."

"That doesn't make me feel better," Frank the New said as he watched Rachel frantically examine every inch of her son.

"You sure we can't go down there? I bet Rachel would feel better if she saw an angel."

"Don't be so sure about that. Angels can freak

people out. Just ask the shepherds on Christmas Eve."

"I thought that was a good story. Good tidings of great joy and all that."

"Not the way I heard it," Gabriel Too said. "Harold the Third had to try ten times before he got a shepherd who didn't run for the hills."

"Harold the Third? I thought those were Herald Angels, you know, *a-l-d*. 'Hark the Herald Angels Sing,' et cetera."

"Common myth," Gabriel Too said. "They're the Harold, *o-l-d*, angels because they're all named Harold."

"Huh," Frank the New muttered. "I guess I learn something new every day." Frank the New glanced down the street.

"Hey—is that Sam sitting there?"

"Where?" exclaimed Gabriel Too, sounding frightened.

"There . . . at the end of the street." Frank the New pointed. "Looks like he's watching Rachel, making sure she's okay."

"Sam doesn't do anything for free," Gabriel Too said, then squinted as he put his hand up to shield his eyes from the sun. "Oh, geez. You're right. It is Sam! Quick, we better hide." Gabriel Too glanced quickly around, looking for a hiding place.

"You said that when Sam first came. Are you afraid of him or something?"

"He's only a killing machine. He knows a hundred ways to destroy you, and that's just with his thumb and pinky."

"So if he's so dangerous, why don't we just take him out right now?"

Gabriel Too, mouth slack, stared at Frank the New. "Did you hear anything I said about him being a lethal weapon? Anything?" Gabriel Too's voice went a little higher, the hint of fear in it.

Frank the New frowned and studied Gabriel Too's face. "How did you get your wings again?"

"Not by committing suicide by throwing myself at a fallen Wrath angel, that's for sure," Gabriel Too said.

"No, seriously. I vanquished the Antichrist. What did you do?"

Gabriel Too stuck his hands in his pockets and mumbled something to his feet.

"What was that?"

"I *said* I transcribed a hundred copies of the Old Testament. By hand."

Frank the New blinked twice. "You were a *monk*?"

"Second century," Gabriel Too clarified.

"You didn't kill any demons."

"No."

"Or fight evil?"

"The evil of illiteracy," Gabriel Too said.

Frank the New shook his head slowly as if he couldn't believe it.

"Hey—I had to do all that writing by candle-light. We didn't have electricity back then. It was hard on the eyes. Besides, it was good training for my current work—taking notes." Gabriel Too held up his yellow legal notepad.

"Oh, brother," Frank the New said, rolling his eyes. "No wonder you are such a sissy."

"I am not."

"You are. You won't even take on a *fallen angel*. He doesn't even have wings."

Gabriel Too went stock-still with fear. "Oh, I think he looked at me— He looked at me!" Gabriel Too was now in full-on panic mode. "Come on, we've got to hide—*now*."

Frank the New shook his head slowly. "You are such a monk."

Ten

After Rachel had poured enough water on Cassidy to irrigate a small farm, she calmed down to the point that Constance and Nathan could get her to sit on the couch. She watched as Father Daniels wrapped her son in a white linen cloth.

"Won't hurt him," he explained. "But will put a curb on the fire breathing. Should've done it earlier, but didn't realize he was that kind of demon."

"There are different kinds?"

"Oh, sure. Mostly, they're divided into the seven deadly sins, but each demon has a unique set of powers. Some breathe fire. Others fly. There are lots of powers and some have a lot and others have a few. Just depends."

"Oh," Rachel said, her head still a little foggy. She still wasn't sure she was processing all this. On the one hand, she'd always known her son was different. She just never thought he was *this* different.

"I know this is hard to take in," Constance said.

"Oh, stop handling her with kid gloves," Father Daniels scoffed. "She can take it." He held Cassidy in his lap, and sat across from Rachel. "Okay. You're tough. You've got to hold yourself together."

Rachel nodded.

"The only thing this boy has on earth right now is you, and if you break down, he's a goner, okay?"

Rachel nodded again. "But what am I supposed to do? I can't raise a demon. I don't even know what to do with one."

"Well, then, kill him."

"What?" Rachel cried, shocked, as she leapt to her feet. "No."

"Fastest way to get rid of a demon, and believe me, if you think he's a handful of trouble right now, wait until he's a teenager. Might as well just burn the town down in advance."

"Father, if you even *mention* the thought of harming a single hair on my son's head, I *will* kick you out of my house." Rachel set her mouth in a grim line.

"Father!" exclaimed Constance.

"What? I'm just helping her set priorities. Now she knows the boy is still her son, whether or not he's half demon. I was just reminding her of what's important."

"I don't need reminding," Rachel snapped, her anger slow to drain away.

"Everybody needs reminding, sister," Father Daniels said.

"You could've done that in a nicer way," Constance

chided, as she reeled Rachel back in and guided her back to her seat.

"Yeah, well, I'm not nice." Father Daniels chomped on his cigar. "Anyway, nobody's killing anybody." He gave a meaningful look to Cassidy. "Yet," he added.

"So what do I do?"

"Since he *is* half human, we can try to train him to fight the demon side of his personality and hope he doesn't grow up to be a monster."

"You're saying he has an angel on one shoulder and a devil on the other?" Rachel asked, hugging Cassidy tightly.

"More like two devils, but maybe one isn't as bad as the other," Father Daniels said.

Rachel slumped down onto the couch and put her chin on Cassidy's head. "How did this happen? I just don't know how this happened."

"You married a demon is how it happened," Father Daniels said. "Happens way more often than you think."

"Father—how about a little tact?" Nathan suggested.

"Tact is for sissies. There's no time for tact. We're in the war of good versus evil. Man up!"

Nathan rolled his eyes.

"Can we exorcise Kevin's half?" Rachel asked.

"Not without killing Cassidy," Father Daniels said. "But it would help to know what kind of powers Kevin has. If we could find him and he'd tell us, then it would help us know how to go about fighting Cassidy's evil half. Not to mention, we should figure out who's after Kevin and why, and whether or not they'll be back for you or the boy."

Rachel stuffed down the panic in her throat and focused on Father Daniels. "So, finding Kevin would be a good thing for Cassidy?"

"Could only help," Father Daniels said.

Rachel was not the kind of woman to sit idly by and wait for fate to sort itself out. If God saw fit to throw her a curveball in the form of a half-demon son, a husband demon on the run, and the kitchen sink while He was at it, she wasn't about to take it lying down.

"Where are you going?" Constance asked, worried, as Rachel turned abruptly and headed for her front door.

"Just stay and watch Cassidy," Rachel said. "And don't let Father Daniels lay a finger on him."

"I'm not going to hurt him!" Father Daniels shouted back. "Geez!"

"And keep Cassidy away from the curtains," Rachel called, jumping into the driver's seat of her minivan.

"Rachel—where are you going? You need to think about this. If you know where Kevin is, then we should all go. It could be dangerous and—" Nathan hadn't finished his sentence before Rachel had turned over the ignition and was backing out of the drive.

"Don't worry—I'll be fine," Rachel shouted back. "I'll call you if I find anything."

"Rachel! Rachel, *wait*," Constance yelled. "Where are you going?"

Rachel hadn't even gotten to the end of her street before her cell phone lit up. Constance was calling. Rachel pressed the ignore button and kept driving. She wasn't going to let Mega-Mart get away with both pushing her father's hardware store out of business *and* being the epicenter of evil in Dogwood County. She was going to go there to get some answers. She was so intent on the drive, she didn't notice Sam, on his motorcycle, following behind her.

A few minutes later Rachel swung her minivan into the Mega-Mart parking lot, under the garish blue and white sign that was big enough and tall enough to be seen from the Interstate, and parked at the closest space she could find, about eight rows from the door. By the looks of the parking lot, nearly the entire population of Dogwood County was inside the store, which explained why sales at her hardware store had been dropping by leaps and bounds all year. She looked at the giant cinder-block building with new eyes. She'd always hated it, but now that she knew true evil lurked there, she half-expected to see a giant 666 pop up on the forehead of Mega-Mart's mascot—the enormous smiley bear face that sat on top of the building. She looked at the huge yellow face for a second or two, but no horns appeared on it. She wondered for a split second if it was a good idea to go in there alone. Rachel quickly pushed away her doubts. What were they going to do to her with a store full of witnesses?

She swung open her door and put her purse resolutely over her shoulder. She was going to march in there and demand some answers. She didn't know how she was going to get them, but she'd figure that out as she went. Rachel walked past a pimply kid in the parking lot, wearing a Mega-Mart blue vest, who was gathering carts. He let several of them slip out of his hands and bump into a new SUV parked near the door, and Rachel thought he did it on purpose. She kept walking, and sucked in a deep breath as she followed a blue-haired woman through the automatic doors. She'd never been inside, as she'd kept her promise never to set foot on the property that every year ate away a little bit more of her family business. Immediately she was struck by the massiveness of the place and the glaring fluorescent lights. Once she managed to adjust to the wattage, she began noticing all the neon yellow smiley faces.

"Nineteen ninety-nine for a full wrench and socket set?" Rachel cried, running to a nearby display. "How can they *do* this?"

She glanced up and saw one of the men who'd come to her house earlier that afternoon. He was riding a forklift carrying giant boxes of Pampers, and stopped it suddenly, glaring at her with unabashed surprise. She dropped the wrench set and started heading toward him. Instead of standing his ground, he abruptly hopped off his forklift, abandoning the diapers, and walked quickly toward the back of the store. Without thinking about it, she followed him down the baby wipes aisle, trying not to notice the fact that the supersized box of wipes was cheaper than it was at Kroger, where she normally shopped.

Rachel kept losing him and then finding him, weaving in and out of one aisle after another, until she nearly ran smack dab into a woman and her shopping cart.

Rachel was in mid-apology when she realized the woman was her mother.

"Mama! What are you *doing* here?" Rachel demanded. Of all the people she expected to run into at Mega-Mart, her own mother was not one of them. Gladys, who had the good sense to look guilty, blushed.

"How can I resist a giant tub of popcorn for a dollar ninety-nine?" she asked, holding up a big silver tin from the cart, which was overflowing with other odds and ends, including the new wrench set.

"Mom! Wrenches and sockets? You can get this at the hardware store," Rachel said, picking up the pack.

"Yes, but for nineteen ninety-nine?" her mother asked, arching her eyebrow.

"That's not the point. I'd expect a little loyalty. What would Daddy say if he were still alive?"

"Well, he's not here, so I don't know." Her mother eyed Rachel's empty arms. "Where's Cassidy? Has that no-good Kevin finally come home?"

"No, he hasn't. Cassidy is with Constance." Rachel glanced up and saw that the Mega-Mart employee she'd been chasing had ducked down the sporting goods aisle. "I've got to go, Mama. I'll explain later."

With that, she left her mother and turned the corner at kids' bicycles. She came face-to-face with her husband, Kevin, who was wearing the Mega-Mart employee uniform while sitting slouched against a box of spare bike tires and smoking a cigarette.

Kevin, plainly shocked, let his mouth slide open into an O and didn't even have the chance to put down his smoke before Rachel lunged.

"You no-good piece of . . ." Rachel hissed, fingernails out and sharp. Kevin jumped up, dropping his cigarette. He threw up a protective hand, sending her flying back without actually laying a finger on her. She tumbled into a giant stand of Nerf footballs, knocking them over and sending neon green and pink footballs bouncing in every direction. She was about to go rolling after them into the center aisle when two strong hands grabbed her quickly and set her straight on her feet. She whipped around in time to see Sam. He was wearing the same snug black T-shirt and jeans, and the same slight frown.

"Are you always in trouble? Or is this just an unusual day for you?" he asked her, setting her back up on her feet.

Before Rachel could answer, Sam had swept by her, putting his body between her and Kevin.

"Do yourself a favor," Sam growled, locking eyes with Kevin. "Don't run."

Kevin didn't look like he was planning to run. Casually, he stepped on his still smoldering cigarette and put both hands in his pockets.

"It took long enough for you to find me," he told Sam, sounding altogether not as scared as he should be.

"I have some questions for you, too, whoever you are," Rachel sputtered, still reeling in shock from being flung aside like a sack of potatoes. "Like, for starters, if you could fling me across the room, why the hell didn't you fix our running toilet? It's been running for three years."

Kevin and Sam ignored Rachel.

"You're coming with me," Sam said, taking a small step toward Kevin.

"Okay, see, that's where I think you're wrong," Kevin said.

Before Kevin had finished his sentence, Sam had him by the throat and was holding him high, his head banging into a big red Huffy hanging from the ceiling and his feet kicking air. Kevin struggled against the grip, grabbing Sam's wrist with both hands. Kevin concentrated a moment and then breathed a stream of fire straight out of his mouth. Just like Cassidy. Sam, however, didn't flinch.

"Demon fire doesn't work on me anymore," Sam said, a slow smile working the corners of his mouth. Rachel gave Sam a hard look. So he knew about the Mega-Mart demons and was immune to fire? Just who—or *what*—was he? "Come on. I'm taking you in. You can come quietly, or I send you right back to hell now." Sam took a holy wafer out of his pocket and waved it in front of Kevin's face.

"Wait!" Kevin wheezed. "I've got a deal for you. I've got information on someone you're dying to collar."

That sounded more like the Kevin Rachel knew. He was always looking after himself, and always trying to make deals, which is why he hadn't taken out the garbage in three years. He was always promising to do other things instead, like wash out the gutters or change Cassidy's diapers for a week. Naturally, he never got around to fulfilling those promises.

"Don't believe him," Rachel said, jabbing her finger in her husband's blue Mega-Mart vest.

"You're lying," Sam said flatly, and started to drag Kevin away.

"I'm not—I'm not, I swear. It's Azazel I'm talking about."

Sam stopped in his tracks. He hauled Kevin up by one arm so they were eye to eye. "The fallen angel that Satan has been looking for for centuries? The one who has topped his most-wanted list for a thousand years? *That* Azazel?"

"The same. I know where he is. You can bring him in. Think about the satisfaction of that!"

"Tell me," Sam said, shaking Kevin hard.

"Not here," Kevin said. "Too many listeners. Meet me at Branson's in an hour. I'll tell you there.

Here, I'll give you collateral." He reached up his sleeve and took out a small silver bracelet lined with three red rubies. "You keep this and we'll meet up at Branson's."

Sam seemed to consider the bracelet. He took it, and then set Kevin down. "Fine," he said. "Branson's. Not an hour. Twenty minutes."

Rachel did a double take. "Are you serious? You're just going to let the little rat go? We can't trust him."

Sam said nothing, his eyes raised and fixed on a point somewhere above her left shoulder. Rachel turned in time to see Bill, the man who'd just nearly set fire to her living room, heading up the aisle along with three new employees she hadn't seen before. They all looked to be barely out of their teens, with shaggy hair in their eyes and acne on their faces. Bill's glance flicked briefly to Rachel before settling on Sam.

"Sam," Bill said, giving him a slow smile that didn't quite reach his eyes. Beside her, Sam stiffened a little but said nothing.

The three employees behind Bill fanned out, effectively blocking the aisle. She turned around to see if Kevin was going to join them, but discovered he'd up and disappeared—into thin air.

"I'm surprised to find you here," Bill said now, his face an emotionless mask. Something about the dull blackness of his eyes made Rachel's skin crawl. And the adolescent thugs on either side of him didn't look any friendlier. "Does this mean you're finally going to choose sides?"

Rachel glanced at Sam, watching his expression carefully. Just who—or what—was he? "No," Sam said, voice casual but stance tense.

"Oh, Sam, that's disappointing," Bill said, making a clucking sound with his tongue. "Why not? You're already doing Satan's bidding."

"I work for myself," Sam ground out.

Bill sent him a dubious look. "Whatever you say." Bill spread out his hands. "Well, you know the rules, then. If you're not with us, you're against us."

"There are a lot of witnesses for a petty grudge match," Sam said. His eyes rocked back and forth to the Mega-Mart shoppers who were pacing up and down the main aisle behind Bill.

"Maybe you should've worried about collateral damage *before* you came here."

Sam casually stepped in front of Rachel, putting his body between her and the Mega-Mart thugs. Rachel bristled a little. She was growing tired of the testosterone overload. Besides, they didn't have time for boyish spitting matches. Not when her soon-to-be ex-husband was on the run.

"Free bicycles!" she shouted at the top of her lungs. "Aisle nineteen! Get all the free bicycles you want while they last."

Both Bill and Sam whipped around, and she could feel their curious stares boring into her, but she didn't care. She just kept shouting. Within seconds, her plan worked, and the aisle was flooded with greedy shoppers looking for a steal. There wasn't room enough to walk, much less fight, with all the customers and their carts crammed in, trying to yank bicycles off the walls.

"Wait—no!" Bill shouted, trying to stop the customers from raiding the sporting goods aisle. There were just too many of them. Even his adolescent helpers couldn't stop the onslaught. "These aren't free!"

"Come on, let's go," Rachel said, tugging on Sam's arm. They pushed their way through the back of the aisle, and slipped out around the bend and through an emergency exit door before Bill or his helpers could stop them.

Sam had her by the wrist and was tugging her in the direction of a black Harley parked on the sidewalk next to a big display of bottled water.

"Whoa—whoa, I'm not going anywhere with you until you tell me just who the hell you are," Rachel demanded, digging in her heels.

"I used to be a good guy," he said.

"And now?"

"Not so much," Sam said. He glanced backward as two Mega-Mart thugs came rushing out of the store. "You can come with me and live, or stay and die," he said flatly.

Given the choice, she jumped on the back of his motorcycle.

"No helmet?" she asked him.

"You won't need it," Sam said, sounding confident as he turned over the ignition and roared out of the Mega-Mart parking lot.

Eleven

Sam revved his engine and pushed it up to a hundred and twenty miles an hour, even as the demons behind them piled into a car and tried to keep up. He didn't know how long they'd stay interested, but he didn't want to find out, either.

The demons behind him howled as he pushed the cycle farther away from them. He was losing them. Good. He hunkered down, the wind whipping in his face, and for a second, remembered what it was like to fly. He pushed the cycle harder and felt Rachel's arms instinctively tighten around his waist, bringing him back down to earth. But he didn't mind. He liked the feeling of her and felt a kind of attraction that he hadn't felt in centuries—if ever. The girl at the hardware store had been dead wrong. Rachel was anything but homely. She was beautiful. The kind of beautiful that came around maybe once every few hundred years.

Sam's attention was drawn back to the road

where a demon materialized in front of them. A tele-porter! Only Sam could see it, as it was wearing a cloak to make it invisible to human eyes. The demon grew rapidly in front of them, the size of its jaws mutating to ridiculous proportions. If they kept on this same path, they'd be swallowed whole.

Inwardly, Sam cursed, then slammed on the brakes, turning the motorcycle away from the wait-ing jaws of the demon. Instantly the bike went down on its side. Rachel screamed in fear. Her leg would've been crushed, but Sam was too quick. He whipped her into his arms, curled his body around hers, and rolled deftly along the asphalt into the woods. He still had enough strength to keep her safe.

They came to a stop in the brush along the side of the road, and Sam looked up in time to see his mo-torcycle speed into the waiting mouth of the demon. His radiator was filled with holy water for just this sort of predicament, and when the demon snapped its jaws shut, his eyes bugged out and he started to smoke. His skin began to bubble, and within sec-onds he'd blown up like an overfilled water balloon. Sam glanced backward. The other demons who'd been following them had watched their partner ex-plode and decided to call off their chase. Demons were nothing if not predictable. They were easily spooked.

"They're gone," Sam told Rachel, who sat up, dazed, a small twig in her hair.

"Who's gone?" Rachel echoed. "And what the hell just happened?"

In the tumble, her sundress had blown upward, revealing all of her calf and most of her thigh, and Rachel was too stunned to notice. He was gripped by the sudden desire to reach out and touch the skin above her knee, wanting to see if it was as soft as it looked.

"How are you not dead?" she asked, amazed, poking at his chest and his arms. "There's barely a scratch on you. And how am I not dead, either?" She patted herself, looking for bruises or wounds, and found none. She met his gaze, her brown eyes questioning. "What *are* you? Because you're not human. That much is for sure." She stood on unsteady legs, smoothing out her dress as she put a little distance between them. "Are you a demon, too? Because I've had my fill of those things." Rachel backed away a step or two, holding up her hands and making a cross with two fingers.

"I'm not a demon," Sam said calmly.

"Then what are you?"

"I am—was—an angel."

She glanced at the tattoo on his arm, took in his jeans and black shirt and ruffled dark hair, and then threw back her head and laughed.

"You? An angel?" she managed to sputter as she gasped for air. "An angel!"

"Why is that so funny?"

Rachel bent over and slapped her knee. "Angel!"

"Fallen," he corrected.

Rachel's laughter died out. "Fallen angel? Like Satan?"

A frown flit across Sam's face. "Not exactly," he said.

"So you're a *good* fallen angel? What's that? Like a used car salesman with a conscience?"

An amused look crossed his face. "Something like that."

Rachel's shoulders relaxed some. Her dark brown hair was a bit of a mess—but a sexy mess—the wind having whipped it out of her ponytail. He had the strong urge to try kissing her again, but he knew she wouldn't like that. Not one bit. And the fact that she wouldn't made him want to do it all the more.

She gave him an assessing look.

"So what do you want with Kevin?"

"Satan will pay me for his return," Sam said.

"So you do work for Satan."

"I work for myself," Sam growled.

"Touchy for a guy who lost his wings," Rachel said. "So why do you keep saving me?"

Sam considered this a moment. Even he wasn't sure. "Old habits," he said, even though this wasn't true. He couldn't very well tell her that he hadn't met a woman like her since being marooned on earth.

She nodded. "Well, I guess I should be grateful for those, then," she said, and rubbed her neck. "You could make the landing a little softer next time, though."

Sam couldn't help himself. He laughed.

"So, how are we going to find my no-good husband?" Rachel asked him.

"What do you mean 'we'? We're not going to do anything." Did this woman never learn? This game was dangerous. Sam suddenly grew serious.

"Of course we are. I need to see him. I'm not going to let you go without me."

Sam set his mouth in a thin line. "You most certainly will." He focused as much of his persuasive energy as he could in her direction. But none of it seemed to work.

"I'm afraid you don't know me that well," Rachel said without blinking an eye. "But I'm not easily intimidated. I grew up with older brothers, and I'm not at all scared of your tough guy act."

Sam just shook his head. He was completely at a loss. He didn't know what to do with her.

"But it's too dangerous," Sam said.

"I held my own at the Mega-Mart," Rachel said, raising her chin a little in defiance.

"You were lucky, that's all. Demons are not to be played with. Drawing all those people could've backfired, you know. Bill could've killed them all without another thought."

By the look on her face, Rachel hadn't thought about that. "Well, he didn't, and we got out of there, and I'd say it was quick thinking," Rachel added swiftly. "Now, are you going to keep lecturing me, or are we going to go after my husband?"

"We don't need to find him. He'll be at Branson's, like he said."

"How can you possibly believe what he said?"

"See this?" Sam asked, holding up the ruby brace-let. "It's like a demon's social security card, only much more important. He can't go anywhere in the demon world without it. And if he doesn't get it back within five hours, he'll start to completely fade from this world."

"Hmpf," Rachel grunted, unconvinced. "So fine, we go to Branson's. I've always wanted to see the inside of a biker bar."

"*We* aren't going anywhere," Sam said. "You are going home. *I'm* going to Branson's."

"You can't be serious."

"This isn't up for discussion," Sam said, eyes hard and determined.

"I know that look," Rachel said. "It's the same one my brothers got when they were about to stuff me into a closet to keep me from following them outside to their boys-only treehouse. I'm guessing you're not above stuffing me into a closet somewhere?"

"Now you're catching on."

Rachel fell silent and crossed her arms grump-ily across her chest.

Sam glanced at the sky, as if reading the time. "I have to go," he said.

"Sure, fine. Leave me in the middle of nowhere. It's only a mild step down from a closet."

Sam hesitated. He didn't like the idea of leaving Rachel alone, and then he caught himself. She wasn't his problem. She was interesting, no doubt, but he didn't have time for hobbies. He had a job to do.

Still, he found himself relieved when he saw, far

in the distance, a sheriff's truck heading their way. He focused and saw it was Sheriff Nathan Garrett behind the wheel. He wasn't there by accident, Sam deduced in a quick read of his face. He listened hard and heard Nathan on his cell phone, telling Constance he'd found Rachel.

"Sheriff is coming to pick you up," he said.

"How do you know that?" Rachel stared where he had looked, but she couldn't see anything.

"Constance told him where you'd be," Sam said, eavesdropping on the conversation some more.

"The Sight," Rachel said, sounding a little awed. "I'll be damned, she *does* have it."

"Tell him to take you to your minivan at Mega-Mart and keep him close for a couple of days," Sam said. "I don't think the demons will try anything more in daylight, but nighttime is a different story. Don't let him take you home. Go to Constance's house. Or a hotel. Or, better yet, a church. And once you get there, you stay there."

"But—"

"Don't argue," Sam said. "I've got to go."

And with that, he disappeared in a blur, speeding down the road on foot, faster than most cars, leaving Rachel behind him, her mouth slack in surprise.

Sam spent the entire run over to Branson's thinking about Rachel.

He couldn't remember the last time someone hadn't just bent to his will automatically. Rachel wasn't going to bend to anyone's will. Not his, and he guessed not that demon's she'd been married to, either. Sam smiled to himself. Pan had been in well over his head choosing Rachel's life to jump into. He was guessing he hadn't had an easy time of it these last five years. He smiled wider.

Then he thought of her stomping into Mega-Mart, and the smile on his face disappeared. That priest she'd been talking to should've kept her away from there. She had no idea of the kind of danger she was facing. Of course, he doubted that knowing would prevent her from doing what she felt needed to be done. Rachel had that unique combination of honest determination and bravery that was uncommon among angels and even rarer in humans.

It was that spark that drew Sam to her. She reminded him of the better part of human nature, the one worth protecting.

Of course, the last thing Sam needed right now was a distraction. He should be hunting Azazel, not saving damsels. No matter how bewitching they were.

He slowed his speed as he approached the bar, and walked straight to the entrance at a human's pace. Inside, the bar was dark and smoky, as usual. Sam didn't even need to blink before his eyes had adjusted to the light, one of his many leftover powers. Angels had to see in the dark, because that's usually where demons hid.

He smelled Kevin before he saw him, his nose taking his eyes to the corner of the bar, where

Kevin sat very still in a booth in the corner, a barely touched beer in front of him. Kevin wasn't the only demon in the place. There were two others holed up in the corner near the pool tables swindling money from two pretty angry-looking bikers.

On his way in, Sam gave a nod to J.D., who nodded back. He tilted his head over to where Kevin was sitting. Sam gave J.D. a slight nod.

Kevin glanced up at Sam, relief all over his face, and that could mean only one of two things: either he was just plain dumb, or he was being hunted by something much more dangerous than Sam.

"I knew you'd show," Kevin said, relief in his voice as he nodded for Sam to take a seat. "You're the only one who can help me."

"Who said anything about helping you?" Sam growled. Doing favors for demons rubbed Sam the wrong way.

"You help me, and I help you," Kevin said evenly, flashing a knowing smile.

Sam considered the strong possibility that the demon was bluffing. Demons weren't known for honesty.

"You don't know anything about Azazel," Sam said, standing up and preparing to leave.

"Wait," Kevin said, reaching out faster than Sam expected and grabbing his arm. "That's why they're after me, or didn't you know? I found his tomb. I know where he's buried."

"Maybe he should stay buried," Sam said. "He's a very dangerous Fallen."

It was no accident he was at the top of Satan's most-wanted list. Before he lost his wings, Azazel had designs on raising a mutant army and taking on Heaven *and* Hell. He almost succeeded.

"You could bring him in," Kevin said. "Complete your record. No one has ever gotten him before. You'd have Satan's eternal gratitude. Maybe he'd set you free—give you what you want—eternal life without the strings."

Sam waited a beat or two, considering.

"All you have to do is not turn me in, and I'll give you everything you need to know."

"I'll think about it."

"You'll *think* about it? Come on, I need a commitment."

"That's the best you're going to get." Sam stood as if to leave, and Kevin frantically grabbed at his arm.

"Wait, no wait, I guess it will do. Fine. My wife Rachel carries the coordinates of Azazel's pit. She doesn't know she has them, but she keeps them with her at all times." Kevin's eyes stretched to the back of the bar, and suddenly he went white, the words drying up on his tongue. "She found me," he spat in a low whisper. "You have to protect me."

Sam turned slowly, but he didn't see anything, and more important, he didn't smell brimstone or rot, either, which meant it was one of the good guys, or something very different altogether.

"Protect you from what?" Sam asked, still looking. That's when he happened to catch a glimpse of Rachel Farnsworth standing near the bar, blinking as her eyes adjusted to the dim interior lights.

"You can't mean her . . ." Sam mused, as his eyes were drawn to her clingy sundress and strappy sandals. Her bright yellow dress and fresh, clean scent were attracting more than his attention, he noticed, as several of the bearded bikers near the bar gave her a slow once-over. How did she get here? He specifically told her to not to follow him, and yet here she was. In clear defiance of everything he'd said.

On the other side of the room, the two demons who'd been pool sharking took notice of Rachel for the first time, and Sam didn't like the way they were looking at her. He felt his stomach flip. She was in danger here.

He glanced over at J.D., who was busy pouring whiskey for the crowd on the other side of the bar. He was too distracted to notice or look out for Rachel.

Sam turned back to Kevin, but he was already on his feet, heading toward the restrooms in the back.

"Wait!" Sam leapt up, too, deciding to let Rachel fend for herself for the next minute. Surely she wouldn't get into too much trouble in sixty seconds. It was only when he reached the restroom door that he felt something cold and slick at his feet. He glanced down and saw a trickle of water running past his shoes. Instead of running out of the bathroom, it seemed to be running to it.

Odd. A water demon, perhaps? He thought they were only legend. It was rumored they were among the oldest kinds of demons, but when Satan took over the demon army he had all of them purged. Fire was his weapon of choice.

Sam swung open the bathroom door in time to see Kevin trying to scuttle out the bathroom window. He was almost free, too, when a giant whoosh of water from the toilet under him exploded beneath his feet, sending up a tower of water like a fire hydrant under pressure. A bit of water splashed on Sam, and he noticed with surprise that it was salt water, not regular tap water. Water demon. Definitely.

The tower of salt water swept Kevin off his feet, shot him into the air to the ceiling and then just as quickly sucked him back into the toilet, where he disappeared with a slushy-sounding flush.

"Dammit," Sam cursed, watching his bounty literally slip down the drain. He took a step closer, but the water started to bubble again, and Sam took a step back. He had no experience fighting water demons.

That's when he heard a cry from the bar, and his thoughts flew immediately to Rachel and the two demons who'd been eyeing her entrance earlier. He rushed out of the bathroom, his eyes quickly finding her yellow sundress in the leather-clad crowd. She had a gang of at least six men standing in a semicircle around her, but she didn't look as scared as she ought to be. His muscles tensed as he strode to her, ready to do what it took to get her the hell out of there in one piece. It was only when he was closer that he realized the cry he heard wasn't from Rachel at all, but from one of her onlookers, and that Rachel was putting on some kind of show.

Sam watched in disbelief as Rachel, with one shot glass lined up in front of her, bent over and without using her hands, grabbed hold of the glass with her mouth and gulped down some dangerous-looking amber liquid in one swig. A cheer went up from the crowd and money exchanged hands, and Rachel, a triumphant look on her face, declared, "See? I told you—didn't lose a drop."

One of the tougher-looking guys with a full beard and a chest full of tattoos slapped a twenty-dollar bill on the bar. "Double or nothing?" he offered.

"How about nothing?" Sam growled, grabbing Rachel by the arm and tugging her away from the bar.

"What do you think you're *doing*?" Sam hissed in her ear, angrier than he'd been in decades.

"Looking for *you*," she said, matter-of-factly. "I was just killing time with the regulars until you showed up."

"You could've been hurt."

"By who? Jimmy?" She nodded toward the bearded guy. "He wouldn't hurt a fly. Besides, I can take care of myself." Her brown eyes flashed with a steely resolve. Grudgingly, he had to admit she handled Branson's better than he would've expected.

Most women would've run for the door, not challenged the bar to a drinking contest.

"Where's my no-good, soon-to-be ex-husband? You didn't let him get away, did you?" Rachel asked, her lips set in a determined line.

"Not exactly," Sam said, focusing on her full bottom lip.

A glass crashed to pieces somewhere at the back of the bar. Sam turned in time to see a wall of water splashing out of the bathroom door, sweeping up tables and people in its path like a rolling ocean wave. Sam saw a man try to pop his head up above the water but get quickly sucked back down.

The water demon wasn't satisfied with just Kevin, Sam realized quickly. It planned to drown them all. He glanced at the bar, but J.D. wasn't there. Neither was Lizzy. They were both on their way to the door, having already seen the water even before Sam did. In a perverse showing of joy, J.D. actually pumped one fist in the air as he ran out of the building and shouted "Saint Thomas, here I come!"

Sam grabbed Rachel, pressed her against his chest, and made for the exit with superhuman speed. He didn't care who saw him. It would be the only way to outrun the demon.

Just as he made it to the door, the water lashed out and over, taking out one of the support beams near him, sending half the ceiling crashing down around them. Above their heads, a large metal light fixture fell, and he heard Rachel scream, her eyes wide in terror. Sam kept moving, curling himself protectively around Rachel, and the beam bounced off his back, rolling into the rising waters. In another two steps, they were out the door. Sam whipped Rachel onto a nearby bike, facing him, her legs still wrapped around his waist.

"What just happened?" Rachel asked, dazed.

"Just hold on," Sam commanded as he powered up the motorcycle that wasn't his by simply touching the handlebars. It roared to life and they sped off into the street just as the water crashed out of Branson's, taking out the first row of parked cars and half the driveway.

Twelve

"What in the name of Christmas holly was *that*?" gasped Frank the New as he and Gabriel Too floated high above a completely submerged parking lot.

"Water demon," Gabriel Too said knowingly. "Now this is *really* getting interesting." He quickly grabbed the notepad from his pocket and started scribbling.

"But Rachel . . ."

"She's fine. Sam will take care of her."

"And what about Kevin! It *ate* him. Wasn't he our assignment? What are we supposed to do now?" Frank the New started to pace the empty air.

"Hold onto your tighty whities," Gabriel Too said, holding up his hand. "I've got this covered." He tucked away his notepad and then dug deep into one of his pockets. He pulled out a box of Philadelphia Cream Cheese.

"What are we supposed to do with that?"

"Oops—wrong thing," Gabriel Too said, sheepish, as he dropped the cream cheese back into his pocket and dug around some more. He pulled out a box of paper clips, a small package of Kleenex, and some duct tape. "Nope, nope, nope," he said, putting them all back. He dug deeper, almost up to his armpit, and then pulled out a shiny gold mobile phone. "Ah-ha! Here it is."

"You are a joke," Frank the New said, shaking his head sadly.

Gabriel Too tapped some numbers on the touchscreen keypad and put the phone to his ear.

"Gabriel Too, reporting from the field," he said, looking upward and doing a little salute. "Yes, sir. We found the target, sir. He's been eaten. By a water demon." Gabriel Too paused, listening. "We are positive, sir. It was definitely a water demon. Uh-huh. Yep. Follow Rachel. Yes, we can do that, sir. Right away. Gabriel Too out."

Gabriel Too looked up in the air, saluted, and then hung up the phone and put it back in his pocket.

"What's with the salute?" Frank the New asked.

"Up in heaven, they can see us any time, but when we call, they make a point of pulling us up in the communications room."

"Communications room?"

"It's like *The Situation Room* for CNN, but with more screens."

"There's a place with more screens than *The Situation Room*?"

"Anyway, Peter says we have to follow Rachel

now. But don't worry, we won't get a pay cut for los-ing Kevin."

Gabriel Too started to fly off in the direction Sam and Rachel went. Frank the New followed.

"We get *paid*? I thought this was a volunteer job," Frank said.

"Everybody gets paid—except for candy strip-ers and stay-at-home moms."

"But what do we get paid in?"

"Time off and tickets," Gabriel Too said. He reached into his pocket and pulled out a roll of small golden tickets that, aside from the metallic sheen, looked like the kind you might find coming out of a Skee-Ball machine at Chuck E. Cheese.

"What do you use these for?" Frank the New asked, holding Gabriel Too's roll of tickets in his hand.

"Everything," Gabriel Too said. "You should see the prize room. It's got everything you ever wanted. I'm saving up for a ruby-encrusted Pac-Man arcade machine."

"What are you going to do with that?"

"Put it on my cloud in Heaven. It'll go right in my classic game collection. I already have Atari and Nintendo 64 sets up there."

"They have anything else besides arcade games?"

"Like I said, anything you want."

"A manual that can teach me how to use angel dust?"

"Well, maybe . . . they've got a lot of books." Ga-briel Too paused as if hit by something. "Hey, wait a minute. It's my job to teach you that. And, no, you can't try to figure it out behind my back. And how do you know about angel dust, anyway?"

Frank the New shrugged. "Everybody knows about it."

Gabriel Too let out a long, frustrated sigh. "Okay, fine. I guess we can start with your lessons. Look in the bottom right corner of your left pocket."

Frank the New dug around in his pocket and pulled out a fistful of white dust. "Cool! I am mighty and powerful!" he shouted, waving his fist as the two drifted over a supermarket.

"Careful what you sprinkle that on," Gabriel Too said, a little too late, as chunks of dust fell down into the Safeway parking lot. Below them, a shopping cart sitting in the middle of a parking space suddenly transformed itself into a giant pumpkin carriage with wheels. Melba Bree, an eighty-eight-year-old retiree, stopped in front of the pumpkin and stared for a long while at the giant carriage before she shook her head and sauntered off toward her silver Buick. She thought she would ask her doctor about side effects of that new blood pressure medication he'd given her.

"I told you to watch it!" Gabriel Too scolded as he whipped out more of his angel dust and sprinkled it on the pumpkin. In short order, it had morphed back into a regular shopping cart.

"Sorry," Frank the New said, sounding sheepish as he put the handful of angel dust back in his pocket.

"Be careful with that dust. A little bit of that goes a *long* way. It's extremely concentrated."

"What can it do?"

"Pretty much anything—as long as it's good," Gabriel Too said. "You can't do evil with it, obviously. But you have to concentrate when you use it on what you want it to do, otherwise you're just going to get a bunch of pumpkin carriages, flowers, and bunny rabbits."

"Bunny rabbits?"

"The Easter Bunny was no accident," Gabriel Too said. "Angel dust takes a long time to master. You don't just wake up one day proficient in all angel powers. It takes time."

"How much time?"

"Oh, maybe a century or so."

"A *century*? It's going to take me a *century* to learn how to use angel dust?"

"Give or take a decade," Gabriel Too said. "What? Don't worry. I'm a great teacher. I'll have you in tip-top shape in fifty years or so."

"Fifty *years*?" Frank the New just shook his head. Having just been recently mortal, it still sounded like an awfully long time. "So why don't I at least start practicing now? What can I sprinkle on next?"

"Whoa, whoa, whoa, amigo. What's the rush?" Gabriel Too said, holding up both hands.

"Well, seems like if we're on assignment, maybe I need to know how to use it in case we have to fight a demon or something."

"Fight a *demon*? We're Watcher angels. We *watch*. That's it."

Frank the New rolled his eyes. "So you keep saying."

"Right now we've got to follow Rachel, and it looks like Sam is taking her to church." Gabriel Too nodded downward as Sam pulled into the First Baptist Church's parking lot off Route 9. He parked his motorcycle and then carefully carried Rachel to the front doors.

"Hmpf," grumbled Frank the New. "Can't I just sprinkle *something*?"

"No."

"How about that tree down there?"

"Nope."

"The squirrel?"

"NO. Seriously, put the dust back in your pocket. You're not ready yet."

Frank the New jutted his lower lip out in a pout. "Fine," he sighed. "When will I be ready?"

"When I say so."

"And when is that?"

"When I *say*."

"Now?"

"No."

"How about now?"

"How about you stop asking or I will *never* show you how."

"Fine," Frank the New said, sighing and crossing his arms.

Thirteen

Rachel must have fainted, because one second she was being teleported out of Branson's and the next she was waking up, smothered in something warm that smelled both spicy and sweet, like cinnamon. It took her another second or two before she regained enough of her senses to realize she knew that smell: Sam.

She shot straight up to sitting and realized she had been lying on a hard bench, with Sam's leather coat draped over her front. That's when she saw a giant winged angel hovering above her head and she nearly slid off the bench and onto the floor. She steadied herself on the bench, heart thumping in her chest, as she began to realize the angel wasn't real—it was a statue made of stone. And the bench beneath her wasn't a bench at all but a pew. She was in a church.

"Don't worry," said a low voice in the row behind her. "He won't bite."

She turned and found herself staring into the stark blue eyes of Sam, who was sitting casually, one tattooed arm laid out on the pew, his ankle resting idly on one knee. He didn't look injured, and yet he'd taken the full weight of a metal beam of lights to his head and back, a blow that should've killed him. But there he sat, a smug smile on his face, and not a single scratch on him.

"So you really are an angel," Rachel said, speaking her thoughts out loud. She hadn't truly allowed herself to believe before, but he certainly wasn't human, that was for sure. Human beings didn't move at the speed of light and take steel beams to the head like pillow fights at a slumber party.

"Fallen," Sam corrected.

"So what are you, then? Good or bad?"

"Neither," he said. "Both."

"That certainly doesn't clear things up," she said. Rachel took in Sam's big arms and wavy dark hair and tried to imagine him with wings and a harp. She simply couldn't. Rachel frowned, but Sam's smile only grew bigger. He seemed to be enjoying this. She shifted some, to get a better look at him, and a branch with flower petals fell off her lap.

"Dogwood flowers?" she asked, picking up the small branch.

"They repel demons, just like crosses and the Bible," Sam explained.

Rachel stopped cold. She remembered Kevin's aversion to dogwood blooms, and Cassidy's allergies.

"Do you know the story of the dogwood tree?"

Numbly, Rachel nodded her head. Just about everyone in Dogwood County knew the story. You couldn't go to a festival or church in the spring and not hear the pastor talk about dogwood tree lore.

"Jesus' cross was supposed to be made from a dogwood tree," Rachel said. "But the tree felt badly for having been the means by which Christ died, so Jesus took pity on the tree and said it would no longer grow big enough to make crosses."

"You left out the part of that story where Jesus infused all trees with the power to repel evil. Dogwood tea is lethal to your average demon, and few can tolerate its smell."

Rachel nodded again. "I have a dogwood tree in my front yard, and it didn't keep those men—or whatever they were—out of my house."

"It would have if we had forced them to drink dogwood tea," Sam said. "Aside from that, it's just a small annoyance."

"So why here? Why Dogwood?"

"It's an ancient battlefield," Sam said simply. "There's always going to be a clash of powers here. That's why the dogwoods bloom twice a year."

Rachel remembered that Father Daniels had tried to tell her something of the same sort. She was still finding it hard to believe. The idea of Dogwood, in the middle of nowhere, East Texas, being pivotal in the fight of good versus evil just made no sense. Of course, that was before she'd found out her husband was a demon and the man who'd saved her at least three times in one day was an angel. Or, correction, a *fallen* angel.

"But you're okay with these?" She waved a dog-wood blossom around. Instantly Sam sneezed.

"I'm not as susceptible to them as your garden variety demon," Sam said. "But they're a little like rag-weed to me."

"So you're allergic to dogwood, but you're fine with churches?" Rachel gestured to the crosses around them.

"I haven't fully gone over to the dark side yet. I could still be redeemed," Sam said, a half smile tug-ging at the corner of his lips. It was clear he thought it was a long shot.

"I didn't think there was a Switzerland in the war of good versus evil," Rachel said.

"Just think of me as Geneva, if it makes you feel better."

"So who's after us? Wait, I think I know." Ra-chel thought for a moment, her memory suddenly dredging up a picture of Branson's under water.

"The water? That was a demon?"

Sam nodded.

"Was it . . ." Rachel almost hated to say the name. "Kevin?"

"No," Sam said.

"Oh." Rachel thought about this a moment, not sure if she should feel relieved or not. Still, she was glad her soon-to-be ex hadn't just tried to murder her. "And Kevin? Where is he?"

Sam didn't answer this question right away,

and instead changed the subject. "Are you hungry?"

"Are you trying to distract me?"

"Maybe."

"Well, it won't work. Besides, food can wait. I want some answers."

"I was afraid you would say that." Sam leaned back in the pew and crossed his arms, looking resigned.

"So where is he?"

"I don't know."

"You let him get away?"

"In a manner of speaking," Sam said in an evasive tone, not meeting her eyes.

"Where do we start looking for him?"

"Your guess is as good as mine."

"Are you ever going to give me a straight answer?"

"Probably not."

Rachel blew out a frustrated breath. "Well, I don't get tired of asking questions, you know. I can keep at this all night," she warned him.

"I can keep at this all century," Sam said evenly.

Rachel blinked twice fast, and then gave an appreciative laugh. She knew when she'd been had. "You fallen angels don't play fair."

"We definitely don't," Sam agreed, leaning forward and showing her his even white smile. Between his dazzling grin and his distinctive smell, Rachel was quickly losing her ability to think clearly.

"If you're not going to tell me about Kevin, then you ought to tell me something else."

"Like what?" Sam asked, unfolding his arms and leaning forward.

"Something about you. Like what you can do."

A slight frown creased his forehead. "You don't really want to know that."

"Oh, yes, I do," Rachel said. "I know you can run fast, and you're strong, but *how* fast? And *how* strong?"

"Fast enough," Sam said. "Strong enough."

"Show me." Rachel gave Sam an expectant look, and he seemed to waver a second. She pounced on his hesitation. "What? Are you scared you aren't as strong or fast as I think you are?"

The dare seemed to work. Sam's blue eyes grew serious.

"Is this"—he started, and then, before he even completed his sentence, he was on the other side of the room, at the top of the altar, leaning against the podium—"fast enough?"

Rachel had seen only the hint of a blur and then he was on the other side of the room. So she hadn't imagined it at Branson's. When he'd picked her up, he'd been so fast, he'd flown from one side of the room to the other.

"And what about—"

"Strength?" he finished for her, and suddenly Rachel was suspended six feet in the air, Sam having rushed back across the church in a blink and lifted up the pew she was sitting on, holding it casually with one hand, looking as if the solid oak pew and her added weight caused him no more trouble than lifting a roll of paper towels.

"Okay, I'm convinced," Rachel said, clutching at

the pew to keep from sliding off. "You can put me down now."

Sam gently laid the bench back down on the cement floor and sat down beside her. "Scared?" he asked her, as if it were a dare.

"I don't scare *that* easily," she said. The proximity of him suddenly made her nervous. And his spicy sweet smell was even stronger now.

"Well, you should," Sam said. "I've never met a woman so oblivious to danger."

"Like when?"

"Like when you were daring those thugs at Branson's to a drinking contest. Or when you got into Bill the demon's face. Or when you recklessly followed me after I specifically told you not to because it was too dangerous for you. Or when you—"

"Okay, okay, I get the idea," Rachel said, waving her hand. "Let's get back to you. Why did you lose your wings?"

Sam became instantly serious. The half-teasing smile that lit up his eyes disappeared, and he suddenly grew somber.

"I don't talk about that."

Rachel, not one to be deterred, continued. "Did you forget to go to church? Did you kill somebody? What happened?"

"Nothing like that." He glanced away.

"Don't tell me you fell in love with a mortal woman? Like in that Nicolas Cage movie."

Sam glanced sharply at her. She knew she'd hit on something.

"Whoa. You did! You fell in love with a woman. That's it, isn't it?"

"I didn't fall in love," Sam said, eyes hard.

"But there was a woman involved." Rachel sounded excited.

"Yes," Sam said. "There was a woman involved. God wanted me to kill her and her baby, but I didn't."

"Baby? Did you say *baby*?"

Sam nodded, then got a distant look in his eye. "I wouldn't do it, so God took my wings."

"That hardly seems fair. Why would God ask you to do something like that?" Rachel couldn't imagine the God she thought of—the benevolent, forgiving, father figure—ordering one of his angels to do such a thing.

Sam shrugged. "You have to ask Him."

Rachel paused a moment, not sure how to ask her next question.

"If my son is . . ." Rachel started, but couldn't quite get herself to say "half demon." She began again. "If he really is, well, part of him, or some of him, or . . . if Kevin . . ." Rachel faltered. Sam glanced her way again, listening. "What I mean is, do you know if Cassidy is evil?" By now her voice was just a whisper. She couldn't believe she'd even asked the question. She *knew* her son, and he wasn't evil, but now that he could breathe fire maybe that would change things.

Sam leaned forward, his sharp blue eyes on hers. "First of all, he's half human, remember that. He has a soul. And he has free will. He can choose his own path," Sam said. "And something else you might not know, all of us—from demons to angels—can change our destinies. There are defections between the two sides all the time. Angels fall, but demons can rise, too."

Rachel visibly slumped in relief, blinking back tears, even as one escaped and rolled down her cheek. Sam leaned forward then, faster than she could see, and wiped the tear away. His hand brushed her cheek and it felt warm and strong, and at this moment she really, *really* needed warm and strong.

"His best hope is you," Sam continued, fixing her with his clear blue eyes. "You are a strong and capable mother, and will show him the right way."

Rachel hadn't had a compliment in a long while, and it took a second or two to register. The last person—or being—she expected it from was Sam, who took surly to a whole other level. But there wasn't anything surly about him now. His face was sincere and honest.

Rachel saw that his features really were perfectly symmetrical—his eyes and nose and mouth all perfectly proportioned. His jaw was smooth and strong, and now that he wasn't frowning, she saw his forehead was completely free of wrinkles. At that very moment, he looked like he could've been an angel—a beautiful one, at that. His skin was so perfect, it almost looked like stone, and for a second she wondered if he and the stone angel above them shared that in common.

Curious, she reached out a hand to touch his face,

something she would've never been bold enough to do had she a) not been under the influence of his strong and dizzying scent, and b) had he not just given her the best pep talk she'd ever heard.

His eyes widened a little in surprise, but he didn't flinch, and he didn't move her hand, either. His jaw was hard, but nothing like stone. It was warm and alive. Her finger now traced the line of his jaw, and he had no stubble, she realized, his chin smooth and hairless. She was looking at his lips now, full and slightly parted, and had a very strong urge to touch them, too.

Deliberately, she moved her fingers up from his chin and rested them on his bottom lip. It was softer than his cheek and felt surprisingly human. Her eyes flicked up to Sam's, the clear blue of his irises even more intense now, as they met her stare. She couldn't read them, but they seemed to be moving toward her. Her hand fell away from his lip and suddenly she felt his arm come around her back, pulling her still closer. His scent was everywhere now, and she couldn't breathe it in fast enough. She could barely remember who she was, or where she was, and all she cared about was getting closer to him.

Her eyes fluttered shut, and his lips brushed hers, and all she could think was *more, more, more.* He tightened his grip, and she could feel how strong he was, and yet how soft.

"Excuse me?" came a hesitant voice at the back of the chapel. "I was just about to lock up. May I help you?"

Sam moved quickly, and suddenly the embrace was over. Rachel opened her eyes and saw a bewildered-looking Pastor Jonathan standing at the vestibule, clearly trying to decide if he should call the police. He was new to Dogwood, having only arrived at the church a few weeks ago. Rachel was suddenly glad of that, as she didn't need him blabbing around town that he saw her there making out with some stranger. Sam was now on his feet, walking purposefully toward him. His scent was suddenly gone, as was his warmth, and Rachel felt the emptiness like a cold draft.

Sam clapped his hand on the pastor's shoulder. "We need a moment, Pastor," he said. "We came here to pray."

Rachel wondered just what kind of praying that might be. The pastor, however, seemed to start to believe Sam. His confused look changed to one of understanding and acceptance.

"Of course," he said, nodding. "You need to pray."

"We'll be here a while," he said.

"Yes, of course, you'll be here a while," the pastor echoed. "Please. Stay as long as you like."

Rachel wondered if that was the angel version of the Jedi mind trick.

"We'll need some food as well," he added.

The pastor didn't even hesitate. "We have sandwiches left over from our senior Bible study class," he said quickly. "Let me get them for you." And with that, the pastor quickly shuffled away.

Sam turned slowly, approaching Rachel with a

cautious look on his face, the frown back firmly in place, his blue eyes once again guarded and cautious. He was careful to sit opposite her on a pew across the aisle, and Rachel couldn't help but feel the sting. First he was practically mauling her, and now he was acting like she was contagious.

"Was it something I said?" Rachel asked lightly, but inside she was more than a little hurt. He'd closed up on her again, putting her at arm's length. She thought she'd seen a glimmer of a different Sam there for a second, but he was now long gone.

Sam didn't answer, and he didn't look at her, either; instead he stared off into the distance, signaling their conversation was over. Fine, she thought. His smell now less imposing, she started to come to her senses. The last thing she needed was to go around kissing fallen angels. Hadn't she just been married to a demon? What was her problem? Did she have a thing for evil guys?

"I ought to get my head examined," she muttered under her breath as she dug around in her purse and plucked out her cell phone. In seconds she'd dialed Constance.

"Hello?" Constance answered, sounding a little winded.

"How's Cassidy?" Rachel asked immediately, turning her back on Sam. If he was going to ignore her, then she would do the same. She turned her attention to her phone. She could hear a loud and blaring beep echoing in the background, along with shouts from Nathan.

"What is that?" Rachel asked, starting to get worried.

"It's just the smoke alarm," Constance said. "Nothing to worry about. Cassidy's fine."

"*Smoke* alarm? Did he start another fire? What about the cloth that Father Daniels gave him?"

In the background she heard Father Daniels cursing and then shouting, "I *will* use the holy sacrament on you, boy. Now come *back* here."

"Don't worry; we've got it under control," Constance said, the fire alarm blaring in the background, a series of high-pitched screeches.

"It doesn't sound like things are under control," Rachel said, unable to contain her skepticism.

"We're fine. Really. Uh, Cass—don't set fire to the carpet! No, Cass! No!" And with that, Constance hung up, leaving Rachel staring at her phone.

Fourteen

It took every last ounce of Sam's willpower not to look at Rachel, to pretend that he didn't hear the light beat of her heart from across the church or smell her sweet, inviting scent.

Every part of him wanted to hold her to his chest and not let go.

The scariest thing was that he hadn't decided to kiss Rachel, his body had, taking control in a way he'd never experienced before. Even now, as he gritted his teeth, he wasn't sure he'd be able to keep himself away from her.

He tried to make sense of what it meant, and then decided it didn't matter. He had to stay focused on finding his next bounty, which at this point looked like it would be Azazel. If he wanted to stay powerful, he'd need a recharge from Satan, and soon. He couldn't afford distractions.

Even as Rachel's voice floated over to him, he tried to keep his mind on other things. He resorted to reciting the Old Testament in his head in Latin.

She clicked her cell phone shut and stood, and Sam realized her conversation was over and she was moving toward him. He deliberately didn't look at her, even as he saw from the corner of his eye the gentle sway of the hem of her dress and the smooth pale line of her calf.

"You can stay for sandwiches," Rachel said to the side of his head as she slung her purse over one shoulder. "But I'm going home." And with that, she started walking resolutely down the aisle, toward the exit.

It took Sam a moment to process the fact that she was leaving. He hadn't expected that. There were a million reasons he needed to stop her, but all he could think of was that water demon. It could be waiting outside for her, for all he knew. She could be walking into a trap.

He sprung to his feet and in seconds was in front of her, blocking her path.

She glanced up at him, annoyed.

"Move," she hissed at him, annoyance turning to anger. "My son needs me."

"It's not safe."

"I don't care."

The expression on her face told Sam she had made up her mind and wasn't about to be dissuaded.

Sam searched his mind for an argument she'd understand.

"You won't find Kevin if you leave," Sam said, grasping at the first thing that leapt into his mind. This wasn't exactly a lie. She wouldn't find him if she left, but she wouldn't find him if she stayed, either. Given the water demon's performance earlier, Sam guessed Kevin had been completely absorbed by the stronger demon and wouldn't be found by anyone ever again.

Rachel stopped and looked up. "What about Kevin?"

"You have questions for him," Sam continued. "He might be able to tell you about Cassidy. Like how to help him."

Rachel hesitated again. Sam could see his argument working on her. But then she seemed to decide to keep going.

"If you leave, you *will* die," Sam said. "That water demon is out there, and demons are always stronger at night. It could be waiting outside those doors right now."

Rachel stopped, her hands on the doors leading outside, and paused.

"Do you really want to make your son an orphan?" Sam asked.

Rachel turned and met Sam's gaze. She grabbed her phone from her purse and started dialing.

"Constance—it's Rachel. Things here are taking longer than I thought, and Sam thinks we are in danger if we leave before sunrise. Are you sure you're okay if I don't come home for a while?" she asked and waited for an answer. "Things do sound better—I don't hear that alarm anymore. What? Oh, good. Okay. If you're sure. I'll call later when I know something more."

Rachel dropped her phone into her purse and glared at Sam.

"Cass is asleep, so I guess I can stay—for now," she said. "But I had better get some answers—and soon."

"Fine," Sam said.

Abruptly Rachel spun on her heel and stomped in the opposite direction, back toward the altar. She sat down, threw her bag in her lap, and crossed her arms, staring off toward a stained glass picture of the Virgin Mary. Rachel looked more beautiful than ever now that she was mad—her cheeks slightly flushed, and her brown eyes flashing fire. As a precaution, Sam took a seat on the opposite side of the church and stared at the wall. He began his mental recital in Latin again, resisting the urge to look at her.

The pastor came back with the sandwiches, and Rachel took one wordlessly, eating it quietly without glancing over at Sam to see if he was eating, too. He wasn't. He didn't need to, just like he didn't need to sleep. At least, not yet. Not until he was fully mortal. And he was doing everything he could to stave off that day. He was struck by a sudden thought—maybe the desire he felt now for Rachel was a harbinger of his mortality. It was a sign, just like his weakening strength. Sure, he'd impressed Rachel with his display in the church, but that was only one hundredth of the strength he'd originally had. Every day put between him and his last bounty meant a little more slipped away.

A long while had passed, he guessed, because a little bit of light began trickling in through the stained glass windows, casting bits of colored light on the floor. Rachel was curled up on her pew, asleep. Time passed quickly for him. What was a few hours in the scheme of millennia? They seemed only like a few minutes. Dawn was coming outside, and it would soon be safe for them to leave. Most demons didn't do well in sunlight. They usually chose night for their most direct attacks. Of course, Sam didn't know if the same rules applied to water demons, since he'd never gone up against one before.

Rachel stirred a little, shifting in her pew. She looked so completely peaceful while sleeping. Her head was lying on a hard hymnal, and Sam wanted suddenly to cushion her head with his jacket. He'd wake her up, no doubt, and she wouldn't be pleased to see him. He had to start thinking about his next step, and stop scrutinizing how her chest rose and fell with each breath. He needed to get her to tell him what she knew about Azazel.

Kevin had said she carried the secret coordinates of his location with her at all times, even though she didn't know it. Sam glanced over at her purse, resting just out of her reach. He looked back at Rachel, and she was still asleep. In seconds he'd grabbed the purse and searched through all the contents, down to every last receipt in her wallet, and had it back and orderly before Rachel had even exhaled two more breaths. There was nothing in it to give him a clue about Azazel. She was supposed to carry it on her at all times on a ring. He glanced down and saw her hand resting gently by her side. On it was a single platinum wedding band and a solitaire engagement ring. *A ring*, of course, Sam thought, staring at Rachel's left hand. Her wedding ring. It was in front of him the whole time.

Seeing if his hunch was right, though, could take some finesse. As gently as he could, Sam lifted her hand, trying to move quickly before she woke up. He almost had the first ring off, when her eyes fluttered open.

A look of surprise and then annoyance passed across her face.

"Now I *know* you're a fallen angel," she said in a sleepy voice, even as her eyes focused sharply on his. "You want to tell me what the hell you're doing trying to steal my wedding ring?"

Fifteen

First he comes on to her, then he gives her a cold shoulder, and now he tries to lift her only valuable jewelry? Rachel couldn't figure him out. He didn't even have the good sense to look embarrassed at being caught. He simply ripped her rings right off her finger and held them up to the light.

"What the hell do you think you're doing?" Rachel declared as she leapt up. Sam, unperturbed, simply held them aloft, away from her, as he studied the inside of the platinum bands. He peered at the inscription, frowning as he turned it this way and that, and he managed to ignore the pounding Rachel was doing on his back. And then, just as quickly, he dropped the rings back into her hand.

"The numbers on the inside of the band, what do they mean?" he asked her.

"They're our favorite psalms; mine is 36:6–9: 'Your love, O Lord, reaches to the heavens, your faithfulness to the skies . . . with you is the foun-

tain of life; in your light we see light.' And Kevin's
was—"

"112:2? 'His descendants will be mighty on
earth; the generation of the upright will be blessed,'"
Sam recited from memory. "*That's* a demon's favorite verse, eh?"

"Are you sure that's the right psalm? I could've
sworn it was something else."

"I used to be an angel, remember? We know the
Bible by heart. In all languages. Standard protocol."

Rachel glanced at the ring again, and the numbers were there, clear as day. She grabbed the Bible
from the pew in front of her and rifled through. In
Psalms, she found that Sam was right.

"Strange."

"Those aren't psalms," Sam said. "A demon
wouldn't care about that. But he would care about
recording coordinates."

"Coordinates for what?"

Sam didn't answer, he simply took the rings from
her hand again. This time he held her diamond up
to the light.

"There," he said, looking at the small stone. "It's
right there in the diamond. We just need someone
to extract it."

"Extract what?" Rachel asked, dumbfounded.

"The map," Sam said simply.

Rachel had no idea where they were headed or
why, because Sam had stopped giving any answers.
He had simply hopped on the motorcycle and waited
a beat for her to climb on and then they were off,

roaring down the highway with Rachel's hair in her face. When they stopped, she saw they had pulled into the parking lot for Bob's Exotic Pets store, located almost at the southern-most border of Dogwood County.

Sam nudged the bike's kickstand out, steadied the cycle, and then turned to Rachel.

"Wait here," he said.

Rachel glanced up at the big sign and then back at Sam. "You going to try to pawn my rings at a pet store?"

"Just wait," Sam grumbled. Rachel crossed her arms and stood by the bike, watching as Sam disappeared behind the worn aluminum door with the cracked window. The big window up-front sported an aquarium filled with once-neon-colored rocks, now faded from years in the sun. On top of the rocks sat a plastic treasure chest and bright white plastic skeleton, but with no fish and no water, and one very sad-looking tree frog, who sat hunched in a corner staring at the plastic skeleton.

Rachel could not imagine what on earth could've brought Sam here. No one shopped here that she knew of. There was a rumor that there might be a puppy mill at this store, or even dog fighting, but nobody had ever proven anything, and few people that Rachel knew ever ventured out this way. There were five other places closer into town that sold dog or cat food for much cheaper, and no one that she knew of was interested in "exotic" pets. Half the county's population owned horses or cows, and that was just about as crazy as people got around there.

She waited a few seconds, shifting her weight from one foot to the other. After about a minute had passed, she decided she was going to go in after him. The door swung open easily, and inside she was hit by the smell of dried dog food and cat litter. The first thing she saw was a teenager sitting behind the counter, his nose buried in a Hellboy comic book, oblivious to just about everything else. The store had at least six wide aisles, and the tile floor beneath her feet was a grungy gray. By the look of it, it probably hadn't been mopped since the Reagan administration. The store seemed mostly empty and quiet, except for the occasional squawk coming from the exotic bird aisle. Rachel saw no immediate sign of Sam and began checking each aisle for signs of him.

At the end of the reptile aisle, at the back of the store, Rachel found him, standing with his back to her in front of a giant glass cage holding the biggest python she'd ever seen outside of the Discovery Channel. It was massive, its body at least a foot or more thick, its coils wrapped around so many times she had no idea how long it was, but she guessed it was at least twenty feet. It was a gleaming brown and green, and its pink tongue flicked against the glass as its head bobbed up and down. If Rachel didn't know better, she would have thought the snake was talking to Sam.

Rachel inched forward down the adjacent aisle to get a closer look. At the end of the aisle, she ducked behind a stack of hamster cages and peeked around. She could see just the hint of Sam's profile as he faced the snake, and now that she was closer, she could hear that the snake was, indeed, talking.

"Now, Sssssam. You know I don't do favorssss—essspecially for Fallensss."

Rachel processed a talking snake without so much as an added blink. In a one-to-ten scale of weirdness she'd experienced in the last twenty-four hours, a talking snake was hardly even a three.

"Oh, Lilith," Sam said, in a voice that sounded like he knew her well. "For me? For old times' sake. Please?"

"I hate it when you usssse that Fallen charm on me," sighed Lilith the Snake, raising her head higher and flicking her long pink tongue against the glass. "You are too damn pretty for your own good. Adam has nothing on you."

"Is that a yes?"

Lilith the snake sighed and dropped her head a little. "Only if you promise me seventy percent of Azazel's bounty."

"Thirty."

"Sixty."

"Forty."

"Fifty."

Sam considered this. "Deal," he said.

"That means you can't kill him," Lilith reminded him.

"I'll do my best," Sam said.

"Fair enough," Lilith said. "Okay. Let me ssssee it."

Sam reached up and dropped Rachel's engagement ring into the cage. Lilith caught it on her tongue, then flipped it up in the air, where it floated just above the snake's head in the cage. In another second Lilith's eyes started to glow a deep red and then a light shot out like a laser, hitting the diamond in the ring setting and reflecting light all around them. The light started to take shape and then came together in a kind of three-dimensional map.

Sam let out a laugh as he recognized the landscape. "The Grand Canyon!" he exclaimed.

Rachel stepped forward a little to get a better look at the red glowing map blazing from her ring, and without realizing it, accidentally toppled a small can of fish food sitting on the shelf in front of her, which hit the ground with a smack and caused both Sam and Lilith to look in her direction. Instantly Rachel's ring fell to the bottom of Lilith's cage, the map disappeared, and Lilith slapped her tail murderously against the glass.

"Descendant of Eve!" hissed Lilith, venom in her voice. She hit the glass hard with her head, desperate to attack.

"Rachel—run," shouted Sam as he grabbed her by the arm and pulled her toward the exit. Behind them Rachel could hear the sound of glass shattering and the snake screeching, "Die! Die! Die!"

The two ran past the kid at the front counter, who—white earbuds in his ears—hadn't heard the commotion. He turned the page of the Hellboy comic and didn't look up as Sam pushed her hard straight out the front door. She staggered into the parking lot but quickly regained her footing.

"That was very dumb," he told her, steering her away from the store. Rachel turned to look, just as the snake hit the pet store door with a sickening thud. She hit it several times more, but the glass didn't budge. "You're lucky she can't cross the seal and come out here, or we'd both be dead."

"What the hell was that?"

Through the large window at the front of the store, Rachel could still see Lilith's shadow, her enormous snake body writhing at the window, looking for a way out.

Sam sighed and ran his hands through his hair in exasperation as he walked to the motorcycle. "That was Lilith. She used to be a woman. In fact, the very *first* woman."

"What about Eve?"

"Eve was the second. Lilith came first, only she wasn't made from Adam's rib. She was made from the same stuff as Adam, and never let him forget it. Adam didn't like her bossiness, among other things, and Lilith didn't much like Adam, either, so she flew out of the garden."

Rachel watched as Lilith's shadow seemed to calm down a bit as she grew tired of trying to escape the store. The snake started a slow retreat away from the door.

"How did she fly?" Rachel asked, swinging her leg over the back of the bike.

"Said God's true name out loud and just sprouted wings and flew. Resourceful, that Lilith. God told her she had to go back or all of her children would die. But she didn't care. She wasn't going back."

"She must've really hated Adam."

"Well, he was kind of a prick at times. So, Adam, now alone, asked God for a different mate, and God sent him one—Eve. Lilith didn't take it very well, as you can imagine. Well, she was recruited by Satan, traded in her wings for a chance at revenge, and became the snake that tempted Eve. Except that she was hoping Eve would die, but she didn't, and instead went on to populate the world. This is particularly annoying to Lilith, who wants all of Eve's descendants dead."

"That's the entire human race."

"Bingo."

"What about the kid in the store?"

"He was a demon."

"Oh." Rachel considered this a moment. "So Lilith—this ancient demon snake—hangs out at Bob's Exotic Pets?"

"She takes in bounties, which is how I know her. And she's particularly adept at figuring out codes, like the coded map locked in your ring. But you were lucky she didn't incinerate you. It was very dumb going in that store."

"How was I to know that Bob's Exotic Pets was so dangerous?"

"Next time, *just do as I tell you.*" Sam turned over his bike's ignition and the engine roared to life.

"And, as a rule of thumb, avoid exotic pet stores in the middle of nowhere."

"But what about somebody who just wanders in the store? I mean—does Lilith just kill them?"

"Yep."

"But that's crazy."

"The world is a crazy place." Sam backed the bike out of its parking space.

"So what was that about the Grand Canyon?"

"Doesn't concern you," Sam grumbled, revving the engine. "I'm taking you home."

"Home! But what about Kevin?"

Sam said nothing, just pulled his bike back onto the highway.

Sixteen

They couldn't get to Rachel's house fast enough, as far as Sam was concerned. Sam couldn't wait to be free of this most troublesome woman. She was always getting into messes of her own making, and she'd probably cost him Lilith's friendship—his best contact in the demon world.

Of course, that didn't explain why he felt a little disappointed when he pulled onto her street, less than two blocks from her house. Rachel might be a pain, but she kept things interesting. After a couple of thousand years wandering the earth, it was rare that he found something that surprised him. But Rachel confounded him at every turn.

They rounded the corner of her street, and Sam slammed on the brakes, skidding the bike to a screeching halt in the middle of the tree-lined street twenty yards from her house.

"What the . . ." Rachel sputtered, seeing what he saw.

Rachel's house had been completely and totally leveled, and bits of brick and half-smashed furniture lay strewn across her yard. No other house on the street look damaged. It was as if a tornado had dropped out of the sky over her house, demolished everything in it, and then lifted up again without touching another building. Giant pools of water lay in her yard, and all the debris in and near where her house used to stand was soaking wet.

"Cassidy?" Rachel squeaked, almost as if she couldn't believe her son could be capable of that kind of destruction.

"Not him," Sam said, shaking his head. "This is the work of the water demon."

A fire truck and ambulance were sitting on the street in front of the place her garage used to be, as well as a county sheriff's truck. Several of her neighbors were standing on the sidewalk, gawking.

"Cassidy!" Rachel cried, panic in her voice now as she realized her son hadn't caused the destruction and might be a victim of it. She leapt off the back of Sam's motorcycle and started running blindly toward her house.

"No, Rachel, wait!" Sam shouted after her, but it was too late. She was halfway there. He abandoned his bike and went after her, grabbing her by the waist before she knew he was even by her side, and suddenly she was kicking and screaming. Her neighbors glanced over, but Sam didn't care. He couldn't be sure the water demon had gone; it could still be waiting for Rachel. And there was no doubt in his mind now that Rachel was the thing's target. Perhaps it was trying to prevent Sam from finding Azazel, or maybe it just wanted to make sure that anyone close to Kevin died with him, but Sam knew with razor certainty that the monster would keep trying to kill Rachel until it succeeded. And based on its performance at Branson's, this particular demon didn't care about witnesses, either. Most demons didn't openly show their powers like this one did. It was an unwritten rule in Satan's army. Satan preferred stealth, and acting showy with power was likely to get a demon executed for showing up their demon in chief.

"Rachel?" Constance Plyd stepped out from behind the ambulance, carrying Cassidy in her arms. Rachel went limp with relief in Sam's grasp. Surprisingly, he found that he, too, felt relieved her son was okay. Sam let her go so that she could wrap her boy in her arms. She buried her face in his shoulder.

"How did you escape?" Sam asked Constance, curious to know if the prophet's powers were greater than he thought. He'd not known prophets to be particularly strong demon fighters.

"We didn't. We were at Nathan's when it happened," she said, nodding back to the sheriff, who was talking animatedly into a CB radio he'd pulled from the driver's side of his truck. "He has a swimming pool in his yard, and since Cassidy kept lighting things on fire, we thought it would just be safer there. Besides, the fire station is two doors down."

"Oh, thank God," Rachel said, recovering a little, as her boy wiggled in her arms.

"Did you see the demon?" Sam asked.

"It's gone already," Constance said. "Father Daniels had just gone back to the church when I saw it in a vision. We came as soon as we could. There was a river of water running down the street."

"And it left you—and Cassidy—alone?"

"It just disappeared in the storm drain without touching us."

Sam nodded again. So the demon didn't care about Cassidy. Just about Rachel. Interesting. Maybe it didn't know Cassidy existed. That would be a stroke of good luck. He still didn't know what the water demon was after, but the fact that it had devoured Kevin's house made him wonder if the water demon could be after Azazel, just like he was. Maybe it was a bounty hunter.

A big, camouflaged Hummer rumbled down the street. As it came to an abrupt stop by Rachel, Father Daniels stuck his head out the window. He eyed Sam and then Rachel.

"What is it with you and the sinful?" Father Daniels asked, thumbing his hand at Sam.

"Nice to see you again, Father," Sam said.

"You two know each other?" Rachel asked.

"I ran into him in Mexico in 1967, back when I was doing missionary work."

"You look different," Sam said.

"And you look exactly the same," Father Daniels

said. The two men stared at each other a minute, an unspoken hostility between them.

"Well, come on, Rachel," Father Daniels said, turning to her. "What are you waiting for? Get in. I've got some information on this water demon. Leave the boy. We've got to go to my church, and he won't like it there very much."

"We'll take him," Constance offered.

"But . . ."

"Come on. It's important."

Reluctantly, Rachel handed Cassidy back to Constance and climbed into the giant SUV. Sam made a move to follow her.

Father Daniels smacked his door. "Not you, Fallen. Just her."

"I'm not going to leave her alone," Sam growled, climbing into the backseat beside her.

"Oh? Altruistic again all of a sudden?" Father Daniels asked, looking in the rearview mirror.

"Just drive," Sam commanded.

Father Daniels wound the Hummer through the curvy back roads that led to St. Mary's Church, the only Catholic church in the county. The Catholic Archdiocese of Dallas kept it open not because they hoped to draw converts, but because they needed an outpost in Dogwood County, where demon activity had been on the rise in recent years. Since demons had taken over the DMV and the Mega-Mart, the demon-per-capita rate was now higher here than even Los Angeles, which was a cause for worry no matter how you sliced it.

"Do you know who's trying to kill Rachel—and why?" Sam asked.

"No, but I think I might know who this water demon is," Father Daniels said. "There have been rumors. Rumors that Tiamat might be making a return, but I didn't think it was possible."

"Tiamat?" Sam had thought Tiamat—the Babylonian creation goddess—was a rumor, nothing more.

"She was before even your time," Father Daniels told Sam as he steered the Hummer toward the small parking lot at the back of the church. "But the church has records of her. Proof she existed." Father Daniels parked his Hummer and climbed down. Rachel and Sam followed him as he turned toward the front door.

"Who is she and why does she want to kill me?" Rachel asked.

"Tiamat is a Babylonian goddess of water and chaos, who is rumored to be mother to the original eleven demons, who have since spawned the ones we know today," Father Daniels explained as he swung open the front door. The three entered the church, and Rachel's eyes flicked up to the large white crucifix hanging above the altar. Jesus had his crown of thorns and his eyes were staring up to heaven. "Tiamat was supposed to have been killed by one of her sons, and God used her body to create the heaven and earth."

"God used her body? I don't remember that in Genesis," Rachel said as they walked down the main aisle, stained glass on either side of the narrow rows of pews.

"You won't find it there," Father Daniels said. "Genesis is just one version of creation. There are many others."

"How many?"

"More than you can count," Sam said. "And no one knows which one is true."

"The Big Guy likes to keep us guessing," Father Daniels explained. He cleared his throat and continued, "It's said that Tiamat didn't die, that a part of her lived on in the water, as a water demon, with only a fraction of her former power. When the war began in heaven and Lucifer fell, she didn't take sides with Satan, but she never asked to be redeemed, either. Sound familiar?"

"A free agent," Sam said. Just like he was.

"As if there really is such a thing," Father Daniels scoffed under his breath.

"I'm warning you," Sam growled.

"And I'm warning you both," Rachel said loudly, in her best mother- disciplinarian voice. "Cut it out, or I swear, if I get killed by this thing I *will* haunt both of you."

The thought of an angry Rachel following them into the afterlife quieted both men.

"Father, proceed," Rachel commanded.

"She's been dormant for thousands of years," Father Daniels said. "Something—or someone—has brought her back."

"Do you know of her weaknesses? Any way to stop her?"

"The last time she was on a rampage, it took her

own grandson to contain her, and he was a powerful demon himself," Father Daniels said, stopping, as they were now at the feet of Christ. Father Daniels stooped and pulled up a door in the floor, revealing a secret cache of weapons.

"Whoa." Rachel's jaw dropped. The secret door revealed stacks and stacks of guns, knives, and even a couple of crossbows.

"She's not a normal demon, and normal exorcism tactics won't work on her," Father Daniels said. "But I might have something in here."

He crouched and started pulling out weapon after weapon. Rachel jumped when he threw a belt of grenades by her feet.

"So this is why you buy all those bullets from my hardware store," Rachel said, sidestepping a semiautomatic rifle that he piled on top of the stack of knives he'd tossed on the ground.

Sam frowned. "We don't need these," he said. "I'm stronger than all of them."

Father Daniels gave him a doubting look. "Sure you are, until the last payoff from Satan you got wears off, which judging by the look of you, could be any day."

Sam pulled himself into a defensive position. "I'm plenty strong for the both of us."

"Well, Fallen who doesn't care about weapons, why don't you go into my office over there? I've got a book on the shelf about water demons. It might have some information you can use."

Sam hesitated a moment, wondering if it was best

to leave Rachel alone with the priest, and then decided there would be no harm in it. He turned, without a word, and headed for Father Daniels' office.

When he was gone, Father Daniels grabbed hold of Rachel's wrist and tugged her down.

"We don't have much time," he whispered. "But that Fallen you're with can't be trusted. He used to be in the Wrath regiment, and those guys are half-crazy as it is. But Sam has been working for Satan for a thousand years."

"He says he's neutral," Rachel said, voice low.

"Pish posh, no such thing," Father Daniels said. "You lie with the devil, you get demon fleas, and he's full of them. You cannot trust him. He's only out for himself, no one else."

Rachel's eyes flicked to Father Daniels' office door. She could just see Sam's back. He was assessing the books on the shelf. "But he lost his wings because he spared a woman's life," Rachel said. "That wasn't selfish."

"That was the last unselfish thing he's done, and that was at least a thousand years ago," Father Daniels said. "You can't trust Fallens. I mean, none of them ever turn out to be anything but bad. There's Lucifer, of course. Then Azazel—"

"Azazel? I heard that name—Lilith mentioned it."

"You saw Lilith?" Father Daniels sucked in a breath. "And lived to tell the tale?"

"Barely. Who is Azazel, anyway?"

"He's the most notorious fallen angel since Lucifer," Father Daniels said. "He seduced half the women of Rome."

"He was a player angel? That's it?"

"He used the women to sire giant mutant children for him who would make an army he could use to march against God and Satan."

"Oh, I see."

"He almost succeeded, too. But he was stopped just in time."

"I'll bet anything Sam is going after Azazel. Lilith told him he could find Azazel in the Grand Canyon."

"Look, kid, Sam is bad news. I ran into him a long time ago, and he nearly cost a lot of lives going after one of his bounties. He got blinded by the addiction he has to his own power, and he didn't care who got hurt, as long as he got the demon he was looking for."

"But—"

"Just trust me, he's a bad seed, and it's only a matter of time before he joins the devil's army and actually becomes a demon," Father Daniels said as he thrust a small vial into her hand. "This can help you protect yourself. It's a high concentration of dogwood tree oil, and it will sap a Fallen's strength." Father Daniels closed Rachel's fingers over the vial. "It's best if he swallows it. It should start to work in seconds."

"I thought Fallens weren't that affected by dogwoods."

"Not a potion this strong. Dogwood blooms

they can handle, but not something this concentrated."

"But, Father, I—"

"Just take it," he said in a voice that left no room for argument. "And be careful. You can't trust him, no matter how sexy his eyes are."

"I never said his eyes were sexy," Rachel exclaimed.

"You didn't have to," Father Daniels said. "Now take my advice, and get free of him as soon as you can. He's no good for you."

Seventeen

"Rachel is *one* measly human woman," Casiphia cried through gnashed teeth. "How does she keep escaping?" Casiphia flipped a long strand of dark hair off her shoulder as she paced anxiously in the hotel room she'd rented on the south rim of the Grand Canyon three nights ago.

"Patience," said Pan, who was still in Kevin's body and lounging on a chair that was made out of an Indian feather headdress. He was most certainly *not* dead or devoured by Tiamat. The entire room and hotel was Indian and cowboy–themed, including the actual saddles glued to the top of the stools in the hotel bar. "We don't really even need her as collateral. Sam bought the story. He's coming here to open the tomb, and he's bringing Rachel with him. We can snag her here."

"I'd rather have her in hand," Casiphia said, her red lips drawing themselves into a pout. "Sam has a thing for her, it's obvious. And we need Sam to play along, and if he decides not to, then we can use her for insurance. Having her as a bargaining chip would make me feel a lot better. I don't want anything to screw this up." Casiphia abruptly stopped pacing. "I shouldn't have left it to a water demon."

"Hey—the good Lady T did her job," Kevin said, holding up what looked like an oversized jelly jar, the kind that would normally hold jam or sweet tea. It was full of a murky-looking liquid that seemed to roll and move in many directions at once. "It wasn't her fault Rachel wasn't at home."

"A demon with half a brain would've known that *before* she leveled the place," Casiphia said with disdain.

The water in the jar started to boil a little, prickled by the insult.

"Now, now, she didn't mean anything by it, girl," Kevin said, soothing the jar with a little pat. "So tell me again why we need Sam?"

"I never told you in the first place," Casiphia snapped. "But I need Sam to open Azazel's tomb. He's one of the only beings who can. The lock can only be opened by a fallen angel who hasn't yet pledged allegiance to the devil."

"And there certainly aren't many of those around. I only know of Sam."

"Exactly."

"So why so hot for Azazel?"

Casiphia shrugged, as if she couldn't care less, and turned to freshen her makeup in the nearby mirror, but Kevin could see through it.

"Oh, I see. You actually *love* him."

"He had a grandiose plan to take on Satan and God. I admire his ambition."

"Hmmm. So you're tricking Sam to come here and release Azazel for you. Man, that's cold. I have to admit, I think you're more evil than I am."

"As if that would be hard," Casiphia sniffed, unimpressed. "You actually lived with a woman for years, happily married, and didn't even manage to do anything bad while you were—unless you count boinking that girl, what's her name?"

"Vanessa."

"Right, and she was what? Eighteen? The legal age of consent. Oooh. The scandal!"

"So sue me," Kevin said. "I happened to like domestic life. It wasn't so bad."

"You have to be kidding."

"I'm not. And Rachel wasn't a bad wife. I still say being married was better than being on Satan's most-wanted list and having to hide out in places like this." Kevin motioned around their room, then nodded toward the headboard made of steer horns and buffalo hides.

"Pffft," Casiphia said. "Satan will be no match for us, once Azazel is free. We've got him running scared. You just have no backbone."

"Well, I can definitely see how you're on your way to becoming the ultimate evil one," Kevin added. "You're a natural."

Casiphia sent him a sharp look, and for a second her eyes glowed red, and the lip gloss in her hand suddenly sizzled and popped as it melted in her hand.

"Why doesn't that sound like a compliment?" she asked, warning in her voice.

Immediately Kevin backtracked. "Oh, it is, of course it is," he blubbered quickly. "I mean you're deliciously, diabolically evil—the best kind. Some of us have to work at being evil, like me, for example, but it's effortless for you. I envy the natural talent."

"That's better," Casiphia said, tossing the melted lip gloss in a nearby trash can. "Now, go out and buy me another one of those. It was my favorite kind."

As Kevin reluctantly got to his feet, Casiphia nodded to the glass canister filled with murky water next to him. "And would you please find a place for Tiamat somewhere outside this hotel room? It smells like dead fish in here."

Sighing, Kevin grabbed the glass jar and left the room, wishing, not for the first time, he'd just stayed undercover as Rachel's husband. She might not be a perfect wife, but even Rachel never ordered him around this much.

Eighteen

Rachel was beginning to think that things could simply not get worse. First, her husband drains their bank account and leaves her. Then, she finds out he's a demon, and her only son is a fire-breathing half demon. She's being pushed around by a sullen fallen angel who smells ridiculously good and is a walking bad boy cliché with enough personal magnetism to make her throw caution and her own good sense to the wind. And now she's being hunted by some kind of mother-of-all-demons who just hours ago destroyed her house and all her worldly possessions. It was almost laughable, except it was her life.

On the bright side, she thought, when the bank came to repossess the house on Friday, they'd find a heaping pile of rubble. In some ways, that seemed fitting.

"What did I do to piss off this demon anyway?" Rachel asked Sam as the two of them sat in the cabin of the plane that was taking them to Arizona, where the next chapter of this little nightmare adventure would begin. "What was her name? Tina? Tagamet?"

"Tiamat," Sam corrected. "And I don't know."

"And why are we going to Arizona again?"

"To find Kevin."

"I don't think I believe you," she said.

"That's your prerogative," he said, then fell silent.

Through the PA system, the pilot told everyone to buckle their seat belts for the landing.

"Isn't this rough for you? Having to take an airplane when you used to fly?"

Sam gave her a sharp look and then glanced around to see if any of the other passengers had heard. Rachel doubted it. They were in first class, and everyone had earphones on. She didn't know how he managed it, but with a few words and a smile, Sam not only got them onto this booked flight, but got them upgraded to first class. It seemed like she wasn't the only one affected by his clear blue eyes and his spicy sweet scent. Even the stewardesses were fawning over him, sending him glass after glass of champagne that didn't affect him much one way or another. She, on the other hand, might as well be invisible. She had to ask twice just to get a Diet Coke.

"Do you ever stop asking questions?" he asked.

"Nope. Here's another one. Lilith mentioned somebody named Azazel. Who is he?"

Sam ground his teeth together.

Sam sighed. "He's a fallen angel who has topped Satan's most-wanted list for a thousand years."

"So you do work for Satan."

"No, I don't."

"Father Daniels said—"

"Oh, right, of course. Father Daniels." Sam rolled his eyes. "What else did he tell you?"

"That you're bad news for me."

Sam moved closer to her, his voice barely above a whisper, his breath warm on her cheek. "Do you believe him?"

Rachel's heart sped up a little as the smell of cinnamon filled her head and made her a little woozy.

"I don't know," she mumbled, suddenly unsure of herself.

"Well, he's right," he said, his blue eyes clear, a cocky half smile on his lips. "I am no good for you."

"Champagne?" asked a flight attendant, suddenly breaking up their conversation as she handed Sam another flute. He took it with a smile, and Rachel seized the opportunity to try to gain control of her senses.

She put her hand into her pocket and felt for the vial Father Daniels had given her. When would she use it? Or how? She had no idea. She squeezed her fingers around it and then let it go. She supposed she would know when. She would just have to wait and see.

By the time Rachel and Sam made it to the Grand Canyon, the sun had just set, and with no moon out, it was hard to see much of anything. Rachel felt a pang of disappointment, since she hadn't taken a trip out of state in years and had never seen the Grand Canyon except on a postcard her mother once sent while on a trip with her church group.

"We have to find shelter for the night," Sam said, abruptly steering the jeep they'd rented back toward the highway. Rachel was grateful to be riding in a car and not his motorcycle, where she'd had to cling to him for dear life, since he tended to pay no attention to any rules of the road.

He wasn't bothering to obey the speed limit now, but Rachel didn't mind. Sam had the top down, which helped disperse his spicy sweet smell, and so for the first time in hours she could actually think clearly without distraction. And she had plenty to think about. She was deeply worried about Cassidy—not just his current fire-breathing state, but also his safety, given there was a homicidal demon on the loose. Sam insisted Cassidy wasn't Tiamat's target, but Rachel still couldn't help but worry. She glanced down at the cell phone she held in her lap and considered calling Constance again. She'd made three phone calls since the plane had touched down, and she could tell Constance was getting a little annoyed. Every time she called, she found out Cassidy was fine, but Rachel couldn't shake the nagging feeling of worry. This, after all, was the first time she'd ever taken a trip without Cassidy, and she didn't like knowing that a couple of state lines sat between them.

She'd left Constance with practically a bible of instructions, from how to put Cassidy to sleep to the number for the local poison control hotline in case he got into something toxic. Despite Sam explaining more than once that Cassidy—as a half demon—could probably drink a bottle of Drano with little effect, Rachel still saw him as her vulnerable baby boy. Sam, on the other hand, seemed more worried about the safety of Constance and Nathan. He gave them a few tips on avoiding being burned by demon fire and left them with the suggestion that they have Father Daniels bless the water in the swimming pool, just in case of an emergency.

Sam glanced at Rachel and, seeing her grasping her cell phone, said, "He's fine."

"I know, but maybe I should call just to make sure he went to bed."

"If you call, then you'll probably wake him up," Sam said. "He's fine. Trust me, it's Constance and Nathan you should worry about."

Rachel frowned and stared out into the dark night. Despite the bright stars in the sky above, she found the darkness around them murky and oppressive. This was probably because there was an ancient demon hiding out there in the shadows who wanted her dead. The thought sent a shiver down her spine. She glanced over at Sam, and remembered the strength and speed he showed at the church. Instantly she felt better about things. At least she didn't have to face whatever was after her on her own.

Sam pulled the jeep into the parking lot of a nearby lodge, one that sat practically on the edge of the canyon. A NO VACANCY sign flashed from the office window.

"It looks like they're full," Rachel said, nodding toward the sign and then to the rest of the parking lot, which was packed with cars.

Sam just shook his head and gave her a cocky half smile, as if she were missing something obvious, and swung out of the jeep. Rachel followed, curious to see just what kind of angel power of persuasion he was going to use this time.

There was a woman behind the counter in the lobby, young to be working the night shift, Rachel thought. She put her age somewhere in the mid-twenties. She was pretty, with light blond hair and a smooth complexion. She had her head bent down over a magazine, and the minute the doorbell dinged behind them, she held up a hand without looking up.

"Sorry, but we don't have any free rooms," she said, sounding bored.

Another second or two passed and Sam's scent filled up the lobby. The girl glanced up from her copy of *Us Weekly*, looking at first confused and then a little dazed. Rachel watched as Sam walked up to the counter and leaned against it so that he was as close to her as possible. The girl, still a little disoriented, didn't back away. In fact, she leaned forward, her eyes wide, and smiled.

"Are you *sure* you don't have any rooms at all?"

Sam asked and smiled. He was using the charm he showed at the airport, but there was something about his voice that was different. Could it be possible? Was he actually . . . *flirting*? Rachel expected another showing of his Jedi mind trick abilities, but this was new. She hadn't seen flirting before.

Sam put his hand on the girl's magazine and slowly trailed it down to the counter as his eyes flicked down to her name tag. "It would really mean a lot to me if you could squeeze me in, Krista."

The girl giggled, giddy. "Actually, uh, I think we might have *one* room, although my manager doesn't usually like for me to rent it, because he sort of considers it *his* room, for when he wants to do whatever it is he does in there, but I could make an exception this one time . . ."

"I'd really appreciate it if you would," Sam said, resting his hand ever so lightly on the girl's arm to show he was earnest. The girl nearly jumped from the touch. It looked like she was considering leaping straight up and over the counter and into Sam's arms. She actually had a kind of dreamy look on her face, like she was in the presence of a superstar, like Brad Pitt or George Clooney, and she was completely oblivious to the fact that Rachel was standing there, right beside him. What if she had been his girlfriend? Or his wife? The girl didn't even notice she was there. Rachel felt like clearing her throat, but decided against it. After all, the whole point was to get a room, and whatever Sam was doing seemed to be working.

For a second Rachel wondered if she was like that around Sam. If her brain went straight out the door, along with her ability to know she was being conned. The girl behind the counter was already digging out the keys for the new room, and in her haste to give Sam what he wanted, forgot to even ask him for a credit card or ID.

Sam took the keys with an easy smile. "Thanks, Krista," he said, letting his hand brush hers. "I really appreciate it."

She giggled and turned a furious shade of pink, and as Sam and Rachel turned away from the counter, she called after them, "I'm on shift until five a.m., so if you, uh, need anything, just, uh, call the front desk."

Rachel rolled her eyes.

"Was all that really necessary?" Rachel asked, annoyed. "Couldn't you have just ordered her to give you a room? What's with the flirting?"

Sam just gave Rachel a sly smile. "Jealous?"

"No," Rachel snapped, sounding more defensive than she intended.

"She didn't have a weak mind," Sam said. "So I had to try a different approach."

"Just how many approaches do you have?" Rachel asked.

"Would you like to find out?" Sam quipped, an amused smile tugging at the corners of his mouth. Rachel realized he was still in superflirt mode.

"Stop flirting with me," she growled, annoyed, as she crossed her hands across her chest and tried not to be affected by the size and presence of him in the close quarters of the elevator.

"As you wish." Sam leaned back against the railing of the elevator and glanced up, an amused look still on his face. Rachel did her best to ignore him.

Their room was at the end of the hall, far from the elevators, and by the time they got to it, Rachel just wanted to take a hot bath and try to forget the last forty-eight hours. Of course, after she walked into the room, all thoughts of relaxation fled her mind. There was one king-sized bed in the middle of the room, and its headboard was made entirely of horseshoes fused together to look like hearts. The bedspread had cowgirls with short skirts and impish smiles, and there was a red silk heart-shaped pillow in the middle of the bed. She supposed this was the western version of the honeymoon suite.

"How are we going to do this, exactly?" Rachel asked, meaning the sleeping arrangements, but Sam jumped a little. "I mean, who gets the bed?" she asked, gesturing toward it.

"I don't sleep," he said almost curtly, the flirty half smile now gone. He was in one of his moods again. He sat down on a nearby chair and folded his arms, a frown on his face.

"Do you shower?" she asked, nodding toward the bathroom. She herself hadn't showered in two days and felt about as fresh as a pair of old gym socks.

He didn't respond, just half-shrugged, glancing away from her, and so she took that as her cue to take dibs on the bathroom. She told herself that a shower—even if it was in the Lovebirds Room— was the thing she needed to feel a little like her old self again, the self that didn't know about moody fallen angels or ancient water demons or any of this crazy stuff. She'd had about enough of crazy for one week.

Nineteen

Sam could hear the shower water running, and every drop that hit the shower floor felt like it was hammering on his own head. He told himself he had to keep his eyes on the floor, no matter what. He traced the Navajo pattern in the carpet, but could only keep his eyes there so long before they glanced quickly to his left, landing squarely on the bathroom door.

The problem was Sam could see through walls. It was a power that came in handy as an angel. After all, you didn't want to appear to someone who wasn't the right person, and so being able to see through buildings helped a lot. It wasn't an unlimited power. He couldn't see to the other end of the earth, but he could probably see a good twenty feet through pretty much anything, even steel or granite. Technically, he could see through clothes, but they were such a thin layer that he would end up seeing straight through a person's skin. If he wanted to see someone naked, a shower was his best bet. And, now, here, less than four feet from him, Rachel had slipped out of her clothes and into the steaming shower.

He should've just told her he had angel sight, and then maybe she would've showered in a robe, or not showered at all, but somehow he just conveniently forgot to tell her, and he couldn't help but wonder if part of him had hoped for a situation like this.

He forced his eyes back down to the carpet again and decided to spy on his downstairs neighbors. The room, however, was empty, so he tried the room next door, where he found a man flipping through channels on TV and nothing at all to hold his interest. His eyes flicked back to the bathroom door again and before he could stop himself, he was glancing beyond the door, inside. Steam had covered the glass shower door and fogged up most of the mirror, so all he saw was a flesh-colored silhouette. Still, even this tantalizing glimpse was enough to cause stirrings in him he hadn't felt in years, and the urge came on him so strongly that he felt like the wind had been knocked out of him.

He could see past the shower door if he concentrated a bit more, but instead he clenched his fists, stood, and turned away.

He marched over to the door of the hotel room, ready to leave and go somewhere—anywhere— where he wouldn't be tempted to spy on Rachel, when a strange sound in the hall downstairs caught his ear. He glanced quickly at the floor and saw a group of three bulky angels moving fast down the carpeted hallway. And they weren't just any regular angels. They wore the black SWAT-like uniforms of the Archangel Special Forces.

For a second his heart skipped a beat. Were they after him? Could the Big Guy have called in the ASFs to stop him for good?

ASFs were usually only called for really big problems, and Sam doubted he was the world's biggest problem at the moment. Besides, if they were going to take him, they could've done it when he'd been in the jeep driving across the desert from the airport. There would've been much fewer witnesses than a hotel full of people. ASFs struck fast and hard and used surgical precision to eliminate their targets in order to cause as little commotion as possible. They were the ones God sent when the Pestilence horseman of the Apocalypse got free and ran loose on earth in the Dark Ages. He managed to stay out long enough to start a plague and kill half of Europe before the ASFs got him and sent him back. They took him down without a single human witness, and that's how they liked to work.

Coming into a hotel full of people meant they were risking exposure. Whatever they were after was big.

Maybe it was Tiamat, he thought. Maybe she was here.

Sam paused, hand on the doorknob. Should

he follow them and find out? Or would that leave Rachel vulnerable to attack if Tiamat *was* lurking nearby somewhere? The angels in black were moving quickly. He had to make a decision now.

He turned the knob and rushed out to the hall, keeping his eyes on the floor. He had to find out what the angels were here for, and he promised himself he wouldn't go far in case Rachel was in danger. The Special Forces Angels moved at a speed he could barely keep up with, a not-so-subtle reminder that Sam was most definitely weakening and losing his powers. The angels in black stopped at the end of the hall, fanning out like a SWAT team, giving each other silent signals as they prepared to storm the room at the end of the hall. In a silent swoosh, all three angels burst through the door in a fury of black, securing the room in a matter of seconds.

Sam watched from above as the ASF leader grabbed the demon they apparently were seeking and whipped him around. Sam nearly lost his footing when he saw the man's face: it was Kevin Farnsworth.

Impossible. He was eaten alive by Tiamat before his very eyes. And yet, here he was, walking and talking and in the grip of a very angry-looking Special Forces Angel.

"Where *is* she?" the angel said now, voice like steel, as he tightened his grip around Kevin's neck.

Kevin looked scared. Legitimately scared, and he should be. ASFs were not the kind of angel who showed mercy. Most of them were former Wrath angels.

"I don't know. She told me to get this, and I did, but when I came back, she was gone," Kevin babbled, holding up a small bag. Another angel ripped into it, and inside there was a single narrow tube of lip gloss.

The commander nodded at the third angel, who was hanging back, and he whipped out the door. He moved so quickly, Sam couldn't follow him, but he was back in a nanosecond.

"Parking lot is clear," the angel said, reporting. "No sign of Praying Mantis. Or Surfer."

"Praying Mantis is a good code name, but Surfer? Tiamat isn't a surfer," Kevin said.

Sam sucked in a breath. Tiamat was there.

"That's pretty lame, guys." Kevin barely got out the last word before the commander had squeezed the air out of his windpipe.

"Tell us where Casiphia is," he demanded, and his wings, which had been tucked neatly behind his back, popped open, hovering above Kevin's head like a white menace.

"I told you, I don't know," Kevin squeaked out. His face was quickly turning red as he clawed at the commander's fingers and kicked his legs, trying to get free.

"If you don't know, then you're of no use to us." The commander cocked his fist back, preparing for a death strike.

"Wait!" Kevin cried, desperate. "I know her plans."

The commander paused a second. "So do we," he said, and then with surgical precision he rammed his fist straight into Kevin's chest and the entire demon quickly turned to dust. It was a special death move of the ASFs. The demon's soul had been sent on an express train back to hell, where he probably had a lot of explaining to do.

"And *you*," the commander said, raising his eyes to Sam. "Eavesdropper."

Sam looked for a quick exit, but couldn't find one. In a blink, all the angels had ascended through the floor and surrounded him. They all gave him hostile stares. ASFs did not like Fallens, mostly because they had to clean up the messes Fallens tended to make.

"Sam, I thought that was you," the commander said, hands on his hips. "I see earth time hasn't sat well with you. You look like shit."

"Ethan, good to see you, too," Sam said sarcastically, recognizing the angel before him as one who used to be his commander. Ethan was hard-nosed and by the book, and never had second thoughts about following orders, mostly because Ethan was ambitious and cared only about getting ahead. He would kill his own brother to get a promotion. Sam pretty much hated his guts, and by the look on Ethan's face he could see the feeling was mutual.

"What are you doing slumming with the ASF? I thought you'd be on the joint chiefs by now," Sam said, a smirk on his face.

"I'll do the talking," Ethan said, peeved. Apparently Sam had hit a sore spot.

"What? Got passed up? Didn't kiss the right ass?" Sam's mouth curved into a cocky smile.

"Shut up," Ethan added, stepping into Sam's personal space. "I won't take back talk from a soldier too chicken to do his own job. You're a coward, Sam."

"And you're a shallow, glory-grabbing snake, Ethan, who wouldn't know free will if it bit you on the ass."

Ethan's cheeks flushed red and he balled his hands into fists. "Next time you see us coming, you should run the *other* way. My team doesn't like Fallens, do we?"

A grumble of agreement rumbled through the other ASFs. Sam glanced around at the serious faces before him. Once they'd been comrades. Now they were enemies.

"Next time we see you, we might just take you out for the fun of it. Hold Order be damned."

"Hold Order?" Sam echoed, surprised.

"Yeah, somebody up there likes you. Someone high up," Ethan grumbled.

"Is that a fact?" Sam asked, grinning.

"Prepare ascension," Ethan growled, turning his head. The three angels crossed their hands across their chests and closed their eyes. Instantly they swept straight up through the ceiling, disappearing into tiny blips in the night sky.

He stared at the sky long after they'd disappeared. Sam wondered who up there liked him. Maybe it was the J-Man. He always had a soft spot for lost causes.

In a flash out of the corner of his eye, he saw the two Watcher angels who'd been tailing him for the last week hovering over the hotel roof. If anyone knew what was going on, they would. He rushed to the stairs and took them two at a time.

Twenty

"I *told* you we'd miss something good, but *noooooo,* You were busy grabbing McDonald's at the drive-through."

"What? Stress always makes me hungry," Gabriel Too said as he whipped out the brown McDonald's bag from his other pocket and started to dig around in it. He pulled out a few fries.

"Well, I hope it's worth it, because we missed the Special Forces guys," Frank the New said, nodding to the now empty sky. "I've never seen them work."

"They're total jerks, anyway," Gabriel Too said, shrugging.

Frank the New rolled his eyes. "Uh-oh, you might want to go hide somewhere, Gabe," he added, glancing down and seeing a very determined-looking Sam staring up at the two angels.

"Ahhhhh!" Gabriel Too shrieked as his eyes met Sam's.

"Okay, Watchers," Sam growled, his voice full of menace. "You'd better tell me what's going on, or things are going to get really ugly very quickly."

"I'm getting some lousy training, that's what's going on," Frank the New grumbled.

"Shut up!" Gabriel Too whispered. "Don't make him angry."

"Damn right don't make me angry," Sam said. "You do that and I will report that you've been falling down on your jobs." He nodded toward the empty burger wrapper tucked in Gabriel Too's hand. "Eating instead of watching? Your lieutenant angel won't be happy to hear about that."

"See? Told you that was a dumb move," Frank the New said.

Gabriel Too ignored him. "You can't tell on us. You don't even know who our lieutenant is."

"Wouldn't happen to be Lieutenant Mark? I know him personally," said Sam. Gabriel Too turned a paler shade of white. Sam continued, "I'm sure a Big Mac isn't a falling offense. Although I hear they're cracking down on gluttony these days. You never know."

"What do you want to know?"

"Why is Tiamat trying to kill Rachel?"

Frank the New and Gabriel Too looked genuinely baffled. "Don't know," Frank the New said, shrugging.

"Um, because she was jealous of Rachel's moxie?" Gabriel Too offered. He gave Sam a weak smile.

Sam, exasperated, sighed. "Who's Casiphia?"

"Um . . . dunno," Gabriel Too said, shaking his head and spreading his hands.

"Do you have any relevant information at all? Anything you can tell me that's worth a damn?"

"I have something," Frank the New said. "A little piece of advice. One of these days you're going to have to choose a side, you know. You keep pretending you're one of the good guys, but you can't just pretend. You have to *be* one. Because being a pretend good guy is the same thing as being a bad guy."

Sam frowned.

"What are you *doing*?" hissed Gabriel Too. "You're going to make him mad."

"I don't care if I do; someone has to say it."

"Put a muzzle on your friend, or I'll do it for you," Sam snapped at Gabriel Too, and then he jumped up and grabbed the McDonald's bag from Gabriel Too's hand.

"Hey! That's mine."

"Not anymore," Sam said before he disappeared back into the hotel.

Twenty-one

When Rachel stepped out of the bathroom, her dark, damp hair wrapped in a towel and wearing a fresh pair of yoga pants and comfy cotton T-shirt, she expected to find Sam sitting in a chair and glaring, but instead she discovered an empty hotel room. She should've been relieved, but she found herself disappointed. She glanced at the desk, but there wasn't a note left for her. Not that she expected a surly fallen angel to be courteous enough to leave messages. Especially when most of the ones she'd been getting from him lately had been mixed. He had more mood swings than her great-aunt Lucille, and she was famous in Amarillo for sitting on her porch with a loaded BB gun and shooting at any kid who was daring enough to try to step on her lawn.

Rachel unwrapped the towel from her head and combed her fingers through her hair. She couldn't help but wonder if Sam hadn't just stalked off somewhere. What if he'd taken up that hotel clerk's offer? What if he wanted to see just how far his charm would get him? Rachel didn't see any reason why he shouldn't pursue just about any offer he had. Why not rack up the conquests? After all, he didn't have anything to lose.

And the hotel clerk had been more than willing. She had practically done a striptease on the lobby desk. He wouldn't have any trouble convincing her to spend some quality time with him. Rachel hit a particularly rough tangle in her hair and yanked a little too hard.

"Ow," she said to the empty room. She stopped combing through her hair and let her hands fall into her lap. She didn't have a reason to be jealous of Sam. He'd barely even kissed her on the lips. Not to mention, he was the least of her worries. Or should be. And yet, here she was, imagining him with his arms wrapped around some young hotel clerk.

She forced herself to put the image out of her head. He probably wasn't with the hotel clerk. He didn't seem that interested after they had gotten the room, she reasoned. So, he was probably just off on one of his brooding, need-to-be-alone walks or something. Then again, what if it wasn't just Sam being Sam? What if he was in trouble? Maybe he had gone after the demon who was trying to kill her. Maybe just now he was in the climax of some kind of life-and-death fight.

The image of him in a fight was far worse than the one of him with the hotel clerk.

She forced herself to think of something else. She wondered what Cassidy was doing at the moment. She wanted to call. She glanced at the clock. It was half past midnight, and far too late to risk it. She'd already called at ten; he'd been asleep, and Constance had been quite annoyed, since it had been her tenth call of the day. She would just have to assume Cassidy hadn't turned the street to ash. Yet.

Thinking about her baby boy possibly setting the town on fire was not a pleasant distraction, and so she quickly turned her thoughts elsewhere. Of course, then she started thinking about her demolished house, and whether or not the insurance would cover demon attack (*Does that count as an act of God or no?* she wondered), and pretty soon found herself thinking about Sam again. Frustrated, she blew out a breath and stood, grabbing the TV remote from the bed and flipping on the television. Of course, what she found there wasn't any help, either. Every station seemed to have either an angel or a devil movie on. She flipped through *Michael*, *Angels in the Outfield*, and *The Devil's Advocate*.

She flipped to CNN, and even they had a feature story about someone claiming to have seen an angel hovering over a McDonald's drive-through. She turned up the volume.

"I swear it was an angel, with wings and a robe and everything," said the pimple-faced teenage boy in a McDonald's uniform. "He asked for extra special sauce."

Rachel jumped up and started pacing the room. An hour or so later, when she'd convinced herself that Sam had been killed by a demon and she was next, the door to her room swung open and Sam walked in, carrying a bag from McDonald's.

Rachel spun and put her hands on her hips. "Where have you *been*? I've been worried sick," she said, sounding a lot like she did when she chastised Kevin for staying out too late after his bowling night on Thursdays.

Sam simply held up the bag. "Hungry?" he asked her.

She glanced at the McDonald's bag in his hand and then back at the TV. The angel story had looped back around and was replaying.

"That wasn't you, was it? Angel in the drive-through?"

Sam glanced at the screen just as they put up a drawing of what the teenager and two other people at the drive-through claimed to have seen. The picture was like any angel you'd see on a Christmas tree. Wings, white robe, gold rope belt, and matching sandals.

Sam frowned. "I don't have wings," he reminded her, and dropped the bag on the table. Rachel realized she hadn't had dinner and was famished, and she dug into the hamburger and french fries like a starving woman. She glanced up, mid-chow-down, and saw Sam wasn't eating. He was just sitting on the bed, watching her intently. She realized she must look like a pig without even the benefit of lipstick, and swallowed her mouthful of Big Mac with as much dignity as she could muster.

Sam was studying her now, his frown deepening on his face, and Rachel couldn't tell if he disliked her in particular or the fact she was shoving a dozen fries in her mouth at once. Kevin had even once told her she ought to enter one of those hotdog eating contests because she could get at least ten in there without even trying.

Sam sat down and crossed his arms. He didn't look her in the eye. Rachel decided she'd had enough of his moping. He disappears and scares her nearly to death and then he goes all Grumpy Dwarf on her. No way. Not this time.

"What is your problem with me anyway?" she snapped.

Surprised, Sam raised his head. "What?"

"Your problem. *With me.*" Rachel had her hands on her hips now as she felt her temper rise. "You seem to care enough about me not to let me die at the hands of some demon, but when it comes to sitting and having a conversation with me, you act like I'm bad luck or something."

Sam shifted uncomfortably but said nothing.

"What? Am I too loud for you?"

Sam sighed. "It's not that."

"Then what? Spit it out." Rachel stared at him, hard. She used the same steely-eyed look of death she'd used on her brothers when they wouldn't tell her where they'd hidden her Barbies. Or when Kevin claimed he was too tired to take out the trash. They all caved eventually, and it looked like Sam would, too.

"You are so different from anyone I've ever met," he said.

"Is that a compliment or an insult?"

"A compliment," Sam said. "In some ways you also remind me of the first Rachel."

"The first?"

"Wife of Jacob? You know he had to work for fourteen years for her father before he agreed to let Jacob marry her."

"That's a long time."

"Well, Jacob thought she was worth the wait."

His scent was back in the room. That, combined with his clear blue gaze, was enough to make her completely lose her train of thought.

"You didn't answer my question," she managed, doing her best not to succumb so easily to his charms. "What's your problem with me?"

"I don't have a problem," he said, which was clearly a lie.

"If you're not going to be honest with me, then I'm leaving," she said as she walked across the room, grabbed her jacket, and headed for the door. She could feel the vial in her pocket where she'd left it. If he tried anything funny, she would use it, she decided.

"Wait," Sam said, grabbing her arm. "Don't go."

"I'm . . ." Rachel was about to say "leaving" when suddenly Sam had pulled her close and was kissing her, full on the lips. Her first instinct was to push him away, but that thought was soon completely overtaken by another desire altogether. So close to him, his scent was nearly overwhelming, and her anger vanished.

His smell was all around her now, and she could feel his strong arms tighten around her. She felt a little thrill as she deepened the kiss, and soon she was sitting in his lap, her hands in his hair. He responded now, taking control, flipping her back on the bed and putting some but not all of his weight on her as the urgency of the kiss turned into something more. He was like no man she'd ever touched before, and she realized with a start, that was because he wasn't, technically, a man.

It had been so long since she'd felt this kind of need, and she wondered if living with a demon for the last five years and a baby for the last year had permanently destroyed any hope of her ever feeling desire again. She hadn't had sex in ages. It had been so long that she had just about forgotten why it was so important in the first place. And yet, now, so close to Sam that she could practically hear his heart thud in his chest, she realized she wanted him, and wanted him in every possible way, and while part of her knew this was wrong, another part told her she was tired of being the responsible one, the mother who took care of things, the wife who picked up the pieces. She was going to do something reckless for a change, because she wanted to.

She remembered, dimly, that this was what all the fuss was about. And, boy, what a fuss.

She was tugging on his shirt, and it came off quickly. But just as suddenly as it did, Sam pulled away, breathing hard, and wouldn't look her in the eye.

"We can't," he said.

The disappointment was like a slap.

"Why?"

"I'll hurt you."

"You can't hurt me," Rachel said, her hands moving up his chest.

"But I can," he said, stopping her hands. He sounded sad.

"Please." Rachel's voice was soft.

"I'm sorry; I can't," Sam said, shaking his head. "You don't understand. A union between us . . ." His voice faded.

Rachel began to understand that he was telling her this really wasn't going to happen. "But why?"

"It's because of what I am," Sam said and sighed.

"But demons and humans can. But angels and humans . . . can't? I don't understand."

"It's best you don't," Sam said, and turned away.

Rachel felt a rush of emotions all at once—disappointment, anger, embarrassment. She'd practically thrown herself at him, and now he was making it all too clear he wasn't interested. She was just like all those other mindless women he attracted. One more zombie under the influence of his pheromones.

Her hands fell away from him, and she turned away, wishing herself anywhere but here.

"Rachel." Sam's voice was soft as he touched her arm. She shrugged off his touch.

"I get it; no big deal," she said, voice cold.

"You don't understand. I don't want to hurt you."

"Then don't."

"Rachel." Sam's voice was insistent. Sincere. "I want you more than I've ever wanted a woman. And that's the problem." Against her will, he pulled her close, enveloping her with warmth and his compelling scent. Despite her better judgment, her anger was thawing.

"So is this the point where you tell me it's not me but it's you?"

"Oh, no, it's definitely you," Sam said, as he tugged her even closer. "You drive me wild," he said, burying his nose in her hair and taking a deep breath. "I'm not actually sure I can resist you."

Rachel let out a grunt. She was forgiving him. Little by little.

"But if anything happened to you because of me, I couldn't forgive myself," he whispered in her ear.

"I don't understand you."

"The feeling is mutual," he said.

Rachel folded herself into him and sighed. It wasn't as good as sex, she reasoned, but she liked the hug, anyway. They were lying on their sides, face-to-face, and he was holding her tightly. She glanced at the arm hugging her tight. She saw the ring of tattoos in a language she didn't understand.

"So, the tattoos . . . what do they mean?" She traced the one above his right bicep.

"It's my rank and file," Sam said. "All angels have them, to tell you their division and their rank, but it's written in the ancient language."

"Rank and file angels!" Rachel found that hard to imagine.

"Did you think man dreamed up army divisions all on his own? We had them first."

"I see." Rachel traced the tattoo with her finger. Then she ran her hand around his side and to his back. She felt a deep indentation there that went nearly half the length of his back and stretched wider than a palm. In fact, Rachel could fit her whole hand in the width of the scar.

She propped herself up a little.

"Are they from . . . ?"

Sam nodded. "Wings," he said.

Rachel stroked the scar with a gentle caress. The skin there was softer than the rest of him and more sensitive to the touch. He shivered a little as Rachel traced the outline of the puckered, pink skin.

"Did it hurt to lose them?"

Sam nodded. "The wings had been ripped off in one quick surgical slice. I bled for weeks, and the pain didn't ebb for months. But worse than the pain was the feeling that I'd lost something vital to myself, like an arm or a leg."

Rachel fell silent then as she absently traced the line of his chest with her fingers. Sam curled himself around her, and he was warm and strong, and his sweet cinnamon smell closed around her, making her feel safe. She yawned, realizing suddenly how tired she was, and without deciding to, she snuggled into him, closed her eyes, and fell asleep.

The next thing she knew, it was dawn, and the light was streaming into their bedroom. Sam had held her all night, and he was awake when she opened her eyes.

"It's time for us to go, isn't it?" she asked him, sitting up.

Sam simply nodded.

"Give me five minutes to get dressed," she said, padding off to the bathroom.

Twenty-two

Sam watched Rachel sip her coffee from a paper cup she'd snagged from the Grand Canyon Caverns diner. They were sitting in the rented jeep, in front of a human-sized plastic dinosaur, waiting for the first tour of the Grand Canyon Caverns. Sam had memorized the map from Rachel's ring, and this is where Azazel was hidden. Sam had to admire God's forward thinking. He was sure the Big Guy had done this on purpose—buried Azazel in a place that would become one giant tourist trap, so that for all eternity Azazel would be able to hear the footsteps of a million women of all shapes and sizes marching straight over his tomb. He glanced at Rachel. It would be dangerous to bring her too close. He planned to subdue Azazel quickly, but on the off chance he managed to escape, he didn't want Rachel to be the first person Azazel saw.

But Sam couldn't leave her above ground alone, either, not with Tiamat on the loose and him no closer to understanding why the ancient demon wanted her dead. He watched Rachel as she looked blankly out through the windshield, sipping her coffee, and wanted desperately to know what she was thinking. She'd been quiet since her shower this morning, and she was one of the few people he had a hard time reading. Most people wore their thoughts on their faces, but Rachel was more complicated. He couldn't tell from one minute to the next what she might do or say.

"So is Kevin going to be down there? With Azazel?"

"About Kevin . . ." Sam began, thinking about his run-in with the ASF angels.

"What about him?" Rachel's voice was suddenly sharp, her big brown eyes squarely focused on him. Under her stare, Sam faltered. He didn't want to see the disappointment on her face, or see her upset.

"Er, well, I can't be sure he's here," he hedged.

"Well, obviously," Rachel said. "Kevin can't be counted on for being anywhere you think he'll be."

"Exactly," Sam said and dropped the subject. He promised he'd come clean with everything eventually. That is, if they both survived the next few days. He needed her to follow his instructions, and he couldn't be sure she would if she knew Kevin was gone forever.

If anyone on the caverns tour took notice of the tall, strikingly good-looking dark-haired man in the leather jacket and the pretty, slim woman by his side, no one let on. Most everyone on the tour was pushing sixty, and fanny packs seemed to be required accessories. Sam was concentrating most of his persuasive powers on the tour guide, hoping that he wouldn't take notice or remember them. They would be making quite a mess in the caverns, and having anyone who could give the police a decent description of them wouldn't be good. Not that he cared particularly about himself. He doubted there was a jail that could hold him, and there were many places he could hide. But Rachel was a different story. He didn't want her implicated in any way.

As they walked through the low-hanging caves, he scanned the floor for any special marks. They wouldn't be visible to the human eye. They would be just below the surface, where only an angel would be able to see them. About halfway through the tour at a particularly narrow passage that was closed off to tourists, Sam found what he was looking for: a tiny mark about a foot down, marking the door to Azazel's tomb. Remarkable. He didn't expect the hiding place to be so close to the surface, much less on a tour. He reached out and touched Rachel's arm, signaling her to stop. She glanced at him silently as he pulled her away from the retreating tourists.

He dropped to the floor as Rachel watched, and he felt along the rock for a seam, or anything that might make getting to the door a little easier than breaking through solid rock. He had the strength to do this, but it would be loud, and he didn't need that kind of attention. At the south edge, he found a small dimple, which to most people would seem like just part of the natural formation of the rock, but Sam knew it was more than that. It was a keyhole of sorts, designed to accept a drop or two of blood from a particular kind of creature, usually an archangel. They were the ones who had the highest security clearance. His blood probably wouldn't work. But it was worth a try.

"What is it?" Rachel whispered.

"A door," Sam said.

"But how did you know it was there?" she asked.

"There's an ancient symbol, beneath the surface," he said, his mind distracted by the lock. If he couldn't open it, simply bashing into the rock probably would do no good. It wouldn't be your average rock, since it had to be strong enough to keep an angel—at full strength—imprisoned. Sam dug around in his pocket and pulled out a penlight, shining a small beam of light on the lock.

"You can *see* through things?" Rachel persisted.

"Of course."

"See through things like bathroom doors and shower curtains?"

Sam's head snapped up and his attention suddenly focused again on Rachel. Her lips were curled in a teasing smile.

"I didn't spy on your shower."

Rachel just kept smiling. "Uh-huh. And fallen angels are known for their honesty."

She was close enough now to kiss him, but she didn't. Sam had a hard time focusing his attention back on the task at hand when all he wanted to do was take Rachel straight back to their hotel room.

"Are you going to do something about it?" Rachel asked him, and for a second he thought she had read his mind and was daring him to follow through.

"W-what?" he stuttered in surprise.

"The door," she said, matter-of-factly, glancing down. It was clear she had no idea the effect she was having on him. He gave himself a mental shake. He had to stop letting her distract him.

Sam glanced down at the door again, trying to focus his attention there. He would have to try the lock, even if it was a long shot. He put his finger on the little crevice, pushing it against the jagged edge. Like he thought, it was sharp as the hardest steel, and it sliced into his finger. He winced as a drop or two of blood dripped down. He didn't know what would happen if his blood didn't open the tomb, but it could, quite possibly, trigger a protective mechanism that would bring the entire cave around them down in an angry avalanche.

"You're bleeding!" Rachel cried, grabbing his hand. She whipped a Kleenex from her purse and pressed it against the tiny wound. His blood instantly soaked it through, proving it was a little more than just a nick.

"It's nothing," he said, pulling his hand away. Rachel clung to the tissue, as Sam waited, frozen where he was, for any sign of impending doom. A groaning sound beneath their feet made Sam tense, ready to protect Rachel from falling rock. But instead of the walls coming down around them, a second or two later the stone floor beneath them started to move. Somehow he'd opened it. He couldn't quite believe it.

"Did your blood do that?" Rachel asked as the floor revealed a tiny stone staircase headed downward.

Sam nodded, although he wasn't sure quite how it had happened. He took a step downward and then paused. "I don't want you to follow me," he instructed Rachel. She paused, giving him a blank look, and then he added, "It's too dangerous."

"Just what am I supposed to do? Go join the tour?" she asked, a skeptical look on her face as she put an annoyed hand on her hip.

"Wait here, and if anybody, I mean *anybody* comes out or in, you hide here," he added, nodding to a little crevice behind the opening. It was narrow, but he was sure Rachel could hide if she needed to do so.

"Cassidy would barely fit in there," she protested.

"Please," Sam said. "This is important."

Rachel hesitated, but then gave in. "Fine," she muttered, crossing her arms and backing away.

Sam knew she was upset, but he didn't know what he was going to find in Azazel's tomb, and he didn't want Rachel there for a whole host of reasons.

The tomb was dark, and Sam shined his flashlight down the long, winding staircase. He paused now and again to listen for sounds that Rachel might be following him, but he couldn't hear her, and it seemed she was, for once, obeying his instructions. When he got to the bottom, he saw a great stone slab with a man sitting on it, one leg chained to the slab by giant metal links.

Azazel lifted his head, his floppy, dirty-blond hair flipping back from his face. He wasn't wearing a shirt, and he hadn't changed much, despite the passage of more than a thousand years or the fact he'd been imprisoned that entire time. He had the same sharp green eyes, the same dimpled grin, and the same broad shoulders. He had movie star abs, despite having been locked away for two millennia. Sam knew in that moment that Azazel hadn't lost any of his dangerous charms, or his will to use them. He was exactly the same. The look in his eyes wasn't the least bit remorseful or contrite. Being locked up for so long hadn't done a thing to convince him he had been wrong.

"Why, Samsapiel. What took you so long?" Azazel said.

"How did you know my name?" Sam growled.

"Sit down." Azazel grinned. "We have some things to discuss."

Twenty-three

Rachel sat cross-legged on the cold stone floor waiting for Sam to return. She thought about marching straight out of the caverns, getting on the elevator that would take her up to the small diner above, getting into their rental car, and leaving the big lout to deal with his own problems, but then she remembered that he still had the rental car keys. She could call a cab, she guessed, but that would surely take the fire out of her dramatic exit. Maybe Father Daniels was right. Maybe he was nothing but trouble. He had dragged her halfway across the country and then ordered her to hide in a dark cave while he went down and fought one of the world's most dangerous demons. For what? It seemed like they were just doing the devil's work. He kept saying they might find Kevin, but she had seen no sign of him and was beginning to think he wasn't here at all.

She whipped out her mobile phone, thinking she

might just go ahead and call that cab, but it predictably didn't get a signal. She was about to at least go find a place where she could make a phone call when she heard footsteps farther down the cave. She stiffened, wondering if it was part of the cave tour, but then remembered that the tour had gone in the other direction. Either this was a new tour or the old one was walking in circles. In any case, she decided she didn't want to explain what she was doing sitting in front of an angel's open tomb in the middle of a tourist trap. She jammed herself into the tiny crevice, pulling her arms tightly to her sides, and waited. She could just about fit entirely, if she didn't breathe.

The footsteps drew closer, and Rachel could tell they belonged to just one person. So it wasn't a tour, then, she thought, trying to lean out slightly from her hiding place to catch a little glimpse of the path. She saw a slim, pale ankle first, and it was followed by another in matching ballet flats. The shoes belonged to a striking woman wearing a tight-fitting little black dress, which Rachel thought didn't exactly seem like appropriate attire for a Grand Canyon Caverns tour. The woman had long dark hair that went far past her shoulders and a figure that wouldn't quit. Rachel felt a little envy looking at her cellulite-free legs and thin, trim arms. Not to mention her big, pouty lips. Rachel couldn't decide if it was the lips or the disappearing hemline, but something about the woman just screamed sex. Rachel felt a small pang of jealousy as she looked down at her faded mom jeans and plain, brown Gap V-neck. She exuded Toddler Mom.

The woman didn't see Rachel, but she went directly for the descending staircase, as if she knew it was there all along. Rachel thought about shouting a warning to Sam, but she couldn't quite figure out how to do that without warning the woman as well. Besides, Rachel thought a little bitterly, Sam had a way with women, didn't he? A pretty girl in a short dress probably wouldn't be a match for his charms, anyway. She took out her cell phone again and hoped she could somehow get a signal.

"How did you know my name?" Sam asked again, his guard up. He glanced across the four corners of the cave, as if hoping to find the answer there.

"Oh, you'd be amazed at the news I get down here," Azazel said. "I've got my sources. So, you're supposed to be one of the best bounty hunters, eh?" He gave Sam an appraising look. "You don't look that tough."

"Maybe you'll feel differently after I deliver you to the devil," Sam said. "He's only been looking for you for a thousand years."

"She might have something to say about that." Azazel coughed, nodding somewhere behind him.

Sam turned around and saw that somehow he'd missed the sound of the woman who had come in behind him. Her footsteps were so light, he hadn't even heard her, and he hadn't smelled her, either. The mystery woman stepped forward and he had a clear view of her face. It was a woman he hadn't seen in more than two thousand years. A woman he thought was long dead.

"It's not possible," he sputtered, reeling from the fact that he was standing in front of the very woman he'd refused to kill all those many years ago. The woman who'd once crouched before him, holding the baby, in the rubble of Sodom.

"How . . . what . . ." He took a few surprised steps backward.

"The name is Casiphia, and yes, my dear, it *is* possible."

She was wearing modern clothes—a short black dress and flat shoes—and her hair was long and free and curled down her back. She was free of the burns on her leg, but otherwise she was exactly as he remembered her, except now there was a slight red shimmer to her eyes.

"Surprised to see me, I'm sure. I wanted to thank you for saving my life. The baby, of course, was never going to make it. It wasn't mine, though. A neighbor's."

"But Ethan . . . He . . ."

"Has terrible aim with a flaming sword. Besides, Satan saved me shortly after your regiment left. He offered me immortality. All I had to do was a couple of favors—the Holocaust, for example."

Sam felt the room spin. The woman he'd shown mercy to all those years ago had been turned into a demon who had killed millions of innocent people. And then he was hit by another, unmistakable truth—that's why God had ordered *him* to kill her. He wanted to make sure she was dead. The baby had been mortally wounded, but she had superficial burns. Sam knew Ethan was more politician than warrior. He let all of his underlings do the heavy fighting. But Sam had refused, and Ethan had bumbled the job, and now here she was, two thousand years later, one of the devil's most powerful demons.

Sam grabbed the holy wafer he kept in his pocket, and felt his body tense all over. "It's not too late for me to kill you," he said, and then he lunged.

"Oh, I don't know about that," Azazel said, behind him. In a second Sam realized his miscalculation. Azazel's chains were long. He could easily reach Sam, and he did, coming from behind and wrapping his arm around Sam's neck. Azazel grabbed the holy wafer before Sam could shrug him off.

Sam growled and his anger flashed into full-on fury as he swung Azazel forward, freeing himself and pinning Azazel to the ground. He swung hard, hitting Azazel square in the jaw. Azazel's head flipped back, and Sam wheeled back again, preparing to take full advantage, when he was grabbed from behind by a white-hot iron grip.

"Not so fast," Casiphia whispered in his ear, her voice now a sickening hiss. She was strong—too strong—and she whipped him easily away from Azazel. Surprised, Sam could barely keep his footing.

He struggled to grab another wafer from his pocket, but Casiphia pinned his arms back, giving him an impish smile. Casiphia trailed her bright red fingernail down his cheek, leaving a mark. Where her fingernail touched his skin, it burned. He winced, pulling away from her, but she held him fast.

"How sad that now you finally *want* to kill me, and instead you wind up doing me a favor." She nodded toward Azazel, who had gotten to his feet and now had wrapped his arms around Casiphia's waist from behind. He nuzzled her neck lovingly. "You see, while I was a mortal woman, I also fell in love with an angel. Azazel. And I've been trying to free him for two thousand years."

Sam felt like someone had hit him hard in the stomach. He could feel his head become light as he thought about what a pawn he'd been. Casiphia had been using him this whole time to release her old lover. Casiphia sliced into his cheek, and a drop of blood fell onto her palm. She touched the drop to Azazel's chains, and instantly his cuffs sprang open. Somehow she'd known that his blood would open the vault door—and Azazel's chains.

"I should thank you, old man," Azazel said, rubbing his wrists and ankles.

The betrayal hit Sam like a brick wall. His shock melted around the edges, and it was slowly replaced with a hot, white anger.

"I'm going to end you both," growled Sam.

"Oh, I don't think so," Casiphia said. "I think you'll be a good boy and stay put." Casiphia threw him hard against the back wall. The force of impact left an imprint in the rock the shape of his body.

"I would say don't follow us," Casiphia purred,

grasping Azazel's hand. "But I don't think you'll be in any shape to do much of anything for the next few hours, and by then, I think you'll find you won't be going anywhere."

He felt the room spin, and he realized it wasn't just from the bump on his head—Casiphia had poisoned him. She'd left some kind of venom in the scratch on his cheek, which was now making it nearly impossible for him to stand. He tried hard to focus, but the only thing he could see was the blurring image of Casiphia and Azazel leaving the tomb. He pulled himself up and attempted to follow, but the ground moved like water beneath his feet and he stumbled and fell, feeling weak and light-headed. He heard, rather than saw, the stone tomb door close, sealing him inside. The only light was now a pale beam of his flashlight shining up to the ceiling. His eyes fluttered closed, his mind a jumble of incoherent thoughts as Casiphia's poison took greater hold of him.

Twenty-four

Rachel heard people coming up from the tomb before she saw them and took refuge in her hiding place, careful to watch for any signs of Sam. She didn't see him. She did, however, see a man who could've been his brother in the dim lights of the cave. He was as tall and broad as Sam and had that otherworldly quality that Sam had—skin that was too perfect to be real, eyes that were a brilliant blue. Except *this* man was fairer, with blond hair, and had a different air about him altogether. Rachel didn't like him, but she couldn't quite say why. Maybe it was the curve of his lip that seemed to suggest some hidden cruelty, or maybe it was the way he reached out and quite unceremoniously pinched the bottom of the dark-haired woman in front of him, his lip curling into a leer.

He wasn't wearing a shirt, and when he turned, showing her his back, Rachel sucked in a breath. He had the same scars near his shoulder blades that Sam had. He was a fallen angel, too. *So this must be Azazel,* she thought. But where was Sam? Why was one of the universe's most dangerous fallen angels walking free?

She watched as the dark-haired woman bent down and clicked some unseen switch. The door to the tomb rolled shut, and Rachel's heart started pounding. Was there a second exit? Had Sam left that way? Was he still locked in there? Something, she knew, was very, very wrong.

The man kept his eyes on the woman's rear, pure lust showing on his face. Her heart thumping in her chest, she reached into her pocket and felt for the vial that Father Daniels had given her. She didn't know how she would use it, but if she were discovered, she'd have to try.

"Casiphia," the man said, his voice a little thick, as he grabbed her arm and pulled the dark-haired woman toward him.

Where on earth was Sam? Rachel wondered as Casiphia pressed herself fully against the fallen angel, her hand roaming down to his crotch.

The grope session was quickly turning X-rated, and neither one seemed to mind. In seconds he had hiked up Casiphia's skirt and yanked down her underwear. Casiphia just laughed, a throaty, flirty laugh, as he lifted her and spun her around, pushing her back against the cave wall, and proceeded to do things that would be illegal in at least four states.

Rachel was in shock. She'd never seen two people with less modesty her entire life and that included her middle brother, Jonathan, who once streaked through the Homecoming Parade buck naked in front of half the county on a dare. Rachel pressed herself flat against the little crevice that was barely big enough to hide her and prayed neither one of them saw her. She wished she could disappear. She didn't even want to think about what might happen if she were discovered. After what felt like forever, he finished with a grunt and dropped Casiphia to her feet, even as a new tour group approached.

"Was that enough to hold you over?" she asked, a smile on her lips.

"For now," he said. "You'd better have women waiting for me elsewhere."

"Of course," Casiphia said nonchalantly, as if he were asking for a pepperoni pizza. "All of your favorite types—at least a half dozen—waiting for you at a little campsite nearby. I say waiting, but not all of them willingly."

"They'll be willing enough when I'm through," he said. Rachel's stomach turned.

"You only have a night with them. After that, we have to move."

"I'll just need a night," Azazel said, flashing a devious smile. "Did I mention I love you?"

"You might have," Casiphia said coyly.

The sound of footsteps from an approaching tour echoed through the cave. People were coming.

"Come on, we have to go," Casiphia said. She grabbed Azazel's hand, and the two of them walked right by Rachel's hiding spot. She held her breath, but neither one of them saw her. She released it as the tour came through, a small, meandering bunch. She waited quietly until the last person in the tour walked by, and then she dropped on all fours, desperate to find the location of the door.

"Sam?" she whispered to the ground, and then felt stupid for doing so, as if he could hear her through rock.

"Rachel," a weak voice answered her. The voice somehow seemed to be right in her ear, and yet she knew it was Sam, from far beneath her. He sounded hurt. Something was wrong.

"Are you okay?"

All she heard was a moan. Desperate, she fumbled for the little lock she'd seen Sam open. After several long minutes she found it, the small edge that covered the finger-sized hole. She thought about sticking her finger in it, but realized her blood probably wouldn't do any good. Not to mention, she might lose a finger.

She glanced around her, looking for a stick, anything she might use to pick the lock, when she saw a crumpled tissue on the ground—the one she'd used to stem the flow of blood from Sam's finger. She grabbed it and unraveled it, feeling that it was still wet. Maybe it would work. Quickly she wrapped it around a tube of lipstick in her purse, and stuck the whole thing into the small hole in the ground. She waited, praying it would work, and just when she was about to give up, she heard a rumble beneath her feet. The stone door slowly opened, and a weak light from below leaked out.

"Sam!" she whispered again, louder this time, as she sprung down the old staircase, taking the steps two at a time. At the bottom of the stairs, she found Sam lying motionless near the far wall. Her heart dropped into her stomach.

She rushed to his side, putting her hands on his face. He moaned and turned over.

"You're not dead!" she cried, relieved. His eyes flickered open.

"Disappointed?" he quipped, before they fell shut again.

"Sam, can you walk? We need to get out of here. Casiphia . . ."

"I know," Sam groaned, as Rachel tried to help him into a sitting position.

"What's wrong? Are you hurt?"

"Poison," Sam ground out, and that's when Rachel realized Sam's skin was clammy to the touch and he was sweating profusely. There was also an angry red scratch on his cheek.

"Can you walk?"

Sam grunted as he slowly stood, putting a lot of his weight on Rachel. She stood next to him and put his arm around her shoulders. Together, they managed to shuffle a few steps. Sam seemed disoriented and dizzy, and he was having trouble making forward progress. In fact, more than once he nearly collapsed, bringing Rachel to her knees.

"This isn't going to work," Rachel said decisively. "I need to get help."

Sam just nodded, slouching down by the stairs, putting his head between his knees.

Rachel found help in a passing tour guide, and after she threatened to sue for Sam's falling down an unmarked hole (failing to mention that they had actually opened the hole in the first place), the staff members were very quick to help Sam get above ground. They were all a bit taken aback to find stairs in the rock and old chains along the floor of the cave. They were still talking about the discovery as Sam declined medical attention, despite a very adamant tour guide.

Once they got back to their jeep, Rachel took the wheel and spun them back out to the highway. Sam, still looking pale, laid his head against the doorframe, breathing in the fresh air blowing in from the open window.

"Are you going to be okay?" Rachel asked, not at all sure he was. "Maybe we should go to a hospital."

"They wouldn't know what to do with me," Sam said, his voice a hoarse whisper. This was no doubt true. They probably didn't get many fallen angels in the ER.

"Who was the woman with Azazel?"

Sam groaned. "Her name is Casiphia," he said. "She may be more dangerous than Azazel. And it's my fault she lives. I should have killed her in Sodom."

"Sodom?"

"She was the woman I spared. The woman who cost me my wings. We have to catch them."

"The woman with her baby? She's a demon."

"That's why God wanted me to kill her in the first place," Sam grumbled, more to himself than to Rachel. "I have to find them."

"Well, we better move fast. Casiphia has kidnapped women for Azazel."

Sam just groaned as Rachel pushed her foot harder on the gas. The wind blew through the open window, ruffling Sam's dark hair.

"Wait," he said, suddenly. "Turn left."

"There's no left," Rachel said, hitting the brake and scanning the barren shoulder for signs of a road. All she saw were trees from the state park they were driving through.

"There *is*. Turn left."

Rachel slowed to a near stop and obeyed, swinging the jeep out from the pavement, between two large trees and what looked like dirt. Amazingly, she saw tire tracks ahead of hers.

"Told you there was a left," Sam said, leaning a little farther out the window.

"Are you tracking them by smell?" Rachel asked, amazed.

"Demons have a particular smell," Sam said. "Hard to miss."

"And what are we going to do when we find them?"

Sam's eyes hardened. "Send them both to hell."

Twenty-five

"What are we doing, just sitting here? We've got to go help them," barked Frank the New, trying to urge Gabriel Too to his feet. His partner, however, sat on the edge of the Grand Canyon, feet dangling, in no hurry to move.

"No interference, remember?" Gabriel Too spread out his hands to show he was helpless.

"If you didn't plan on interfering, why did you take those?" Frank the New nodded to the long chains sticking out of Gabriel Too's left pocket, the chains he'd swiped from Azazel's tomb.

"I dunno. Thought they might be useful."

"Like when we fight Azazel?" Frank the New started to sound excited.

"Fight? What, are you crazy? We're not going to fight anyone." Gabriel Too shook his head, pushing the chains down into his pocket. "No, I mean, when we're giving our report up in Heaven when this is all over. You get extra points for visual aids."

"You're unbelievable."

"Sam would've been better off just killing Casiphia when God told him to," Gabriel Too said, changing the subject. "That's something you ought to remember, newbie. When He gives a command, He expects it to be followed on faith."

"Like Abraham? And his son?"

"Bad example. That was a little misunderstanding. God technically asked for a sacrificial goat, but it got lost in the translation. Believe me, *that* messenger angel got fired."

"Oh, dear."

"It's a little reminder *not* to fall asleep in debriefing meetings."

"So what now? Shouldn't we be trying to stop that guy—Azazel? He sounds like bad news."

"Even worse than you think. Every woman who conceives a baby with him will die."

"What do you mean?"

"Angel babies are huge and grow rapidly and a mortal woman's body is simply not capable of handling it. When the babies are born, they are supersized."

"Whoa—really?"

"Really."

"Does Azazel know?"

"Of course he does. He's counting on it. Last time he was here on earth he made about ten thousand babies. He wanted an army of giants that he could lead against heaven or hell, whoever attacked him first."

"He wanted to take over the world?"

"Think bigger. Try universe."

Frank the New whistled. "He's a lot worse than Sam, then."

"Yep. A lot worse."

"So we *have* to stop him." Frank the New reached into his pocket and pulled out a handful of dust. A bit of it sprinkled down to earth and turned a few rocks into giant pastel-colored Peeps.

"Oh, yeah, a lot of good an army of marshmallows will do us," Gabriel Too said, nodding down to the candy chicks below.

"If you teach me, then maybe we could do something constructive," Frank the New said. "Quick, show me how to make a flaming sword."

"Er . . ." Gabriel Too looked at his sandals. "No."

"Okay, fine. What about just righteous flames?"

"No."

"A burning bush? Anything?"

"No."

"But . . ." Frank the New stopped midsentence, realization dawning. "Hang on a second. You don't know how to make a flaming sword, do you?"

Gabriel Too put his hands behind his back and kicked an imaginary rock with his gold-sandaled foot.

"Well, no."

"I *knew* it! You probably can barely do more than I can!"

"I can definitely do more than *you*," Gabriel Too said, straightening and putting his hands on his hips. "I can jump-start cars, for one."

"Until I see a flaming sword, I'm not going to be impressed."

Gabriel Too seemed to think about this a moment. Then he snapped his fingers. "Okay, watch this," he said and reached into his pocket, pulling out a small pinch of dust. He rubbed it between his two palms and pretty soon the dust started to grow, taking on a shape not unlike a baseball bat. Then, as Gabriel Too closed his eyes to concentrate, the bat's handle grew into solid wood, and the other end began to sprout leaves and small flower buds. In seconds it looked like a large topiary.

"What are you supposed to do with that?" exclaimed Frank the New.

"You could hit somebody with it," Gabriel Too said defensively as he swung the topiary around a bit. A few of its leaves and petals fluttered harmlessly to the ground.

"Oh, yes, it's quite a weapon if your goal is to decorate a hotel lobby."

"I can make weapons." Gabriel Too frowned. "I just need a little time to concentrate. I don't do well under pressure. Maybe if you turned around so you're not looking at me, it might help."

Frank the New sniffed, unimpressed. "We don't have time for this."

"We do, actually," Gabriel Too said. "We're supposed to wait for the flood."

"Flood? What flood?" Frank the New looked alarmed. "There's going to be a flood? Like Noah-caliber?"

"Not *that* bad. Just wait. You'll see."

Twenty-six

Rachel and Sam drove down the dirt road in silence, Rachel wondering all the while if Sam was going to live or die. She had no idea what demon poison would do to him. After a while, however, it seemed that the effects of the poison were fading. He didn't have his head pressed against the doorframe anymore with his eyes closed as if the room were spinning. He was sitting upright, eyes open, staring dully ahead.

"So how did Casiphia and Azazel get away?"

Sam sighed and closed his eyes. For a second Rachel thought he wasn't going to answer, but then he did.

"They're stronger than me. I'm losing my strength."

"The poison?"

"I was on my way to becoming human anyway," Sam said. "The poison may be speeding things along." He paused. "Slow down," Sam commanded

suddenly as he leaned forward, hand on the doorknob.

"What are you doing?" Rachel was starting to
get nervous, thinking her passenger was going to
leap out of his seat and roll in the dirt like one of
the stuntmen from *T.J. Hooker*.

"Just take the left side of the fork in the road.
It'll take you straight to the Colorado River. Wait
for me there. I won't be long."

"But you're hurt."

"I'm fine. If I don't show in ten minutes, take
the jeep to the airport and fly home and forget anything ever happened here."

"How am I supposed to forget? You got an am-
nesia power you haven't told me about?"

"Just do it." Sam paused. "Please," he added a
little reluctantly, like the word was glued down and
hard to set free.

Rachel had slowed the car to nearly twenty
miles an hour. "But what are you—" Before she
could even finish her sentence, Sam had swung
open the door and jumped out. Just like Rachel
feared he would, except he didn't roll, he just landed
on both feet and kept running. She slammed on the
brakes in time to see him in her rearview mirror
as he slipped into the trees. The passenger door,
however, was still swinging open.

"I could've just stopped," Rachel muttered as
she leaned over and grabbed the open door. "But he
had to show off."

Rachel thought long and hard about driving

on, just like Sam told her to do, but the more she thought about it, the more it just didn't make any sense. He wasn't in his right mind on account of the poison, and he probably wasn't in his right body, either, and there he went, off to fight a demon and a fallen angel who had bested him when he *wasn't* loopy on demon juice. It hardly made sense. Not that Rachel could be much help in that department, either, she reasoned, but if she caught up to him, maybe she could convince him to call off his little suicide mission. It didn't occur to her that going after him was her own brand of suicide mission.

She swung the jeep around and parked it at the spot where she saw Sam duck into the trees. Then she got out on foot and headed into the woods, hoping she'd lay eyes on him soon, and if she didn't, that she could remember enough of her Girl Scout camping training not to get lost.

Sam made his way quickly down the trail that he knew would take him to Casiphia and Azazel. He could smell Casiphia from half a mile away, and her scent was only getting stronger. The poison, luckily, was wearing off, but he still wasn't quite himself. Rationally, he didn't have a chance of winning a straight fight with either of them, but he wasn't being rational at the moment. All he wanted was a chance to try to even the score. Besides, he had the element of surprise with him. That was usually enough for cowboys in Westerns, and it was good enough for him. His pride wouldn't let him admit defeat. He'd never lost a straight fight with a bounty, and he wasn't about to let this one go just because the odds weren't in his favor.

At a small clearing near the Colorado River, he found what he was looking for: two silver antique RVs, complete with two lawn chairs sitting out front. Sam concentrated and scanned the first RV. Inside, he saw Azazel and Casiphia kissing, and neither one was wearing clothes. Repulsed, he quickly looked away. He scanned the adjacent trailer and saw at least six women, all with their hands tied and gags on their mouths.

He started toward Azazel and Casiphia's trailer, but hesitated. He turned back to the other trailer. He could almost hear Rachel's voice in his ear. She would want him to save them. His best chance at winning would be to attack Azazel and Casiphia now, when they were vulnerable, but if he did that and he lost, then the fate of the women would be sealed.

After having a second of indecision, which wasn't like him at all, he decided to free the women first. He silently moved forward and wrenched open the door. A blond woman leapt back in surprise, fear on her face, and then puzzlement. Sam put his hand to his lips to signal quiet, and the woman nodded. Quickly he undid her restraints, as well as the others', and told them in hushed tones how to get to the road. They filed silently out of the trailer and quickly disappeared through the trail into the woods, some running blindly, others taking deliberate and calm steps.

Now Sam took a deep breath and stepped toward the other trailer.

A rustling sound in the woods grabbed his attention before he'd taken two steps. He glanced quickly to his left and saw a woman walking toward the clearing, half in and half out of the shadows. At first he thought it might be one of the six he'd let go, who'd gotten lost or frozen in panic, but the more he stared, the more he realized he knew that overconfident gait. It wasn't a panicked hostage, or an innocent hiker: that woman stomping directly and decidedly into danger was Rachel.

He let loose a dozen or so curses in at least four languages, two of them dead. Then he sighed and hung his head. He should've known she wouldn't take orders, even if he said "please." She was as stubborn as at least three kinds of demon. He peered into the next trailer and saw the two had finished their sweaty dance and were lounging about on the small trailer bed. They wouldn't stay distracted forever. Sam had to get Rachel to safety before they figured out he'd just let Azazel's harem free. If Rachel were anywhere near when that happened, she'd feel the full brunt of Azazel's anger and, most likely, his lust. The thought made Sam feel sick. It was one thing to know he wouldn't survive, but it was quite another to think of Rachel as being hurt in any way.

He took the steps four at a time and managed to head Rachel off before she made it to the clearing.

"What the heaven do you think you're doing?" Sam hissed in her ear, tightening his arm around her waist as he easily lifted her off the ground and pulled her back to the road.

"Trying to talk some sense into you," Rachel said, fighting uselessly against his grasp. "I was coming here to try to convince you not to go through with your suicide mission."

"By making it a double-suicide mission? Do you have *any* idea how dangerous they are?"

"Do *you*?" Rachel countered. "Or do you *want* to die? Is that the plan?"

Sam grit his teeth but didn't get a chance to answer because a howl behind him screeched through the air. Azazel had discovered the empty trailer. Sam picked up the pace, practically flying to the jeep. He considered running her straight on down the road, but decided against it. The poison was still weakening him and he would attract undue mortal attention. He placed her in the passenger seat and swung himself into the driver's seat. He threw the jeep into gear, but, instinctively, he knew it was too late. In his rearview he saw a flash of bodies materializing in seconds. They were Casiphia and Azazel, standing at the center of the trail, fuming. He hit the gas and hoped the six-cylinder engine could outrun them.

Rachel grabbed the dashboard, even as Sam gunned the engine and they sped off down the dirt road at speeds not fit for highway driving, much less unpaved roads. But Rachel didn't tell him to slow down. She whipped back around in time to see

Casiphia and Azazel in pursuit, no more than two whitish blurs on the road behind them, and even as Sam hit the gas, they didn't seem to be putting more distance between them. One of the blurs—Azazel—materialized just long enough to give her a little wink. She shuddered.

The jeep took a particularly rocky patch hard, and Rachel braced herself for another set of bone-jarring bumps.

"No asphalt," she shouted to Sam, "is one of many reasons I hate camping."

Sam just sent her a sidelong glance with the hint of a smile before he threw the jeep into a different gear. The jeep roared under Sam's command, breaking through a small patch of shrubs, and suddenly they were driving up a steep incline, all red mud and rocks, like in one of those Jeep Wrangler commercials she thought were all staged. But apparently the Wrangler could handle the rocks, even if her spine was having trouble. She set her jaw and grabbed the dash to steady herself as the jeep bumped and jostled over the rough terrain.

At the top of the incline they bounced over mostly flat rocks, avoiding several large boulders, and as they turned the corner, Rachel realized with amazement that they had somehow made it to the Grand Canyon. It stretched out before them in a giant zigzag.

"Wow," she breathed, taking a millisecond to take in the spectacle. That was before a rather large rock hit the back of the jeep. She turned and saw that Casiphia was hurling stones at them, a rain of rocks that made Sam swerve abruptly several times, sending them perilously close to the edge of the ravine. A giant boulder fell in front of them, and Sam turned hard to the right, sending them on a path straight into the canyon.

"Look out!" Rachel shouted, but it was too late; they were going over.

Sam, seemingly unfazed, ripped off what was left of the jeep's canopy above their heads and grabbed Rachel securely by the waist.

"Hold on to me," he shouted, before the entire jeep went straight over the side of the cliff. Sam leapt up then, taking Rachel with him, and the two of them were soaring through the air for one heart-stopping minute. Rachel wanted to squeeze her eyes shut, but they were frozen open in shock. Sam threw himself against the side of the cliff, and his outstretched hand made contact with the cliff wall. Rachel heard a hard screeching sound, and realized that Sam's hand was carving a long line into the rock. She glanced over and saw a few shocked tourists on donkeys, walking a steep trail beneath them. Sam slowly came to a stop, with Rachel still grasped tightly to his chest. They dangled for a second or two before Sam swung his body over to a waiting ledge, gently placing Rachel on it. She nearly cried tears of relief when her feet touched hard ground. Sam pulled his hand out from the rock, swatting some extra dirt and dust from it. She noticed he didn't have a single scratch, despite having dug a gaping gash in the side of a mountain. Down below, the donkey-riding tourists started snapping pictures of them, and some applauded Sam's rescue efforts. Sam ignored them. His eyes were fixed high above, where Casiphia and Azazel stood on the ledge looking down at them.

Rachel swallowed hard. This wasn't good. She didn't see an escape route, as the tourists were at least fifty feet below them, as was the slow-moving Colorado River. Sam stiffened beside her as if ready to spring to action, although just what kind of action he planned was beyond her. Unless he could fly, which she knew he couldn't, they were in deep, deep trouble.

Rachel glanced up and saw Casiphia give them a slow smile, then pull something from a bag on her shoulder: a glass jar filled with a murky kind of liquid. The jar gleamed in the sunlight.

"What's that?" Rachel asked.

Sam just frowned.

Casiphia unscrewed the cap and dumped the contents over the side of the cliff, and what started as a Big Gulp–sized cascade soon ballooned into a roaring river.

"Tiamat," Sam ground out. He threw his arms around Rachel and pushed her protectively against the rock face, just as a wall of water hit them.

Twenty-seven

"Oh, dear," cried Frank the New as he and Gabriel Too sat on the edge of the Grand Canyon, feet dangling in. "I see what you mean about the flood. What are we going to do? We can't let Tiamat drown Rachel! And if you say we can't interfere, so help me I will—"

"Calm down. We're going to help. I've got it covered."

"What? With more decorative flowers? Where's that flaming sword, for Pete's sake?"

"We don't need a flaming sword," Gabriel Too snapped, annoyed.

Gabriel Too reached into the pocket of his white robe. He pulled out a harp and set it aside, and then a stick of glitter glue and a packet of Tic Tacs. "Where did I *put* that?" he murmured to himself as he kept pulling out more junk, including a remote control, a small potted plant, and a giant foam "number one" hand.

"What are you doing?"

"Ah! Here it is," Gabriel Too cried, pulling out a small baby food jar. It was filled with a purple-colored liquid. He unscrewed the cap.

"Where did you get Free Will?" Frank the New asked, amazed.

"With yellow tickets," Gabriel Too said. "Told you that prize room was pretty comprehensive. You can never have too much Free Will."

"So, you dump it in the water, and Tiamat remembers that she's got a choice in what she does and isn't controlled by Casiphia." Frank the New looked at Gabriel Too with new appreciation. "You know, I can't believe I'm saying this, but that might well be a genius move."

"Yep, it is," Gabriel Too said, looking smug.

"But I thought we weren't supposed to interfere."

Gabriel Too smiled. "I'm not interfering," he said. "I'm just—oops!" He tilted the vial, spilling its contents into the water below. "Having a little accident. It's a shame I—*accidentally*—spilled that."

"Yes, very accidental."

"Exactly."

"So how do we know if it worked?"

"We just have to wait and see." Gabriel Too reached deep into his pocket and pulled out a pair of binoculars.

"Hey—how long have you had those?"

"A while."

"And you didn't think we could use them before?" Frank the New asked.

"My pockets are big," Gabriel Too explained. "Sometimes I lose things in there."

Sam could feel his grasp loosen from the canyon wall, and despite all his best efforts to hang on, he just wasn't strong enough. The wall of water hit hard and washed them both off their little ledge in seconds. They flew where the water took them, downward, toward the river and the waiting tourists. The donkeys were the first to sense looming catastrophe, and some of them tried to bolt, but it didn't matter. The water was coming, and it was coming fast.

It hit the pack of tourists like an avalanche, sending fanny packs and sunscreen flying, as well as bodies and donkeys in all directions. The water swept them up and carried them along, swelling the river's edges. Sam held Rachel's head above water, even as she coughed and sputtered, arms flailing. He tried to control his body, waiting for the water to take on a life of its own, crushing the breath out of them, but it didn't. It simply ran free, merging with the Colorado and rushing forward at a break-neck speed, as if Tiamat weren't trying to kill them after all. It seemed like she was trying to escape.

Sam lunged at a rock that swept by them, hoping to grab hold. His grip seemed even weaker than usual, and he slipped. Another rock swept past them, and Sam reached out, this time managing to cling to it. He pulled Rachel to the rock and she managed to climb half on it, half off, her feet and most of her bottom half-dangling in the rushing water. Sam surveyed their surroundings. They were at a relatively swallow part of the river, dotted with rocks. He saw that several of the boulders made a path to the shore. That path, however, was quickly being swallowed by the rising water. He had to move fast. He stood and then leaned down, holding his arm out to Rachel.

"Grab on," he said as she reached for him. He concentrated on keeping his balance while he swung her up and onto his back. The move was harder than it should've been. He was definitely losing strength. He grunted with effort, holding Rachel on his back, and focused on making the jump to the next rock. He hoped adrenaline and what was left of his strength would be enough to get them to the other side. He used everything he had to leap from rock to rock. He made it to two before almost losing his footing. He forced himself upright, balancing on the sharp point of the stone even as the waves lapped at his heels.

Above them, Casiphia shouted what sounded like "Get them!" in a screech that was more demon than human. Sam braced for the deluge, fully expecting Tiamat to rear up and drown them, but instead she parted the waters, showing him a dry path to land.

"Thank you," Sam said to the ancient water demon, even as she swept past them down the Colorado River. "I hope you get free."

The water didn't answer, just simply rushed by as Sam made it to shore in four big steps. Sam glanced once back upward and saw that Casiphia and Azazel were arguing, and Azazel was pointing angrily at the water below. They didn't look like they were planning a pursuit. He had to take advantage of their distraction to get Rachel to safety.

"Can you walk?" Sam asked Rachel, helping her to her feet. Rachel nodded. "We've got to go. Find a way out of here."

Sam scanned the cliff face, looking for the best route up. He didn't see much in the way of ledges or crevices he could use as handholds. Not to mention he wasn't quite sure he'd be able to carry Rachel all the way up. And there was no way he'd risk having her climb by herself without a safety rope. He looked backward. The water was rising, and fast. Pretty soon, the entire canyon would be filled. Tiamat was only growing in strength and speed. He didn't want to test her goodwill again. He had to get Rachel out of there.

He glanced farther up, to the top of the cliff, and noticed the two angels who'd been following him the last week, sitting there, feet dangling off the edge. One of them was peering at them through binoculars.

"Why don't you guys make yourselves useful and find us a rope?" Sam shouted up to them. The angels, a little startled by being addressed directly, jumped. The one with the binoculars spoke.

"We can't," he said. "We're just Watchers. We're not supposed to interfere."

"Right," Sam said, rolling his eyes. "Like you guys really follow those rules."

"Um, who are you talking to?" Rachel whispered, glancing up and at the rocks. Naturally, she couldn't see the angels.

"Just a bunch of amateurs," Sam said.

"Who are you calling amateurs?" the one holding binoculars said defensively. "I could fly you two up here in, like, a heartbeat. I'm just trying to play by the rules."

"Forget the rules; let's help," the other said.

"Uh, Sam—the water?" Rachel said, pointing.

"Besides, you didn't say, 'please.' "

Sam sighed, exasperated. "Please."

"What? I didn't hear that," he said, putting his hand behind his ear as if to help catch the sound.

"I said *please*!" Sam cried, louder this time. If he ever got up there, he thought, he'd beat some sense into those angels.

Rachel glanced up, still puzzled, as she was completely shut out of this conversation. As far as she knew, he was talking to rocks. She sidestepped the growing water, pressing herself against the canyon wall and trying to find a foothold to climb up.

"Are you going to talk to yourself all day? Or are we going to climb?" she asked Sam.

"What do you think, Frank? Should we help them?"

"Will you stop talking and start helping?" Frank said, reaching downward to try to grab Sam's hand. Sam reached up, but Frank's hand was too high to reach.

Sam glanced back over his shoulder and saw

that Casiphia and Azazel were nowhere to be seen. They had either taken their argument elsewhere or were regrouping for a surprise attack.

"Could we make a decision sometime *this* century?" growled Sam.

"Gabe, I need help here," Frank said.

"Indeed. Well, fine. We'll help. But it's only accidental help. If anyone asks, I accidentally spilled this angel dust."

"Fine," Sam ground out, not at all sure he wanted to be indebted to a pair of incompetent angels. But he didn't have much of a choice. He didn't want to risk being trapped by Azazel and Casiphia, and he needed all the help he could get.

"Good. Now, up you go." The angel put down his binoculars long enough to sprinkle a little angel dust down the side of the rock, a vine with blossoms appeared, and Sam grabbed it and pulled them to safety.

"Where'd that vine come from?" Rachel asked.

"Angels."

"Where?" Rachel turned her head from side to side, eager to catch a glimpse of a real angel. Sam couldn't help but note the excitement in her voice. Apparently fallen ones just weren't the same thing.

"See? *She* likes us," the binocular-wielding one said.

"Shut up," Sam growled.

"And this is the thanks we get," he exclaimed. "We should've saved her and left him down there to drown."

"That's not very nice. And neither is hogging those binoculars."

"I'm not hogging them!"

Sam sighed and turned his back on the bickering angels.

"Come on," Sam said, grabbing Rachel by the arm.

"But I want to see the angels," she said.

Sam glanced back and saw one of the angels grab the binoculars and throw them down on the ground, and the other leap up, angry.

"No you don't," Sam said. "They're fighting over binoculars."

"They're what?"

"Never mind," he added. "Trust me, it's just not worth it. Let's go."

Twenty-eight

"How could you let Tiamat go? We *needed* her," Azazel said, for the fiftieth time, as they looked at the gushing water that was now flowing straight into the Gulf of California. The two had followed Tiamat across three states and hadn't managed to contain her. With the water around her, she'd grown too strong for Casiphia to ensnare her again.

Casiphia was starting to wonder if Azazel was worth all the trouble.

"I didn't *let* her go," Casiphia spat. "I was trying to stop Sam. He could wreck all our plans. All he has to do is talk to those angels that are all around him and—"

"He doesn't know our plans."

"He can figure them out."

"He's not *that* smart," Azazel said, smug. "And even if he is, what's he going to do about it? He won't fight with demons, and angels won't fight with him. He's not a threat to us."

"And you were always way too overconfident," Casiphia said, even as Azazel's eyes roamed to a nearby woman who was selling handmade seashell necklaces on the beach. The woman met his gaze and smiled shyly. Casiphia nudged Azazel. "Can we focus, please?"

"You can focus," Azazel said, making his way over to the woman. "I'll be right back."

"Not again!" Casiphia stomped her foot.

"You are not one of those jealous sorts? One of *those* types of clingy demons?" Azazel's gaze was sharp.

"I'm not jealous; I'm roasting out here," Casiphia said, fanning her face. "And we're wasting time. The devil's army could be on to us soon, and we need to go back to Texas. I told you, that's where we can raise an army. The Dogwood Festival is this week. We'll have three hundred eighteen-year-olds from all over the state. And they're supposed to be pretty. They're all Dogwood Princesses or something like that."

"I do like royalty," Azazel said, tempted.

"Exactly," Casiphia said, neglecting to mention that neither the Dogwood Queen nor Princesses were actual royalty. It was a statewide festival where teens competed for the honor of being crowned Dogwood Queen for the year. The major perks were publicity and riding in floats in the Dogwood Festival parade.

Azazel paused, as if considering this. Then he made up his mind. "We have plenty of time to get there," he said, continuing toward the woman on the beach. "Besides, it's not wasted time if it's love at first sight."

"Your love at first sights last about ten minutes."

"That's all I need," Azazel said with a leer.

Casiphia was *really* starting to wonder if he was worth all the trouble.

Twenty-nine

Sam hadn't said more than three words on the plane ride back to Texas, and Rachel was beginning to think he'd forgotten she was there at all. Sam had insisted that they drive straight to the airport once they'd managed to find a road and Sam had charmed himself into the RV of a fifty-something woman who played Dolly Parton's greatest hits on a loop. She dropped them off at the airport, and despite looking like they'd just survived a flood and an avalanche, Sam also managed to charm the airline attendant into giving them free seats on board the next 777 bound for Dallas.

Now the two of them were sitting in silence as Sam steered Rachel's white minivan toward her house. In the absence of conversation, she'd had time to figure out a few things. Like, for one, Father Daniels was right about Sam's obsession with self-interest. Chasing one of his bounties had nearly gotten them both killed. Clearly the man had more baggage than DFW International Airport.

But what Rachel couldn't figure out was why he'd bothered to bring her along at all. And then there was the other puzzle: the fact that every so often she caught him staring at her with one of his intense expressions that she couldn't for the life of her read.

Rachel saw they had turned down Constance's street. The familiar shapes of her neighbors' houses zoomed by and before she could blink, Sam had pulled the van into Constance's driveway.

Rachel unlatched her seat belt, but Sam stayed seated, unmoving.

"You should be safe now," he said without looking at her. "Tiamat has escaped, and I don't think Casiphia or Azazel will come after you. I think they have other things to worry about."

"Oh," Rachel said. This was the longest sentence Sam had spoken to her in more than eight hours. She was still processing the sound of his voice when he continued.

"I have to go after them," he said. "It's important that I stop Azazel. He . . ." Sam paused a beat. "He can do a lot of harm on earth."

"Not anything to do with him running off with your old girlfriend?" The words popped out of her mouth before she could reel them back in. She wished she had a faster edit button. Hers seemed to work like her brother's old VCR. It never would rewind anything, and later, when her mom took it in to get repaired, they found it was full of old gummy bears.

Sam gave Rachel a sharp glance. "She's not—"

"Your girlfriend," Rachel finished. "I know." She paused and looked at her hands. "Are you coming back?" she asked him, staring at his profile. She wished there were some flaw she could find, but everything, from the slope of his forehead to the bend of his chin, was perfect.

"I don't know." Sam still didn't look her in the eye. This was starting to get annoying. She was beginning to feel like a one-night stand who had worn out her welcome. First he was all cuddly and now more cold shoulder? Rachel was getting whiplash. Thank God they hadn't slept together, she thought. Who knows how he would be then.

"Okay, then, answer me this one question before you go. You never intended to find Kevin, did you?"

Sam's eyes shifted quickly to hers. She'd managed to break his stoic, far-off look. *Good*, she thought.

"No," he said, looking a little pained as he said it.

"Can you tell me where he is?"

"He's been sent back to hell by archangels, and he's not likely to come back." Sam still looked uncomfortable. But at least he seemed like he was telling the truth this time.

"But how do you know?"

"I saw them—back at the lodge."

"And you waited until *now* to tell me?"

Sam didn't make eye contact, and Rachel swallowed what she was about to say next. Her surge of anger quickly faded, and she just felt empty inside. She glanced up at Constance's front door. She knew Cassidy was inside waiting for her. She now had to raise him alone, and she didn't have the first clue how to do that. How was she supposed to deal with a fire-breathing toddler? She suddenly felt like a fish in skis. She had no idea what she was going to do next.

She shook those uncertain thoughts from her head and lifted her chin a little. Well, she certainly wasn't going to let Sam see her go all boo-hooey. She had enough pride not to lose it in front of him.

"Okay, well, good luck," she said curtly as she swung her legs out of the minivan. "Hope you find them."

Sam looked a little taken aback. Maybe he was expecting a waterworks scene. Well, Rachel wasn't a waterworks kind of girl. She grabbed her bag and took a step away.

"Rachel . . ." Sam said. He had climbed out of the driver's seat and was walking toward her. He looked like he might be about to say something important. Rachel paused, waiting. A tiny flame of hope lit up inside her. Maybe this wasn't good-bye? The hope must've reached her eyes, because Sam seemed to abruptly lose confidence in whatever it was he was about to say. He shifted awkwardly. "You forgot your jacket."

He held up the jacket, which Rachel hadn't seen. Suddenly she felt like a fool.

Silently she reached up to get it, and as Sam handed it over, the little vial of dogwood oil fell out of her pocket and onto the grass.

Sam glanced down, frowning.

"What's that?" he asked, suspicion in his voice as he reached down to pick it up.

Rachel felt her stomach sink. "It's nothing. It's just—"

"Dogwood oil," Sam growled, as if he could smell it through the cap. His temper flared. "Were you planning on using this on me?"

"Well, no, at least not now. I mean, Father Daniels—"

"Wanted you to kill me," Sam finished.

"No, no, no. He said it would just stun you. So I could get away."

"You'd get away, all right," Sam said, turning his back. "A few swallowed drops of that would kill me." Sam thrust the jacket and the vial into Rachel's hands. She took them awkwardly, still reeling from the fact that Father Daniels had lied.

"But I didn't know. I swear."

But Sam wasn't listening. "I should've known better than to trust you," he muttered. He turned his back on Rachel and started to walk away.

"Sam, wait," Rachel called after him, but she was too late. In a blink Sam had sped away, leaving in a blur before she could say another word. She stood there a second or two before turning toward Constance's house, a sick feeling in her stomach.

* * *

It had been centuries since Sam had felt this angry. Or this blindsided.

He should've known Rachel—like all daughters of Eve—would eventually find a way to betray him. Anger—an emotion he'd always had trouble controlling—bubbled up in his throat. He looked around for a demon, or a Watcher angel—anyone he could start a fight with. Finding no one, he knocked over a couple of mailboxes as he zoomed down the street, but it didn't make him feel any better. In fact, it made him feel small.

Eventually his anger drained away, and he realized he wasn't really mad at Rachel. She'd never used the dogwood oil, and she probably didn't know it was lethal to him. He was really mad at himself. He was angry he'd lied to her, and angrier still that he'd put her into harm's way. Casiphia or Azazel could've killed her, and that would have been on his head. The more he tried to protect her, the more he put her in danger. For centuries he had only thought of himself, he realized. The bounties, the deals with the devil, they were all about his pride. His stubborn pride. He wanted to prove to God and everyone else that he didn't need anyone. But now he realized his mistake. He did need someone. Rachel made him realize how lonely—and self-serving—his life had been.

He cut across two yards and a school's playground and found himself on the plot of land where Rachel's house used to be before Tiamat reduced it to rubble. His bike, miraculously, was in one piece

and sitting right where he'd left it in the driveway.
He glanced down and saw today's newspaper rolled
up at his feet. A teaser headline on the top of the
news section caught his eye: Another Pregnant
Woman Killed; Fetus Goes Missing. He reached
down, picked up the paper, and glanced through the
story. According to police, a pregnant woman had
been murdered and the unborn baby taken. It was
the second in a string of similar crimes in southern
California. Unusually large footprints were found
at both crime scenes.

Sam, however, knew it wasn't a murderer. This
was Azazel at work. What Sam hadn't told Rachel
was that the baby of an angel and a human was
a mix called a Nephilim—a fast-growing giant.
Most women didn't survive the quick birth. This
was why Sam hadn't slept with Rachel. He didn't
want to risk even the remote possibility of her becoming pregnant. Azazel, of course, didn't care. All
he wanted was an army of Nephilim that he could
lead and take over the earth. That's what he'd done
nearly two millennia ago, and now it looked like he
planned to do the same now.

Sam felt a stab of guilt. He'd been so short-
sighted. His obsession with power and bounties
had led him to unleash one of the most dangerous
Fallens the earth had ever seen. And now he'd put
the lives of thousands of innocent women at risk.
For now he pushed aside his feelings about Rachel.
He had a job to do.

And there was only one way to stop Azazel.

He'd have to make a deal that he never thought he'd make. He swung a leg over his motorcycle and turned over the ignition. The bike rumbled to life and he steered it toward the Mega-Mart off the interstate.

Cassidy dropped everything he was doing and sprinted toward Rachel, throwing himself in her arms and hugging her tight. To her relief, there wasn't any sign of flames. Constance looked like she hadn't gotten much sleep, but otherwise everything in her house was intact and burn free.

"How was he?" Rachel wasn't sure she wanted the answer.

"He was fine," Constance said, a bit too high-pitched and with a forced cheerfulness that told Rachel she was lying. Still, she appreciated her friend for trying. "He missed you."

Rachel hugged her son a little tighter. Demon or no demon, she didn't care. He was her baby boy.

"I never thought I'd say this, but I kinda like that kid," said Father Daniels as he came out of the kitchen, drying his hands on a tea towel.

"What's he doing here?" Rachel snapped.

"He was helping Cassidy learn to control his powers."

"The kid's a fast learner," Father Daniels said. "Gotta give him credit for that."

"I want him out," Rachel declared.

"But why?" Constance exchanged a look with Father Daniels.

"You lied to me," Rachel declared, standing. "You told me the dogwood oil would only stun Sam. Not kill him."

"Well, if I told you it was fatal, I figured you wouldn't use it. Did he go up in smoke?" Father Daniels looked a bit too eager.

"No. I didn't use it. But he found it and accused me of trying to kill him."

Father Daniels smacked a hand against his forward. "You let him *find* it? Oh, woman. That's your first mistake."

"Constance, tell Father Daniels to get the hell out of your house," Rachel demanded, eyes flashing with heat.

"Now, wait, let's just hear him out," Constance said. She looked at Father Daniels.

"Hear me out what? I said my piece."

"Father," prompted Constance. "Tell her what you told me."

Father Daniels threw down the tea towel and sighed. "Fine. Look, you know I don't trust Sam. When I ran into him all those years ago, he destroyed half a village trying to collar one of his bounties. He doesn't care about anything but himself."

Rachel considered this a minute. "I don't believe Sam would do that."

"Believe it," Father Daniels said. "If there was a choice between saving you and saving his own hide, he would choose his hide in a second."

"See?" Constance said. "Father Daniels was just trying to look after you."

Rachel considered this.

"And," Constance continued, "he has really helped with Cassidy. He's like a new boy."

Rachel sighed.

"I don't know if I can forgive you," Rachel said. "But I'll think about it."

"Well, thanks," Father Daniels said sarcastically. "I swear, no good deed goes unpunished around here."

Cassidy, who looked up at Father Daniels' wrinkled face, giggled.

"Think that's funny, do ya, kid?" the old priest said, giving the boy a poke.

Out of the corner of her eye, Rachel saw that the television, which was switched to CNN, showed some footage of the Grand Canyon.

"Can you turn that up?" she asked Constance, who grabbed the remote from the coffee table and flicked the volume button. Rachel got to hear the reporter talk about a planned water surge through the Grand Canyon.

". . . scientists are purposefully flooding the Colorado River to help flush the river of impurities and help the local fish life reproduce . . ."

"Planned flooding!" scoffed Rachel. "Hardly."

"What do you mean? Did you find Kevin?" Constance asked, eyes wide with concern.

"No, and it's a long story. You won't believe me."

"Try me. I see dead people, remember? And the future. You can't shock me."

Cassidy broke free of his mother's arms then

and jumped on Constance's lap. As soon as he made contact, Constance froze, like she'd gotten an electric shock.

"Uh-oh," Rachel said, shooting out a hand to steady her friend. "Another vision?"

"Dammit, I thought I had that under control," Constance said, groaning as she held her head. Her eyes, focused on Rachel and Cassidy, suddenly grew wide with worry.

"It's Cassidy," Constance said, suddenly alarmed. "He's in trouble."

"What do you mean, 'in trouble'?"

"He's going to be kidnapped," Constance said with a certainty that sent a chill down Rachel's spine.

"Kidnapped?" she echoed.

"By a demon," Constance said. "And her name is Casiphia."

Thirty

"So let me get this straight, you want *my* help in fighting Azazel, and in exchange, what do I get again?" said Marcus the demon and manager of the Mega-Mart off Highway 9. He leaned back in his squeaky office chair and put his feet on his desk. Behind him, a row of black-and-white television screens flickered with images sent from security cameras based throughout the store. One of the screens, however, was running a local news broadcast.

Sam scrunched his nose a little; Marcus's demon smell, like burnt popcorn, was nearly overpowering. He was beginning to regret coming here at all. But he didn't see that he had a choice. It wasn't like he could call the ASFs, or any other angels he knew, for reinforcements. They had made it perfectly clear they didn't want anything to do with him.

"You get the prestige of bringing down one of the most wanted on Satan's lists," Sam said. "It'll surely mean a promotion."

"It's true Satan likes to be the only fallen angel on earth trying to take over the world. He doesn't like competition," Marcus said, waving his hand as if that were obvious. "But what about you? You're not going to come to our side, then?"

"No," Sam said.

"So I am supposed to trust a would-be angel who's not even willing to admit he's already one of us?"

"I'm not one of you," Sam ground out and then immediately regretted it. A flash of annoyance rippled across Marcus's face. Sam tried to calm himself. "What I mean is that we have a common enemy and we should join forces. It's a win-win for you. You don't need me to turn."

"Seems to me, with your temper, that you'd be well-suited for the Wrath division of Satan's army."

"I don't do Wrath anymore," Sam said.

Marcus gave him a knowing nod. "Which is why you're here, begging me for help to find Azazel and Casiphia. Because you want to nice them to death."

Sam managed not to blurt out that he wasn't begging. He never begged.

"So why not ask some of your angel friends to help?" Marcus asked, folding his fingers together in front of him and studying them. Sam clenched his teeth and looked away from Marcus. "Or are they not talking to you these days?"

"Are you going to help me or not?" Sam snapped, his temper getting the best of him.

Marcus slid his feet off the desk, leaned forward, and gave Sam a very evil grin.

"We'll help," Marcus said abruptly, extending his hand. "I suppose this makes us partners."

Reluctantly, Sam took Marcus's hand and shook it, hoping he'd made the right call. He glanced at the TV behind Marcus and saw a story on the news that caught his attention. The graphic on the screen said, "Pregnant Women: A New Target?"

"Turn that up," Sam said, pointing to the screen. Marcus leaned back and twisted the knob. The voice of the perky female anchor flooded the small office.

"The last victim of the alleged serial killer was found early this morning near Fort Worth. Currently, police have no leads, but they say that women in their third trimester should be extra cautious when walking alone or driving at night . . ."

"That's Azazel," Sam muttered, doing quick calculations in his head. He knew the truck stop. It was maybe two hours from Dogwood County. "But why is he here?"

"Maybe for this?" Marcus tossed Sam the morning's paper. On the top of the fold there was a teaser about the Dogwood Festival Beauty Pageant being held that very evening. "You said he had a weakness for fertile young girls, and here they are."

"That's it," Sam declared. "That's where he'll be. Can you get your troops ready in time?"

Marcus just smiled a sly smile. "We're *always* ready."

After strapping Cassidy into his car seat, Rachel had made a beeline for Branson's bar before remembering it had been completely wiped out by Tiamat. Rachel needed help, and fast, and Sam was the only one she knew who could even remotely begin to protect Cassidy from Casiphia. She looked at what was left of the once shady biker bar: a concrete slab and some bits of broken bar stools, hoping against hope that maybe Sam would be here anyway, but he wasn't.

"Dammit," Rachel muttered, hitting the steering wheel.

"Daaaaaabbbit," imitated Cassidy from his car seat. Rachel glanced at him through her rearview mirror and he just smiled at her. He was quite simply too angelic to be half demon.

Rachel focused her attention back on the highway. In one direction was the church where Sam had taken them to hide. She thought about going there, but she wasn't sure if Cassidy would sit still inside a church for very long. Besides, the pastor probably wouldn't take kindly to a fire-breathing toddler on the premises.

In the other direction was Mega-Mart, the place where Constance had foreseen Cassidy being kidnapped. Constance had told her it was in the Mega-Mart parking lot that she'd seen Casiphia grab Cassidy. So Rachel planned to stay away from there at all costs. If she didn't take Cassidy near the Mega-Mart, she reasoned, he couldn't be kidnapped.

Then a police truck swung into the parking lot of Branson's. Rachel recognized Nathan behind the wheel. He put the truck in park and slid out of the driver's seat.

"Hey, Rachel," he said, giving her one of his easy Garrett smiles. "I hear Cassidy might be in trouble. How 'bout the two of you come to the county jail? We'll look after the both of you."

Rachel felt instantly relieved, even though she wasn't quite sure what Nathan or anybody could do to protect her and her son against one of the world's most powerful demons. Still, the county jail was in the exact opposite direction of Mega-Mart. It seemed as good a place as any to hide, and with its cement walls was practically fireproof. Another plus.

"If it makes you feel better, I'll call Father Daniels. He's pretty good with this, uh, kind of stuff."

"Thanks, Nathan," Rachel said, suddenly feeling very grateful.

At the station, surrounded by ten or so sheriff's deputies and watching Cassidy's eager face as he pointed to all the squad cars in the parking lot, Rachel started to feel a little more relaxed. She knew they were dealing with otherworldly demons here, but it was really hard to think about that when Nathan was handing her a hot cup of coffee. She could see why Constance was so head over heels for him. Not only did Nathan have the looks, he also had a gentle way about him that made Rachel feel at ease.

Father Daniels, for his part, was talking to Constance on the other side of the station, the two exchanging whispered words for the better part of the last half hour. Rachel tried not to let this add fuel to her worry and instead focused on Cassidy, who was sitting on the floor at her feet, playing with Nathan's traffic whistle.

"Are you sure you don't mind him playing with this?" Rachel asked.

"It's fine," Nathan said. "It's high-near inde-structible, and besides, I have dozens of 'em."

Rachel knew that nothing was indestructible where Cassidy was concerned but took comfort in the fact that Nathan had replacement whistles.

The Father Daniels–Constance powwow broke up, and the two made their way over to Nathan's office. Rachel tried to read Constance's face but couldn't get much other than that she was nervous. And she had been nervous since she first had the vi-sion about Cassidy.

"Now, little guy," Father Daniels said, getting down to Cassidy's level. "If you're good, I promise I'll teach you how to use a rocket launcher."

"Father!" admonished Rachel.

"Just kidding, son," Father Daniels said, but then when Rachel's back was turned, he gave the boy a little wink.

"Everything okay?" Rachel asked Constance.

"As okay as it gets," Constance said. "I still somehow feel this is all my fault."

"*Your* fault? How?"

"Well, nothing weird ever happened in Dog-wood County until I started getting visions, and now, look, it's like an epidemic."

"Maybe weird stuff was always happening, but

we just never stopped to pay attention," Rachel said. "Besides, without you, we would be flying blind here, so I appreciate the advance warning."

"Some warning. I got a few flashes of Cassidy in the parking lot of Mega-Mart with Casiphia. That's all. I can't even tell you if it works out all right in the end."

"It will," Father Daniels said with a confidence that encouraged Rachel.

"How do you know?" Constance asked him.

"Well in the *end* end, as in end-of-the-world, it will," Father Daniels said. "That's guaranteed. But as for the here and now, well, it's anyone's guess."

Rachel's shoulders slumped. "That doesn't make me feel a whole heck of a lot better."

Rachel's mobile phone blared the Dixie Chicks from her pocket. She snatched up the phone and, seeing an unknown number flash across the front, got a cold feeling in the pit of her stomach. She just knew this wasn't going to be good news.

She flipped open her phone. "Hello," she answered, praying it was a telemarketer.

"Rachel, my dear," a slick and sultry voice purred through the phone. "How *have* you been? And more important, just how are you and my old friend Sam getting along?"

"Casiphia," Rachel barely managed to whisper. Constance stiffened. Father Daniels moved in closer to hear, and Nathan stood, hand on his gun belt.

"Of course. None other," Casiphia said. "And how's that darling little son of yours?"

"You stay away from him," Rachel hissed, every nerve in her body on edge. Her heart was pounding, and she was ready for a fight.

"Here's the thing," Casiphia said. "I've always wanted a little half-breed demon son of my own. They're so hard to find at the adoption agencies. You have no idea."

Rachel only managed a growl this time.

"And to think you've got one right there for me."

"You can't have him."

"Oh, I can, and I will, and you'll bring him to me. Because if you don't, I'm going to kill Sam. Isn't that right, baby?"

A muffled groan into the phone made Rachel's heart drop into her stomach.

"Azazel wanted to just outright kill him, but I'm much more practical. I'd rather torture him first and *then* let him die," Casiphia said. "Or, you could save him. It's your choice. Meet us at the Mega-Mart parking lot in an hour. Bring your son, or Sam dies."

Rachel felt all the blood drain out of her head and her hands went numb with fear.

"Oh, and Rachel? Don't be late." With that, the line went dead.

Thirty-one

Sam was doing his best to concentrate on the task at hand, and not let the smell of the other twelve demons squeezed into the van he was driving distract him. They would be at the beauty pageant well in advance. He would be able to take Azazel by surprise; of this, he was sure.

"What *is* that smell?" one of the demons in the back shouted. "I swear, it's getting worse."

"Shut up, Ian."

"What? I'm telling you, it's seriously rank."

"And *I* said, *shut up.*"

Sam glanced at the rearview mirror and saw two of the teen demons shoving each other. He knew *he* was the one who smelled bad to them. Even fallen angels didn't sit well in demon noses.

"Seriously, that smell is . . ."

Sam was about to turn around and tell them to both shut it, when two angels suddenly appeared on the hood of the van.

"Boo!" cried Frank the New.

Startled, Sam slammed on the brakes, sending the van skidding down the highway. He managed to regain control long enough not to flip the whole thing over and pull along the shoulder.

"Surprised to see us?" Gabriel Too said, unfazed by nearly causing a crash.

"So *that's* the smell," one of the demons behind Sam exclaimed.

"*Told* you," another said, poking his friend in the arm.

"Should we fight them?" yet another asked, perplexed.

"Let me handle this," Sam growled, swinging open the driver's side door and hopping out. He slammed the door and frowned at the angels.

"What do you want, Laurel and Hardy?"

"We resent that," said Gabriel Too, hopping off the hood and flattening out the wrinkles in his robe with his hands.

"Yeah, we're trying to help you," Frank the New said, shaking dust off his robe sleeves. "But if you don't want our help . . ."

"Just spit it out. I don't have all day."

"Grumpy!"

"I'll say."

Sam growled and took a step forward. Gabriel Too flinched.

"Okay, okay," the angel said, holding up one hand and backing away from Sam. "You're going the wrong way. Azazel and Casiphia aren't at the pageant. They're back where you came from. Near the Mega-Mart off Route Nine."

"Yeah, not so smart vacating all the demons from there," Frank the New said. "Azazel and Casiphia now have the perfect hiding place—right under Satan's nose."

Sam sent Frank the New a sharp look.

"Not to mention, they've got a bus full of pageant contestants in the parking lot who think they're going to be auditioning for a reality show," Frank the New added. "And Casiphia is going to kidnap Rachel and her son to use as collateral so you don't interfere until Azazel has bred his mutant army."

Sam felt a chill run through him. "She wouldn't."

"She already has," Gabriel Too said. "She's lured Rachel there by saying she's going to kill you."

"But I'm here."

"Rachel doesn't know that."

"Rachel's risking her life . . ." Sam trailed off.

"To save your worthless one, that's right," Frank the New said. "Unlike you, she's chosen a side in this war."

"I don't believe you," Sam said.

"Well, you'd better start believing us, and soon." Frank the New poked one small finger in the middle of Sam's chest. "Because if Casiphia gets Rachel and Cassidy, she plans to sacrifice them to Satan as a kind of peace offering. So you'd better decide which side you're playing on, champ. This is no time to sit on the sidelines."

A pang of guilt hit him. Sam never intended

to bring danger to Rachel, or her son, and now he might get them both killed.

"Not, of course, that it will prevent Satan from waging war on Azazel or Casiphia," Gabriel Too interjected.

"Well, of course not, that goes without saying." Frank the New waved a dismissive hand. "Satan doesn't honor contracts or peace offerings."

"Guys," Sam interrupted, feeling suddenly suspicious. "Why are you telling me this? Watcher angels aren't supposed to intervene."

Gabriel Too shrugged. "We like Rachel," he said.

"Yeah, she's got moxie," Frank the New added.

"You're breaking the rules for moxie?" Sam asked, perplexed.

"Not really," Frank the New said.

"We got special permission to break the rules," Gabriel Too said. "Somebody up there likes you."

Sam hesitated, trying to decide whether the angels were telling him the truth or intentionally misleading him. In a split second he'd made up his mind. He couldn't risk it. He jumped back in the van, kicking it into gear.

"Hey—where are we going?" one of the demons in back shouted as Sam spun the van around in a hard U-turn.

"Just hold on," Sam grumbled, hitting the gas.

"This is not a good idea," Nathan told Rachel for the hundredth time since they'd set off from the police station. They were riding in the police Bronco.

Rachel had left Cassidy with Father Daniels and Constance back at the station, in hopes that she could somehow save Sam without actually using her son as a bargaining chip. Nathan, however, was visibly nervous.

Given his past experience a few months back, she wasn't surprised. Nathan was no stranger to the paranormal. She'd just learned that he had come face-to-face with the devil and lived to talk about it, but didn't want to press his luck a second time.

"I can't just let Sam die," Rachel said, determined. "He saved my life."

Nathan sighed. "Yeah, I understand. Constance saved mine, and she told me in no uncertain terms that I wasn't supposed to let anything happen to you."

Rachel smiled.

"Anyway, that's why I'm here," Nathan said. "But I don't have to like it. It would be a lot better for the both of us if we just turn around and go back to the police station. Then I can keep you in one piece *and* Constance won't kill me."

"Sorry, Nathan. Can't do it," Rachel said.

Nathan sighed. "I thought you'd say that." He pulled the Bronco into the parking lot of Mega-Mart. It was strangely deserted. In fact, there were only a couple of cars and a giant bus with windows so dark you couldn't see in.

"Did you hear anything about the store being closed?" Rachel asked.

"Nope," Nathan said, his eyes scanning the parking lot for signs of life. He swung the Bronco closer to the store, and they both saw a big sign in the window that said CLOSED FOR EMPLOYEE TRAINING.

"Something's not right here," he added.

"Wait—there," Rachel said, pointing back to the big bus in the parking lot.

Seconds later the door opened and out walked Casiphia—her long dark hair worn high in a ponytail. She was wearing a red, clingy dress and matching heels.

"I don't like this," Nathan said. He leaned forward then and opened the glove compartment, grabbing what looked like a small neon pink water gun. He handed it to Rachel. It fit in the palm of her hand. "Holy water," he added for her benefit. "Works pretty well on most of 'em."

"What about you?"

"I'm covered," he said, reaching under his seat, and pulling out two giant Super Soakers.

"How come I don't get one of those?" Rachel asked.

"You do," Nathan said, giving her one, and taking the pink gun and sticking it in his gun belt.

Rachel looped the Super Soaker over her shoulder. "Now what?"

They watched as Casiphia smiled, then waved them over. Nathan clenched his teeth. "We go see what the lady wants," he said, turning the wheel.

Cassidy had never been this quiet his whole short twelve months, but he knew that it was important at this moment to remain perfectly still. He could do it, too, even though his mother thought he couldn't. He could do a lot of things she didn't know about, but he figured he'd just break her in slowly. She couldn't handle everything all at once. Look how the fire thing had turned out. He'd been practicing that for weeks in secret, but he shows her once and she completely freaks out. Must be a mother thing. They always overreacted.

Cassidy crouched down lower in the back of Nathan's police Bronco and tried to be very quiet. It had been hard sneaking in there, what with everyone looking, but, frankly, that Father Daniels guy just wasn't very with it. Cassidy had gotten away from him easily, and seeing his mama headed for the truck, he'd simply tried out one of his new powers—teleporting. He'd blinked three times and—poof!—he'd ended up in the backseat with Nathan's smelly gym bag and a few unloaded sheriff's rifles.

He wasn't about to let his mama go off somewhere without him again, not when they were talking about Sam. He liked that guy—even if he did smell a little weird—and wanted to see him. He was the only one next to his dad that didn't seem to be fazed by the fire-breathing thing. That was a plus. So, he wanted to see Sam and figured there wouldn't be any harm in tagging along. Of course, Mama would be royally mad when she found out he'd made the ride without his car seat, but he figured he'd give her one of his don't-be-mad-I'm-too-adorable faces and she probably wouldn't be upset for long. If that didn't work, he would break out a new move he'd been saving for when he was really in trouble: blowing kisses. His mom had been trying to get him to do that for weeks. But he'd been saving it for a big day. No way she could be mad at him after he blew her a kiss. No way.

Cassidy poked his little head up to see out the window and saw the truck headed for a pretty lady in white. *That* wasn't Sam. What was the big idea?

Who in the heck was she, anyway?

Rachel felt her stomach cinch up in knots the closer they came to Casiphia, who was giving them a smile that made Rachel's skin crawl. Rachel remembered what Sam had said about her. She'd caused centuries of death and suffering. Well, Rachel could believe it. She tightened her grip on the water gun slung around her shoulders. She would use it at the first opportunity.

Nathan slowed to a stop about fifteen feet from Casiphia. Rachel had her hand on the door latch, ready to get out.

"Wait," Nathan said, just as his seat belt snapped tightly against his chest, flattening him against his seat. "I can't move."

Rachel leaned over and tried to help unlatch the seat belt, but it wouldn't budge. "It's stuck," she cried, tugging uselessly at the latch that simply wouldn't come undone. Just then her own door unlocked itself and swung open. The water gun around her shoulders pulled itself free, the strap breaking in two as

Casiphia flung it straight out into the parking lot. It hit the ground with a sharp crack, sending holy water spewing harmlessly onto the asphalt.

"Dammit," Rachel cursed, whipping around in time to lock eyes with Casiphia, who just gave her a serene smile.

"I'm *waiting*," Casiphia purred, hands crossed across her slim torso.

"Here," whispered Nathan, glancing down to his belt. "Take the pink one. Hide it."

Quickly, Rachel swiped the miniature gun and swiftly put it in her pocket, her back to Casiphia so she couldn't see. With heart thudding, she turned to face Casiphia.

Alone.

Thirty-two

Casiphia's eyes roamed up and down Rachel's body, sizing her up.

"I'm not sure what Sam sees in you," Casiphia said. "Pretty? Barely."

Rachel ignored the insult.

"Where is he?" Rachel demanded in a voice that she somehow managed to keep steady. She could feel the little water gun in her pocket, but she didn't dare put her hand there and risk drawing Casiphia's attention.

"You *do* care for him, don't you?" Casiphia purred, a sinister little smile spreading across her face. "I guess anything is possible. You must go for boring, upright types. Me, I like bad boys."

"So I gathered, since I saw you and your new boyfriend together," Rachel said, taking another step closer. She figured keeping Casiphia talking was better than not. She didn't know how far the water gun would reach. It wasn't big, so it probably only had a range of maybe a a foot or two. She'd have to be close for it to do any good.

"You saw us?" Casiphia asked, curious.

"In the caves," Rachel added. "Neither one of you is very shy."

"Did you enjoy the show?" Casiphia asked, smirking.

"It was surprisingly short. I mean, that boyfriend of yours is supposed to be some legend in the bedroom, right? I thought he would last longer."

A flash of uncertainty and then annoyance passed across Casiphia's face.

"He'd had a dry spell; you can't blame him."

Rachel decided to tread carefully. She wanted to engage Casiphia, but not tick her off.

"Right, but, I mean, what about *your* needs? I was married to a no-good lax of a demon husband for years who didn't care about what I wanted. I just thought Azazel should've been a little more considerate of you, is all."

Rachel took another three steps forward.

"Where is he, anyway?"

Casiphia blanched a little, and Rachel picked up on it. He was with another woman, she knew instantly. Or *women*, she corrected herself, remembering what she'd overheard in the caves.

"He's with someone else?" Rachel clucked her tongue.

"I know about it," Casiphia said. "I don't care. It's just who he is."

Rachel shook her head. "I'm just not sure why

you put up with it," Rachel added. "Why aren't *you* enough? You were beautiful enough to make *two* angels choose you over immortality. You have something . . . special."

Casiphia considered this. Rachel could see she liked the compliment. She took another step closer, her hand hovering ever closer to her pocket.

"Clearly you're gorgeous and you're strong, and all these other women pale in comparison to you," Rachel continued, attempting to casually slip her hand into her skirt. She felt the plastic handle of the water gun and wrapped her fingers around it. She laid her index finger on the trigger and tried to keep her voice steady. "Why would he need anyone else?"

"He needs them to build his army, *duh*," Casiphia said, rolling her eyes. "I can't conceive children as a demon. Couldn't as a mortal woman, either."

So Casiphia was barren? Interesting, Rachel thought. But then her thoughts centered around the word "army." What did that mean? An army of babies? Rachel didn't understand.

"You don't know," Casiphia said, the balance tipping back in her favor. She gave Rachel a sly smile. "So Sam *didn't* tell you?"

"Tell me what?"

"When angels impregnate human women, those women give birth to giants," Casiphia said. "These giants are incredibly powerful and nearly impossible to kill. They also happen to kill their birth mothers during delivery, but that's another story. Anyway, Azazel plans to make an army of thousands in the next few weeks, and then we can take over the earth, and after that, heaven and hell."

Rachel felt her head spin. A mutant army made at the expense of thousands of women's lives? An army that would march over every defense on earth? Why didn't Sam tell her?

Rachel pushed the thought away, trying to keep her wits about her. She had to focus.

"That's why Azazel was buried underground all this time," Rachel said, the pieces falling together.

"Bingo," Casiphia answered, her smile getting bigger.

She sure was chatty for an evil demon planning to take over the world, Rachel thought, and then it dawned on her. Casiphia probably intended to kill her. Maniacal bad guys never told their plans in full to the good guys unless they planned to do away with them, and soon.

Rachel, who was now only two steps away from the demon, tightened her grip on the water gun.

"Sounds like a great plan, but you forgot one thing," Rachel said.

"What's that?"

"Me," Rachel said, taking one more step forward and whipping out the water gun. She held it face level and fired. A fine spray of water shot out about two feet, landing smack dab between Casiphia's eyes. The water hit her face and instantly sizzled and turned to steam, and Casiphia wheeled backward, holding her nose with two hands.

"Arrrgggh," she shouted, doubling over. Right before Rachel's eyes, Casiphia's face distorted, her left eyelid and part of her nose were charred black and smoking. Rachel wondered if this was the moment she melted like the Wicked Witch of the West in *The Wizard of Oz*, or maybe, since she was a demon, she'd just go up in a puff of smoke. Casiphia, however, did neither. In fact, after Rachel had unloaded the ounce or so of the holy water that was held in the tiny water pistol, Casiphia straightened, a murderous look in her eye.

"You shouldn't have done that," Casiphia said through gritted teeth, her left eye now swollen completely shut and the looks of a jagged scar forming across her nose and down her left cheek. Before Rachel could react, Casiphia lashed out, grabbed her by the throat, and pulled her close, so that they were nearly nose to nose. Rachel could even smell the burned demon flesh, a sickening scent like the mixture of burnt popcorn and rotten eggs. "How about I give you a little something in return?"

She raised her hand as if she was going to claw her eyes out, slap her, or just plain knock her head off. Rachel fought with all her might but couldn't free herself from Casiphia's grasp. She shut her eyes and prepared for the worst.

Thirty-three

"Where do you think you're going?" exclaimed Gabriel Too, catching Frank the New by the back of the white robe.

"I'm going to save her," Frank the New declared, trying to wrest himself free from Gabriel's grasp.

"One second, I think I have something almost as good as a sword here," Gabriel Too mumbled as he rubbed some angel dust between his fingers. Instantly a can opener appeared.

"Would you stop fooling around? Sam is *miles* away. He can't make it in time."

"Just a minute," his partner added, rubbing his hands harder together. The can opener morphed into a small kitchen knife with a tiny flame at its tip, smaller than your average Bic lighter. "Ah, ha!" He exclaimed, holding it aloft. "Flaming sword of justice."

"More like Slightly Warmed Pear Knife of You've Got to be Joking."

Gabriel Too waved the steak knife and made a few practice jabs as if trying it out. "I'm getting closer, is all I'm saying."

"But Rachel! We can't let Casiphia poison her. And if you're not going to do anything about it, I will." Frank the New reached into his pocket and grabbed a handful of dust.

"Whoa," Gabriel Too said, grabbing Frank's hand. He managed to contain most of the dust, although some fell on an orange parking pylon below them and turned it into a big orange bunny rabbit that hopped out of the parking lot.

He glanced down at the rabbit. "Oh, sure. You're so much better than me at that, I can see." Gabriel Too rolled his eyes. "Besides, we don't need to do anything. She's going to be fine."

"What? Are you a prophet all of a sudden?"

"No," Gabriel Too said, waving his steak knife.

"Then how do you know?"

"Because I'm wise beyond my years."

Frank the New gave Gabriel Too a skeptical look. "Cut the crap. How do you know, *really*?"

Gabriel Too sighed, giving in. "Look in the police truck, Einstein. See someone you know there?"

Just as Frank the New focused his eyes there, he saw Rachel's boy Cassidy teleport out of the back of the truck and reappear on his mother's back. In a blink, Cassidy had disappeared again, taking Rachel with him to some unseen location. Casiphia, foiled for the moment, just stared slack-jawed at the empty space where Rachel had been standing.

"*Told* you she wouldn't get poisoned," Gabriel Too said.

Thirty-four

Rachel blinked and found herself in the shampoo aisle of Mega-Mart, staring at a row of super-sized Pantene bottles.

"What on earth?" she muttered, even as Cassidy let out a giggle and slid off her back and onto the floor.

"Mama!" he cried, eyes bright with pride—the same look he'd given her after he'd taken his very first steps by himself.

"Cassidy, what did you *do*?" Rachel asked, even though her gut already told her that the only explanation must be that he had just beamed her up and away from certain death.

"Mama!" Cassidy said again and giggled.

She gave Cassidy a fierce squeeze, temporarily forgetting that his being anywhere near the Mega-Mart was bad news altogether, and glad in the moment for just being alive. Cassidy hugged her back but then immediately wiggled to get free, the toy aisle in his sights. He jumped to the floor and sprinted away from her. He was headed directly for a giant ride-on Thomas the Train, when Rachel heard a rumble outside. The rumbling got louder and was followed by a crash that sounded like a trailer toppling off its blocks. Rachel swept Cassidy off his feet, pulled him away from the train, and sprinted toward the front of the store.

She stopped at the glass doors and peered out, hugging Cassidy close to her chest, careful to stay out of view from the outside. She saw Nathan's sheriff's truck first. It was speeding away in reverse in the parking lot, past her line of vision. Rachel glanced in the other direction, trying to see what he was running from, and saw that the oversized tinted-windowed bus was now on its side with its metal side torn out as if there'd been an explosion of some kind. Except Rachel didn't see any smoke. The ground beneath her feet shook, and she heard another rumbling sound, followed by another, and she wondered if they were experiencing some kind of earthquake. Only, Dogwood County didn't sit on any fault lines that she knew of.

A giant shadow fell on the ground, darkening the windows of the Mega-Mart, and Rachel soon saw what Nathan had been high-tailing it away from in such a hurry. A giant chubby foot, the size of a Ford Explorer, stepped right in front of the doors of the Mega-Mart, flattening two shopping carts and a display of geraniums. Rachel fell back, gasping and holding Cassidy tight. Another foot swept past, and then two more. There were at least two of them.

It hit her suddenly: Azazel's children. The giants! They were here already, and they were wrecking havoc in the parking lot of the local Mega-Mart. A third giant flattened a white SUV parked near the Mega-Mart door. Rachel hugged Cassidy close and prayed for a miracle.

Sam couldn't get where he was going fast enough, pushing the van to its outer limits of speed for the past hour. He thought about ditching the van and running on foot, but the fact that he needed his now grumpy passengers to help defeat Casiphia and Azazel stopped him from going it alone. When he saw the exit sign for Mega-Mart, his heart took a little leap. Maybe he could still get there in time. Maybe Rachel wasn't hurt. Then again, knowing Rachel, she was doing something foolhardy at this very moment. Sam pressed the gas pedal flat against the floor and zoomed off the Interstate, the right tire temporarily parting with the pavement as he swerved down the exit ramp.

The Mega-Mart came into view almost immediately, and he nearly hit the brakes. Giants were stomping their way through the giant parking lot. Azazel's children. So he *had* been busy, Sam thought. Of course, these children weren't very old. Mere toddlers, most of them, even though they were the size of ten-story buildings. They would be much bigger when they reached adulthood, which would probably be in a day or so. As of now, the five toddlers Sam saw were causing enough trouble. They had little motor or impulse control, and no adult supervision. One of them fell over, skinned a knee, and started to cry, while another crawled over to the Mega-Mart and peeled off the lighted *M* and popped it in his mouth. Yet another was randomly ripping up light poles from the ground and screaming in delight when he set off sparks.

"What the hell?" cried a demon in the back. "Giant . . . babies?"

One giant toddler careened into the nearby Mega-Mart, fell hard on his bottom, and started to cry.

"And no diapers, either," another demon said, pointing to another who was making a rather large mess near an overturned bus in the center of the parking lot.

Sam scanned the lot but saw no signs of Rachel or her minivan. He felt a rush of hope: maybe she wasn't here after all. After another second he saw Casiphia and Azazel standing in the middle of the parking lot, arguing, with Casiphia pointing to the toddlers, clearly upset, and Azazel seemingly acting as if it were not his problem.

Another van screeched to a stop behind them, with a very angry-looking Marcus hopping out of the driver's seat.

"My store!" he cried as a toddler kicked in a side door with one giant foot.

"Don't worry about that now," Sam said. "There's Azazel."

"Troops, we move out!" Marcus commanded the demons sitting in the backseat and gawking at the toddlers on the loose.

Sam swung open his door, ready to join the fight, when he saw a police truck being lifted by one of the toddlers. He turned and saw Nathan Garrett behind the wheel shouting at the top of his lungs, "Bad boy. Bad, bad, boy! Put me down!"

"Sam!" he heard Rachel's voice call him. It was soft but distinctly there, loud enough for him to hear but too soft to be heard by most. He glanced toward the Mega-Mart window and saw Rachel holding Cassidy. They were pointing at Nathan's truck. "We're fine—help him!" she cried.

He paused, glancing at Marcus. Now was his chance to fight Casiphia and Azazel, but all he wanted to do was run straight to Rachel and make sure she was safe. Sam thought about running to them, sheriff be damned, but he stopped himself. Rachel would never forgive him if he let one of her friends die.

"Where do you think you're going?" Marcus demanded as Sam veered off to the right. "I'll be right back," Sam promised, running at full speed toward Nathan.

Behind him, the demons, still in their Mega-Mart uniforms, piled out of the van and headed toward Azazel and Casiphia.

Sam saw that he wasn't the only one interested by the toddler with the police truck. Another toddler ambled up and decided she wanted to play with the truck, too. She grabbed the truck's front end, even as the first toddler let out a squeal of protest, and held on tight. A tug of war ensued. During the distraction, Sam climbed up the wobbly toddler's knee and managed to crawl out onto his arm.

He made eye contact with Nathan.

"I'm stuck," Nathan shouted, struggling against the seat belt that was keeping him firmly latched to his seat.

"Hang on," Sam said, even as the toddler holding the truck pulled hard against the other baby, causing a sudden shift to the left. Sam made a daring leap and landed on the roof of the truck, just on the other side of a giant baby thumb. He grabbed hold of the windshield wipers as the truck lurched violently side to side between two giant chubby toddler hands. Sam pulled himself up and reached around to the driver's side window, which was open, and took hold of the seat belt. He pulled hard and the entire belt came free.

"Here, grab my hand," Sam commanded as Nathan scrambled out of his seat, taking hold of Sam's hand as they both eased out onto the roof of the car. "And don't look down."

Too late, Nathan glanced down at the six-story drop and nearly lost his footing. Sam righted him and the two slid back down the roof, headed to a toddler arm.

"Mine!" cried one of the toddlers, pointing to the squirming men. Interest in the truck was temporarily lost, and the little girl let go, sending the truck flying downward, away from her.

Sam grabbed the edge of the hood closest to the windshield with one hand and tightened his grip on Nathan with the other, bracing as the truck swung hard, front end down. The strain was more than it should be on his muscles, and Sam felt his strength draining away from him. In his prime, Sam could've carried Nathan and the truck as if they weighed no more than a doll. But, now, things had changed.

Sam had to move quickly.

"I'm going to swing you over to the leg," Sam said, nodding in the direction of the giant, fat thigh near them. "Can you grab on?"

"I'll try," Nathan said, unsure.

Sam swung Nathan to the left, sliding him across the hood of the car, and when he got close enough to the thigh, he saw him grab on to a few downy hairs.

"Got it," Nathan said, surprising even himself. He let go of Sam's hand and started an unstable descent to the ground.

"Ooooh," the toddler cried above him, bending over to get a closer look at Sam and the truck. Sam coiled himself, trying to get up enough momentum to jump over to the leg himself. He was about to make the leap when he felt the truck above him give way. The toddler, on a whim, had decided to drop it. He scrambled up over the falling hood and roof and pushed off from the back bumper, half-leaping, half-falling into the shin of the toddler. He hit the bone hard, and it took all his concentration to wrap his arms around the giant leg as he skidded downward. He hit the top of the toddler's foot with a thud and rolled off over the toes, coming to an ungraceful stop.

Dazed, he shook his head to clear it, and sat up in time to see a giant pinky toe cast a long shadow across his legs. He looked up and saw another giant pudgy toddler foot raised above his head, a few feet away from crushing him flat.

Thirty-five

Rachel had been watching Sam and Nathan struggle with the giant toddler from the window of the Mega-Mart for the last few heart-wrenching minutes. She was seized by the need to do something. But what? And how could she leave Cassidy—even for a second?

She glanced over at Casiphia and Azazel, who had stopped their arguing long enough to battle a van full of Mega-Mart employees, who were trying fairly unsuccessfully to surround them.

Cassidy tugged at Rachel's pant leg and then threw both arms up, demanding to be picked up.

"Sam is in trouble," Rachel said, pulling him up, and they watched as Sam rolled quickly out of the way of the lumbering toddler foot. The foot smashed down into the pavement, making an indention on the asphalt. Sam sprung to his feet, even as Nathan held on to the toddler's leg for dear life.

"Nathan is in trouble, too," Rachel said.

"Tubble," Cassidy echoed, voice serious.

Just then two Mega-Mart employees were flung aside by the giant toddlers and crashed into a row of shopping carts in front of the store. Rachel tried to shield her son's eyes. Demons or no demons, they still *looked* human. And they were most certainly getting their you-know-whats stomped by the toddlers. But then, Sam and Nathan weren't faring much better.

Cassidy wiggled free of Rachel's hand and pulled up to see Sam and Nathan. Nathan was hanging on to the toddler's leg and Sam was on the ground rolling, trying to avoid being stomped to death by a toddler who had walked over and picked up the discarded truck. The boy who dropped it started shouting and crying, throwing his fists in the air. Pretty soon he'd be in full-fledged temper-tantrum mode. In fact, Rachel could sense, by the toddler's body language, that he was about to throw himself on the ground and wail. Even worse, Sam was right in the middle of the chaos. If the stomping toddler didn't kill him, the one about to throw a tantrum would.

"Look out!" Rachel shouted, as if Sam could hear her.

"Out!" cried Cassidy suddenly, alarmed. And then, in the blink of an eye, Cassidy disappeared completely from Rachel's arms and reappeared outside, on Sam's shoulders. In another blink, both Cassidy and Sam disappeared. The toddler holding the truck dropped it then, and the truck smashed into the ground, headlights breaking and bumper bending, but managing to land wheels down on the ground.

The toddler followed the truck, throwing himself into the predicted tantrum. Nathan, who had been clinging to the toddler's leg, now jumped down to the ground and started running away from the giant baby.

Rachel scoured the parking lot and found Sam and Cassidy safe together about twenty yards away. She glanced over and saw she wasn't the only one who'd noticed Cassidy's sudden reappearance. Casiphia had paused in her fight with four other demons long enough to take note. She abruptly leapt up, escaping the fight, and started heading toward them. Rachel realized in a panic that Sam had no idea Casiphia planned to kidnap Cassidy. Heart in her throat, Rachel ran out of the Mega-Mart, hoping to warn Sam in time.

Sam was as surprised as anyone to see Cassidy's new power and hadn't anticipated a one-year-old half demon to be so accurate in his teleporting abilities. Normally demons spend a fair amount of time in various other dimensions before perfecting the art. Still, it might have been a lucky try. They could've easily ended up on the other side of the universe. Or at a toy store. Whatever the demon thought about at the very moment of transition would be the spot they'd end up. If he happened to think of Elmo, then, poof! They'd be on *Sesame Street*.

"Careful with that," Sam warned Cassidy.

Cassidy just flashed him a gap-toothed grin.

He wouldn't be easily dissuaded. He knew he'd just saved the day.

Sam heard his name then, and his head whipped up in time to see Rachel running toward him, yelling. She was oblivious to the danger all around her, namely the toddlers who were stomping holes in the Mega-Mart parking lot with their giant feet and the demons who were fighting them clumsily. Cassidy followed Sam's sight line, and Sam could tell the toddler was planning another trip through space. Sam had a sudden vision of Rachel floating in outer space.

"No," Sam cautioned him. "No *jump.*"

Cassidy looked at him.

"No," Sam added, voice firm. Cassidy paused, eyes questioning. "Jumping is dangerous."

Cassidy nodded as if he understood. Sam knew he comprehended far more than he let on. His demon side would've been significantly more developed than his human side at this age. He'd be able to understand most speech, even different languages.

Sam glanced up at Rachel, who was running quickly toward them and pointing. He couldn't tell what she was saying, but what he did know was that a big white van was heading her way, full of Marcus's troops, who were retreating at breakneck speeds from a curious toddler who had just eaten a lamppost. Sam could tell by the trajectory of the van that it didn't plan to stop or swerve to avoid hitting Rachel. They were in full-on panic mode.

In a split-second decision, Sam put Cassidy on the ground in what he thought was a safe place away from the stomping toddlers. "Stay," he told Cassidy, and then ran for Rachel. He got there just in time to whisk her from the path of the zooming van. Arms around her waist, he came to a stop a few feet away, with Rachel shouting in his ear.

"Cassidy! We have to help Cassidy!"

Sam's head whipped around, and with dawning dread, he realized his mistake. While he'd been saving Rachel, Casiphia had zeroed in on Cassidy, and now she had him. She swept him up in her arms, with Cassidy squirming and fighting, arms out toward his mother. He half-expected the toddler to make another teleporting leap, but he didn't, apparently taking Sam's warning to heart.

Rachel got free and started sprinting, but Sam was faster and outpaced her easily, quickly closing in on Casiphia and Cassidy. Casiphia flew toward a black sedan that had miraculously been left alone by the monster toddlers, and Sam knew he had to reach her before she got inside.

A quick glance around told Sam that the demons were losing the battle with the toddlers. At least five of them had been squashed in the parking lot by heavy feet, and most of the others were running in all directions, trying to avoid being either stomped, eaten, or drooled on.

So much for Marcus's army. Five toddlers had pretty much scattered them in less than ten minutes. And, Sam noticed, Marcus didn't have Azazel captured, either, as the two of them were sparring near a line of shopping carts at the east side of the parking lot. Azazel looked like he had the upper hand.

Sam refocused his energy on Casiphia and Cassidy, now only four or five steps behind them. He would catch them before they got to the car. But then, just as he was about to lunge, he was suddenly caught from behind and lifted thirty feet in the air. He struggled and turned and saw he had been snagged by a giant pudgy hand and was now looking straight into the blue eyes of a baby girl.

"Boo!" she said and giggled at him, eyeing his jeans, T-shirt, and dark hair. She had him by the back of the shirt, and as Sam hung, helplessly, he saw Casiphia jump into the black sedan, tossing Cassidy in the backseat. Below him, Rachel was still running, shouting, her arms outstretched, toward the black sedan.

"Let me go!" Sam shouted at the toddler, who just looked at him and blinked. She got a funny look on her face, like she was about to taste him. He struggled more in her grasp, but it seemed like he was about to be the main attraction of toddler snacktime. He braced himself, hoping this toddler didn't have many teeth, when the sky opened up above him in a streak of lightning and a clap of thunder, and ten ASF angels descended quickly on the scene.

One of them landed squarely on the head of the toddler who was about to eat him, and the others landed on or near the lumbering giants scattered throughout the parking lot. Sam wasn't sure if he should be relieved or worried. God never sent the ASF unless things were really out of hand.

"Figures you'd be here in the middle of this disaster," said Ethan, sounding more than a little annoyed as he clung to the curly bangs of the toddler.

"I was trying to help," Sam said. "And you guys took your sweet time getting here."

"Just try to stay out of the way while the big boys do their jobs, okay?" Ethan said.

"Don't miss this time," Sam growled.

Ethan ignored the taunt and just clapped his hands together. Then he pursed his lips and blew into his palms. His breath started to take shape; it began as a small funnel and started to grow quickly. Soon it would be a full-blown twister.

Sam glanced over and saw that Azazel had defeated Marcus and was now running toward the black sedan.

"You big boys are letting Azazel get away," Sam grumbled, but Ethan didn't hear him, being too close to the wind funnel. And before Sam could repeat himself, the toddler holding him let him go, distracted by the angel on his head and the sprouting tornado. Sam plunged downward, grabbing at the toddler's leg as he went, and managed to slow himself enough so that the collision with the ground wasn't quite as bad as he feared. He grunted on impact, rolled a few times, and then got to his feet, assessing for the first time if he'd been hurt. In his new, weakened state, he didn't know what he could stand. A quick check told him he'd hurt something in his side but nothing too serious—maybe a rib or two. He scanned the lot and found Rachel, still running, even as the black sedan carrying Casiphia and her son pulled out of the parking lot and sped away. She was completely oblivious to everything else except running, including the growing twisters all around that were sucking up giant toddlers.

"Rachel!" Sam shouted, but he couldn't be heard above the wind. He knew he had to get to her, and fast. Ethan wasn't one to show much mercy as a rule.

Rachel was right in between two giant, black funnel clouds. She was unaware she was in any danger, her eyes still fixed on the black sedan, which had skidded to a stop in front of Azazel, giving him enough time to duck into the car. Sam sucked in a breath and started sprinting, hoping to get to her in time.

Thirty-six

Rachel felt two strong arms come around her waist and then she was off the ground and moving at least ten times faster than she had on her own. She knew without seeing his face that it was Sam. She could tell by the spicy sweet scent that surrounded her and the sure way his arm held her. At first she felt relief. Maybe they *would* catch that black sedan after all. Then suddenly a sound like a train roared in her ears, and the path to the car was covered by a whirling funnel cloud—one of the biggest twisters she'd ever seen.

Sam took a hard left and zoomed them straight into the forest, out of the path of the tornado, and in the opposite direction of her son.

"Cassidy!" Rachel cried, not caring that she'd just been saved. "We have to go after him."

"Not now," Sam grumbled, pinning her to the ground. Rachel glanced over and saw for the first time what had Sam so worried: there wasn't just one tornado, there were ten. Ten giant funnel clouds twisting and turning in the parking lot of the Mega-Mart, sucking up everything in their path, from shopping carts to the giant toddlers. A few of them made short work of the actual Mega-Mart building—ripping off its roof and flinging its China-made products all over Dogwood County. In seconds everything had been completely flattened. The first tornadoes started to rise, heading straight up into the blue sky. After a few moments, all the tornadoes had gone, and nothing was left but a giant pile of Mega-Mart rubble.

"What *was* that?" Rachel asked, having never seen so many twisters before. If she didn't know better, she'd say it was her father's work from the grave. He would've flattened Mega-Mart if he had the chance.

"The Archangel Special Forces," Sam said. "They took care of Azazel's offspring. But they didn't take care of Azazel or Casiphia. They got away."

"Azazel! Casiphia! We have to find them." Rachel stood in a panic.

"Don't worry," Sam said, laying a hand on her shoulder. "I know where they're headed."

"You do?"

"Dogwood Festival Ball tonight. You know—the place where three hundred of the state's prettiest girls compete for the title of Dogwood Queen?"

"But that's at least a half hour away. What about Cassidy? We can't leave him with those monsters for that long—he won't be safe."

"He'll be fine. They need him as collateral until the ball is over. They won't harm him until then."

"But how are we going to get him back?"

"I don't know, but we will," Sam said, setting his jaw.

Rachel fell against Sam. His chest was broad and strong, and she felt for the first time like there might be some hope. As Rachel lay her head on Sam's shoulder, he winced slightly.

"What's wrong? Are you hurt?" Rachel pulled away from him.

"It's a rib, I think. I'm fine," Sam said, holding his side and grimacing. Rachel felt her hope drain away.

"Do you heal super fast?" she asked.

"I don't know."

"What do you mean, you don't know? Do you or don't you?"

"I did—once," he said.

"But that was before Casiphia's poison."

"That's right."

"How long do you have before you lose everything?"

"I don't know."

"Come on, let's get you up," Rachel said, holding out her hand.

"I'm fine," Sam said, grunting as he got up by himself, despite what was quite obviously some pain.

"If you ask me, you're already a man," Rachel said. "Stubborn as one, anyway."

Sam just sent her a rueful look.

"Any ideas on how we're going to get to the pageant?" Rachel asked, walking out to what was left of the parking lot, which was mostly broken chunks of asphalt.

"Walk?" Sam offered.

Just then a horn honked at the far end of the Mega-Mart lot. A battered, but still running, sheriff's truck was coming at them, Nathan behind the wheel. He waved out the window and honked again.

"Well, he made it. I'll be damned," Sam said.

"You can say that again." Rachel practically leapt into the front seat when Nathan pulled around. "I've never been so glad to see a Garrett," she said.

"That makes two of us," Nathan said. "I didn't think I was going to survive the twister showdown, but I got lucky, I guess."

"How fast do you think you can get us to the Dogwood Queen Pageant?"

Nathan glanced blankly from Rachel to Sam and back again. "The pageant?"

"That's where Azazel and Casiphia are headed," Sam said. "He wants to make more babies."

"More giants?" Nathan asked, stricken.

"And Nathan," Rachel said, trying to keep her voice level. "They have Cassidy."

Thirty-seven

The 75th Annual Dogwood Festival started out like any other. The dogwood trees along Main Street started to bloom, and then the ones all along Route 4 and Highway 9 followed shortly after, and then the merchants started setting up their tents to take advantage of the hundreds of tourists that would be piling through Dogwood County over the next week. They would sell homemade jam, antiques, lemonade, beaded jewelry, and a fair share of dogwood-tree bowls, chairs, and spoons. The Dogwood Festival was famous across the state, mainly for its ornate coronation ceremony of the Dogwood Queen, a pageant unmatched in the region except by the Rose Queen coronation in Tyler every year.

The title of Dogwood Queen wasn't awarded to the most beautiful or the richest girl in the state. It usually went to a young woman in the Hicks Family—the Hickses being one of the founding families of both Dogwood County and the Dogwood Festival, since Pastor Jeremiah Hicks had supposedly planted the dogwood trees two hundred years ago to ward off evil spirits. Still, it was a great honor to be named a Dogwood Princess, a title which went to a couple of hundred other girls who rode in the parade alongside the queen. The beauty pageant wasn't a contest so much as a big elaborate show, where the girls wore costumes and pranced across the stage and got their pictures taken for display in the Dogwood Festival Museum.

The coronation ceremony was held at the Hicks Auditorium, near the town square, and it would be packed to bursting with all three hundred audience chairs filled. After the pageant, the queen and her royal entourage would alight to waiting floats and then parade down Main Street waving to the crowds. The show would end with a victory lap at the Dogwood High School football field, where another five hundred people would be waiting to cheer the Dogwood Queen.

In short, it was a big deal, because this was the South, so anything involving a tiara was a big deal.

"The county judge is going to have my badge for sure this time," Nathan Garrett said as he pulled up to the Hicks Auditorium, where the Dogwood Queen coronation ceremony would be taking place in fifteen minutes.

"I thought you were elected and couldn't be fired," Rachel pointed out.

"Trust me, the county judge would hold a recall

election in a blink," Nathan said. "You don't mess with the Dogwood Festival. He once had a maintenance worker arrested for failing to properly prune the dogwood trees on the town square. That poor guy sat in jail for thirty days, and that was just for cutting off one too many branches."

"I think your job is probably the least of our worries," Sam said, sliding out of the car and wincing. Rachel could tell his side was still sore, even as he tried to hide it.

Another car pulled up next to Nathan's. Constance and Father Daniels popped out.

"I *told* you to stay away from here," Nathan chided Constance as he hopped out of the truck and folded her into a hug.

"I had to see for myself that you were okay," Constance said, worry still on her face. She turned to Rachel. "About Cassidy . . . I am *so* sorry. He just disappeared. Literally. I was watching him and then *poof!* He just vanished."

"He can teleport," Rachel explained.

"Oh, well, *that* makes babysitting tricky," Father Daniels said. "Would've been nice to know in advance."

"We didn't know until you did," Rachel said.

"So Constance—any visions that might help us?" Nathan asked. "Anything that says we might be winning?"

"Actually, I think things are getting worse," Constance said. "I think the devil himself is coming out tonight."

"I thought he was trapped in hell except for two weeks every century or so," Nathan said.

"He can sneak out now and then," Father Daniels said. "Especially when heavenly Watchers are distracted by other calamities—like those involving fallen angels. And Satan does love a good fight, especially with upstart fallen angels looking to take his place."

"So—wait—he's coming for Azazel? That's a good thing . . . isn't it?" Rachel asked.

"The devil on earth is *never* a good thing. That guy is the original loose cannon," Father Daniels said. "He's not the sort of creature who shows self-restraint."

Rachel felt her hope slipping away. How was she ever going to get Cassidy back?

"So what do we do?" Rachel asked Father Daniels.

"For starters, we have to take care of Azazel and Casiphia before the devil gets here."

"And how do we do that?"

"Maybe we can help?" came a voice somewhere above Rachel's head. She squinted, hard, and saw a kind of white mist floating above them.

"You two again," Sam growled.

"Who two?" Nathan asked.

"Angels," Constance said, looking up.

"You can see them?" Rachel asked, astonished.

"It comes with the Sight thing," she explained and shrugged. Then she glanced back up. "Hey, you look kind of familiar," she told Frank the New. "Do I know you?"

"You sure do," Frank the New said, beaming. "It's me! Frank."

"Frank?" Constance asked, astonished. "As in Frank the Talking French Bulldog?"

"I earned my wings, see?"

"I'm impressed."

"This little reunion is touching and all, but can we get back to the part where we kick some demon butt? Time's a-wasting." Father Daniels tapped his watch impatiently.

"They say they can help," Constance told Father Daniels.

"You can't even make yourself visible to everyone," Father Daniels pointed out.

"Ugh—fine," Gabriel Too said. He shut his eyes and grunted and then started glowing brighter. Frank the New, still unsure of how to do this, tried his best to mimic Gabriel, but only managed to make his head visible. Gabriel Too glanced over at Frank the New and just rolled his eyes. "Newbies," he muttered.

"Hey—there they are!" Rachel said, pointing.

"Well, technically one angel and a floating head," Nathan said.

"Hey—I'm working on it," Frank the New exclaimed. "I'm new at this. Give me a break."

"They don't know what they're doing," Sam grumbled. "They have no plan."

"We have a plan," Gabriel Too said, sounding defensive.

"A very good plan," added Frank the New.

"The best plan ever," Gabriel Too said.

"Best *ever*," Frank the New echoed, and then took a long pause, during which neither angel elaborated on said plan.

Sam just scowled at the two of them. "Like I said, they don't have a plan."

"Okay, well, depends on what you mean by 'plan,'" Gabriel Too admitted. "But, uh, we do have something that could help." Gabriel Too dug deep into his pocket. He pulled out a ball of rubber bands, a can of Pringles, and a box of Yahtzee.

"What are you doing?" hissed Frank the New as the rest of them stared at Gabriel Too's junk with puzzled looks on their faces.

"Wait, that's not it," Gabriel Too said, rummaging around. "Hold on. Almost got it."

"You need a little spring cleaning, boy," Father Daniels said.

Gabriel Too pulled out a Rubik's Cube, a tube of toothpaste, and a roll of Christmas lights. Then he bent down and looked in his own pocket; his entire head disappeared inside as he tossed out more junk. "Wait, I have it. I have it!" he cried, triumphant, as he straightened, pulling himself out of the pocket along with a long, rusty metal chain.

"These were the chains that bound Azazel," Gabriel Too said. "Only Sam's blood will fasten the locks, but you can use them to trap Azazel."

"But how do we get close enough to use them?" Sam asked.

"Well, we'll need bait," Frank the New said.

"And Azazel might want a bunch of the girls in the pageant, but he'll almost certainly *have* to have the queen," Gabriel Too said.

"The Dogwood Queen?" Rachel asked.

"Yeah. Azazel has a thing for royalty. And he always goes for the highest-ranking lady in the room."

"But the Dogwood Queen isn't technically royal anything," Constance pointed out.

"She wears the biggest crown, doesn't she?" Frank the New pointed to his own head. "That makes her royal enough for Azazel."

"Probably true," Sam agreed, nodding.

"Okay—so, I've got an idea," Constance said. "What if I dress up like the Dogwood Queen, we entice Azazel over, capture him, and then use him as bait to get Casiphia? We might even be able to make a switch for Cassidy."

"There's no way I'm letting you dress up as the Dogwood Queen," Nathan said, sounding stern.

"And anyway, I don't think he likes blondes," Gabriel Too said. Constance sent him a look. "What? It's true. Brunettes are more his thing."

"I'll do it," Rachel volunteered, flipping her dark hair off one shoulder.

"Absolutely not," Sam nearly growled, jumping up as if to physically stop her. His insistence caught everyone by surprise.

"I'm the best person to do this," Rachel said.

"No." Sam shook his head.

"It's my son we're talking about," Rachel said,

her mouth drawn in a stubborn line. "And I *am* doing this."

Sam glared at Rachel, and Rachel glared back.

"I do so love it when a plan comes together," Frank the New said.

"Did you just quote *The A-Team*?" Nathan asked him.

"Ahem," Father Daniels said. "We have a lot of work to do, so I think we should get to it."

"What about us? What do we do?" Frank the New asked, rubbing his hands together eagerly.

"You two just stand watch," Father Daniels said, sounding stern.

"But . . ."

"Just do as the priest says," Sam agreed.

"I could've so come up with a better plan than this," Frank the New complained as he and Gabriel Too hovered in the rafters above the pageant stage. The state's prettiest girls rushed about behind the closed curtains, getting ready for their big entrance.

"What? We're Watchers. It's what we do. I don't know why you're complaining. It plays to our strengths. Besides, if you wanted to be taken more seriously, you should've materialized all the way. You looked like a total newbie with your head floating there all by itself."

"What? It's not as easy as it looks. I just need some practice." Frank the New adjusted his sleeves self-consciously and cleared his throat. "Anyway, let's just keep an eye out for Azazel, okay?"

Gabriel Too sighed. "Fine."

"Wait—what's that over there?"

"What?"

"That group of girls—they all seem to be hovering around one person."

Gabriel Too squinted. "That's him!" He peered through the crowd. "He's putting the moves on at least three fifteen-year-olds from Marble Falls."

"You see Casiphia or Cassidy anywhere?"

"Nope—wait. Over there." Gabriel Too pointed at the lighting booth up at the back of the auditorium. Casiphia and Cassidy were waiting there, high above the audience.

"One of us should go tell Rachel, and fast," Frank the New said, nodding to the group of girls below, who were becoming increasingly interested in Azazel. The way they were giggling and flirting, he might as well have been Robert Pattinson.

"You go. I'll keep an eye on him."

"I'll be back in five minutes," Frank the New said.

Thirty-eight

Sam wasn't sure he liked this plan one bit, but he didn't have a better idea, and at least this way he could keep an eye on Rachel. Even if she was putting herself smack-dab in the middle of the most dangerous part of this plan. Not that he'd expect any less of her. He was standing beside her, close enough to do something about it if she did decide to do something foolish. That is, if he could manage to take his eyes off of her long enough to act. She was wearing a dress that was a size too small and entirely too revealing for him to concentrate on much else.

"I don't see why you have to hang so close to me," Rachel said as she stood behind the curtain, wearing a silver sequined dress that was engineered so that it would make even a board look like it had cleavage. She tucked a rhinestone scepter under one arm and then adjusted the heavy rhinestone crown on her head.

"Because Azazel is going to see you soon enough," Sam said. "And I have to be ready."

"I'm prepared," Rachel said, showing Sam the vial of dogwood-tree oil she'd stashed in the dress's built-in bra. "And it's not like I'm going to fall for his charms, you know."

Sam just sent her a doubting look.

"What? I have free will, don't I?"

"Most women choose not to use it when he's around."

"Well, I'm not most women."

"That's for sure," Sam said, his eyes flashing with a kind of reluctant pride. He had to admit, he liked her determination and her courage.

"Okay, then," Rachel said. "So you can give me a foot or two of space. The Dogwood Queen wouldn't have her chaperone so close."

"Hey, guys," Nathan said, walking up to Rachel. "I hope this works, because the *real* Dogwood Queen is royally pissed."

"Better pissed than dead," Father Daniels said as he stood beside Nathan. "Did you tell her that?"

"In a nicer way," Nathan said. "But I still think the county judge is going to fire me."

Abruptly, Frank the New's head appeared in the air about a foot above Nathan. His body, however, was still missing. "We found Azazel," he exclaimed, excited.

"You need to work on your materialization skills," Father Daniels told him.

"Look, do you want this information or not?"

"I do."

"So, he's backstage, and Casiphia and Cassidy

are up in the sound booth." Frank the New nodded up to the back of the auditorium.

"I have to go get Cassidy," Rachel said, pushing toward the sound booth. Sam stopped her.

"It's too dangerous," he said. "I'll go get the boy."

"Why don't you let us take care of Cassidy?" Frank the New said. "We'll be more stealthy."

"You're no match for Casiphia," Sam said bluntly.

"Well, neither are you, in your practically human condition," Frank the New pointed out. Sam raised an eyebrow and Frank the New continued, "Think we don't know about that? We're not totally oblivious. And neither is Azazel."

"Hmpf," Sam said and looked away.

"Besides, you're the only one who will be able to use those chains on Azazel. And we need him taken care of if we want to avoid seeing Lucifer this evening. He'd make a much bigger mess of this whole thing than any of us could."

Sam considered this. He hated to admit it, but the newbie angel was right. "Fine," he said after a minute. "But *don't* screw this up."

"I won't. I swear." Frank the New held up three fingers like he was giving a Boy Scout oath.

"You guys get once chance," Sam said. "If so much as a *hair* on Cassidy's head is harmed . . ."

Frank the New sighed and rolled his eyes. "There's no place for us to hide from your wrath. You'll search for us for two thousand years, if need be, to make our lives living hell."

"And don't forget it," Sam said.

Frank the New nodded his head and then disappeared with a tiny popping sound.

Rachel gave him an appreciative look. "Thanks," she said. "You didn't have to do that."

"'Course I did," Sam said. "I'm not letting anything happen to Cassidy. It's my fault Casiphia took him. I'm going to make things right."

Rachel sent him a grateful look that made him feel warm all over.

"You sure you don't want to wear a shawl?" Sam asked her, glancing down at the more than hint of cleavage she was showing.

"The whole point is to entice Azazel," Rachel pointed out. "I can't do that if I'm wearing a shroud."

"Very well," Sam grumbled, "but I'm staying right here."

"Hey—*you're* not the queen," said one of the contestants, sauntering by in a slinky red dress and heels. She eyed Rachel's sash that said DOGWOOD QUEEN with skepticism. She herself was wearing a sash that said, MISS MARFA.

"Beat it, kid," Rachel said. "Or I'll cut you some really ugly bangs." Rachel made a snip-snip gesture with her fingers. Miss Marfa just wrinkled her nose and walked on. "Azazel better hurry," Rachel said, adjusting her tiara on her head. "I'm not sure how much longer I can keep this up."

Miss Marfa headed onstage. Rachel would be next. A big announcement went over the speakers that everyone would rise to salute the queen. Sam looked hard around them, and found Azazel, interest piqued, heading toward the stage.

"He's coming for you," Sam said as he stiffened beside her. The two walked out onstage, Rachel waving.

"I'll be ready," Rachel said, straightening her crown, as the processional started.

"No time," said Sam, realizing that Azazel was moving fast and would be able to easily snatch her from the stage. "Change of plan. We go to the float."

"What?" Rachel asked, confused. "But . . ." By then, Sam had grabbed her arm and was pulling her offstage. The audience looked confused as Sam picked Rachel up and ran her down the aisle and out the back of the auditorium.

"Hey—wait—where are you going?" cried the stage manager, who went running after them.

Sam said nothing and Rachel just shrugged and sent the woman an apologetic smile as she was carried out the door and into the light of a warm spring afternoon. In the massive parking lot, a line of floats was waiting, most of them decorated with dogwood blooms. Sam leapt up on the nearest float, dragging Rachel with him. He jumped down underneath the petal-laden floor, sneezed once, and started up the engine hidden beneath the confetti.

"Hey! What the . . ." a man nearby yelled as Sam turned the wheel and sent the lumbering parade float into the street.

Rachel grabbed the small metal standing rod

near the front of the float and tried to hang on to her crown and her scepter as Sam pushed the float faster than it was intended to go. Behind them, Azazel was gaining.

"This isn't going to work," Rachel shouted down to Sam.

"Why doesn't this thing go any faster?" he cursed, pushing the accelerator to the floor. Bits of flowers flew off in clumps, and bystanders nearby pointed and stopped to stare. Rachel gave them what she hoped was a regal wave and then grabbed her tiara again before it toppled off.

"Because it's a *parade float*," Rachel shouted down at Sam, whose head and shoulders were the only things visible. The rest of his body was tucked neatly under the float, where the steering wheel and gas pedal were.

Rachel turned and saw Azazel just a few car lengths behind them. They'd be intercepted soon. Sam saw, as well, and shouted up to Rachel, "Give me your scepter!"

Rachel, still grasping the scepter, hesitated. "Why?" she asked. Nathan had told her in no uncertain terms that the Dogwood Queen crown and scepter (seventy-five years old and full of rhinestones) were to be returned without a single ding or she'd have the wrath of the county judge to deal with.

"I need it," Sam shouted, hand out.

"Here," Rachel said, handing it over. In seconds he'd wedged it between the seat and the accelerator, while tying the steering wheel with a rope from the floor. That done, he crawled out of the space.

"I don't know if that's a good idea," Rachel said, uneasy.

"We don't have long," Sam said, putting himself in front of Rachel protectively. In another blink, Azazel had leapt onto the other end of the float.

"Sam," he said with a small smirk on his face, "you must know you're no match for me." In a move too fast for Rachel to see, Azazel jumped forward, and suddenly he and Sam were in a kind of wrestling match, knocking over petals and dogwood branches as they went, bits of sparkling tinsel flying in all directions. Rachel grabbed the vial of dogwood tree oil, but she couldn't use it with Sam so close to Azazel.

The two figures spun so quickly that Rachel could hardly see the arms landing blows. She only heard the sickening thud, thud, thud sounds, and prayed it was Azazel and not Sam getting the worst of it.

The parade float careened dangerously down Main Street, bumping up against parked cars as it went, and Rachel clung to the little stand for dear life as the fallen angels fought each other. She glanced up and saw they were coming upon a turn—a sharp turn—in front of the Dogwood County Courthouse. Sam and Azazel were still locked in a fight, and they were blocking the only entrance to the float's steering wheel.

"We're going to crash," Rachel shouted, pointing to the county courthouse lawn, but she didn't know if either one heard her as the fighting continued. Rachel braced herself for impact, wrapping her arms around a papier-mâché dogwood tree. Beside her, she heard a sickening crack, and suddenly she saw Sam flung high above the float and behind it. There wasn't even time to shout his name before the float crashed into the yard of the courthouse, the front flowers crumpled against the courthouse steps, and Rachel flew off the float, where she hit the grass and rolled, coming to an awkward stop underneath a large blooming white dogwood, petals falling on her head.

Stunned, she sat up and held her head, but she'd lost her crown mid-flight. She was just processing the fact that she was in one piece, that she'd managed to hold on to the vial of dogwood tree oil, and that she should go look for Sam, when a shadow fell across her feet.

"Rachel," said a low, sultry voice.

She glanced up and, with a chill, saw Azazel standing before her, a half smile on his lips. He was holding the Dogwood Queen's crown in his hand.

"I believe this belongs to you," he said, giving a little bow and holding out her crown. Reluctantly, she took it, her eyes flicking back and forth, looking for signs of Sam. Azazel's eyes roamed slowly up her body, appraising. Rachel was acutely aware that the fall had ripped the slit in her skirt higher than it should've been and that the dress was entirely way too low cut. She glanced quickly to the side, wondering if she could make it to the courthouse doors before Azazel could catch her. Given his size and strength, she guessed not.

"Rachel," he said again, smile returning as he finally met her eyes. "Shall we go somewhere a little more . . . private?"

Thirty-nine

"I'm going to teleport Cassidy out of there," Frank the New said. The two angels were hovering near the sound booth.

"*No,*" Gabriel Too nearly shouted, before he got hold of himself and lowered his voice. "I mean, uh, no. This requires finesse and more practice than you've had."

"I think I'm getting better," Frank the New said.

"You are, I'm sure, but just let me do this one, this time, okay?" Gabriel Too bent over, cracked his knuckles, and then let out a long breath of air as he waggled his fingers above the sound booth and made a low moaning sound. He then squeezed his eyes shut and wiggled his fingers some more.

Frank the New looked down, but Cassidy hadn't moved an inch. He was still sitting in the corner playing with a couple of electrical cords while Casiphia paced distractedly in the sound booth, her eyes on the stage.

"Where *did* he go?" Casiphia fumed, referring to Azazel. "He was there just a second ago."

"Cassidy didn't move," Frank the New said. "You sure you know what you're doing?"

"I haven't teleported a demon before," Gabriel Too said. "So sue me. I've only done humans, okay?"

"So, are you sure Watcher angels aren't supposed to intervene because of God's order, or because they *don't know how to do anything*?" Frank the New hissed, frustrated.

"Hey—newbie. I don't see you doing any better."

"I offered."

"Just back up and give me some space. Let me try again." Gabriel Too squeezed his eyes shut and wiggled his fingers again, this time with a little more intensity, and yet Cassidy stayed stubbornly put.

"Who's the newbie again?" Frank the New poked Gabriel Too in the arm. "We don't have much time before Casiphia figures out we're here."

"Don't you think I *know* that?"

"Wait, I have an idea," Frank the New said, snapping his fingers. He reached into his pocket for some angel dust. He sprinkled it on his hand, and instantly a banana appeared. "Darn it, that's not what I wanted." He sprinkled some more dust on the banana, and this time the banana morphed into a banana-shaped phone. "Close enough," Frank the New said, picking up the banana receiver. He dialed and then put it to his ear. Below them, the phone in the sound booth started to ring.

Casiphia stared at it a second, and then decided to pick it up.

"Hello?"

"This is Frank the . . . uh, the stage manager. The Dogwood Queen has left the building, and apparently some guy is after her. We don't know more details than that, but they have *left* the building. Repeat . . . left the . . ."

Casiphia slammed down the phone.

"Dammit," she hissed, turning to Cassidy. "You—stay put," she commanded, flicking her wrist. Suddenly Cassidy dropped the cords and appeared as if he couldn't move. He gave a whine of protest. "I'll be right back."

She stomped out of the sound booth, beneath the hovering angels.

"Not bad," Gabriel Too said.

"Thank you," Frank the New replied, plunking the banana phone into his left pocket. "Now, let's go."

The two angels swooped in and within seconds had Cassidy between them. Cassidy scrunched up his nose as if he smelled something bad, but he didn't scream.

"We're going to take you to see your mama," Gabriel Too said.

"Mama," Cassidy repeated, sounding excited. "Mamamamamama!"

Sam came to in the middle of the sidewalk with an elderly man leaning on a cane bending over him.

The man had a small white dog on a leash that was licking Sam's face.

"You okay, son?" the man asked, giving Sam a gentle nudge with the cane. "You were out cold there for a while."

Sam groaned and pushed the dog away as he sat up. His vision flooded with stars, and a bright, searing pain split his head. That hadn't happened before. It must be his mortality creeping in. Now he was susceptible to pain and blackouts. Great.

He rubbed his eyes and tried to stand, but his legs were wobbly.

"Careful, son," the old man said, steadying him a little with his arm. "You might want to get your bearings before you go after that fella."

Azazel! The last several moments before his blackout came flooding back. Azazel had tossed him from the float, and that left Rachel totally defenseless.

"Rachel!" Sam exclaimed, all the muscles in his body tensing as he glanced in every direction. His eyes lighted on the crumpled remains of the float, which were sitting in two parts on the lawn of the Dogwood County Courthouse. There was no sign of Azazel or Rachel. "Did you see a woman—with a crown? Did you see what happened?" Sam grabbed the lapels of the old man.

The small dog barked twice.

The man glanced down and then up again. "Calm down there, son," he said. "If you're talking about that fella and the Dogwood Queen, they went in the courthouse."

Sam sprang forward, despite the fact he was still seeing stars, and ran to the courthouse. He cursed himself for being so weak. Maybe he should've handed his soul over to the devil. Then he would've been strong enough to defeat Azazel and save Rachel. He wouldn't have been lying on the pavement, useless for however long it had been.

He slammed open the doors of the courthouse and blinked. Normally his eyes adjusted immediately to changes in light, but this time they were a little slower to respond. When he could finally see, he saw two guards unconscious at his feet and three more at the end of the hall. He guessed he should follow the bodies.

Azazel had cleared out the main courtroom, tossing the bailiffs and the judge out like they weighed no more than rag dolls. He swept clean the judge's desk, knocking over stacks of papers and a gavel.

"There," he said, giving Rachel a smirk. "Not exactly a royal bed, but it should do nicely."

Rachel felt a shiver down her spine, and involuntarily took a step backward. He'd left her near the doors. He'd barricaded them inside with the help of a few well-placed benches. Her back hit one of them, and she was suddenly struck by the fact that she and Azazel were very much alone. The courtroom smelled strongly of him—a bit like Sam, only sharper. And the scent didn't seem to have the same effect on Rachel's senses. Instead of feeling weak-kneed, she just felt light-headed and dizzy, like she might throw up.

"Don't be scared, Your Highness," Azazel purred, trying to calm her. "I promise it'll be something you'll remember forever."

Rachel glanced quickly around the room, but saw no route of escape. The only windows were behind Azazel, and she didn't even know if they opened.

"I'm not royalty, you know," Rachel said, quickly taking off her crown with one hand, while hiding the other hand, which still held the vial of dogwood tree oil, in what was left of her skirt. "I was just pretending."

"I know," Azazel said, a smile growing slowly across his face. "Although Sam seems to think so."

Rachel's head popped up suddenly. So Azazel wasn't interested in her for her supposed royal line. He wanted her because Sam did.

"There's nothing between us," Rachel said flatly.

"I've never seen him fight so hard for a woman," Azazel said. "So you're wrong there, Rachel." Azazel took a step closer, and Rachel took a step to the side away from him. She had to keep him talking.

"Why do you care what Sam wants?"

Azazel's fingers traced the edge of the desk. "He's just so *good*," he said, frowning. "He gave up his wings for a *mortal*. Ridiculous. But why all this talk about Sam? How about *you and me*?" Azazel took another step closer.

"There *is* no you and me," Rachel said, shaking her head firmly.

"You can't really mean that." Azazel gave her a

knowing look. She could feel him trying to turn her thoughts to sex, trying to make her attracted to him. But there was no power on earth that could do that. She despised him, for everything that he'd done, and there was no spell powerful enough to change that.

"Trust me, I do mean it. Stay away from me."

For a second Azazel looked shocked. "You really aren't attracted to me, are you?"

"I've seen roadkill that looks more appetizing," Rachel snapped, still moving away from him, eyes flicking this way and that, looking for an escape route. There was a door next to the jury box, on her side of the courtroom, which probably led to the jury deliberation room. Maybe she could get to it before Azazel realized what she was doing.

"Now that *is* a challenge," Azazel said, rubbing his chin as if thinking. "I don't usually force women to have me."

"I don't see why you should start on my account," Rachel said quickly.

"Honestly, it's a mystery. Why *aren't* you even the least bit into me? Every other woman I've ever met couldn't keep her hands off me."

"Maybe you've been spending too much time with the weak-minded ones," Rachel suggested. "You should try hanging around women with half a brain. It would be refreshing." This should have made Azazel mad, but instead he just laughed.

"I can see what Sam sees in you," Azazel said, eyes glinting. "A woman that speaks her mind is a rare thing indeed."

"Says the man who's been in a cave for a thousand years," Rachel grumbled, stepping ever closer to the door. "You'll find a lot more of us nowadays. Trust me, I'm not unique."

"Oh, I doubt that," Azazel said. "I've already sampled a few of you modern women. You are *very* unique."

In the distance, Rachel heard her name being called, and she knew instantly it was Sam. Azazel's attention went suddenly to the door.

"Sam!" Rachel shouted as loud as she could, and then suddenly Azazel was beside her, his hand muffling her mouth.

"Let's not do that," Azazel said, his breath hot on her neck. She smashed the vial against Azazel's cheek, and it broke into pieces, dripping oil everywhere—into his mouth, and burning a hole through his cheek. Azazel shrieked in pain, dropped her, and held his face. Rachel scurried to the other side of the room and hid beneath an overturned bench. A crash of glass at the front of the room drew her attention. She hoped beyond hope to see Sam standing there, but instead in hopped Casiphia, hands on her hips and looking more than a little bent out of shape.

"What the hell is going on?" she demanded as Azazel, still holding his face, looked up.

"What happened to you? Finally found one that fought back?"

"Dogwood tree oil." Azazel coughed, still holding his face. "I think I swallowed some."

"No," Casiphia exhaled, suddenly serious. "No, no, *no.*"

Azazel fell to his knees, coughing.

A banging on the door behind them made them both turn.

"Rachel!" shouted Sam from outside.

"Sam!" Rachel whispered. He seemed to have heard her, because he shouted, "I'm coming! Don't worry."

Of course, he wasn't the only one who heard her. Casiphia was by her side in seconds, pulling her up by her shirt.

"You'd better have the antidote to that poison you just fed Azazel, or I *will* kill you," hissed Casiphia in her ear.

The door rumbled as Sam tried to push it open.

"Fix him," Casiphia commanded as Azazel coughed louder, hunched over his own knees, wheezing.

"I can't," Rachel said. "And even if I could, I wouldn't."

"I swear by Satan—"

"Don't speak of the devil, you fool!" Azazel warned. But it was too late.

The ground beneath their feet began shaking. Bits of ceiling fell to the floor, and chairs fell over in the courtroom. A big crack appeared in the floor, breaking apart the marble tile on the floor like it was cheap plastic. Azazel stepped quickly to one side as the crack crew larger. Casiphia leaned against the wall to steady herself.

From the massive hole in the floor, a hand

reached up and grabbed the jagged edge of cracked tile. A well-dressed man with a handsome face popped out and dusted himself off.

"I have to tell the boys to fix that damn elevator," he grumbled, wiping dust from his suit. "This earthquake business is *no* way to travel."

Azazel's grip tightened around Rachel, who squinted at the man who'd just crawled up from the floor.

"Satan," Casiphia purred, quickly changing gears. "How *good* to see you again."

"As if you are really glad to see me, Cass," the devil replied, rolling his eyes and brushing a bit of dust off his curly dark hair. "I wasn't born yesterday. Starting to regret picking Azazel over me?" He glanced over to Azazel, who was still on his knees, weak and wheezing.

"I didn't pick him over *you*. Never."

"You lie as badly as ever," the devil said, sending her a smile that didn't reach his eyes. He noticed Rachel in Casiphia's grip.

"Rachel Farnsworth," he said, shaking his head slowly from side to side. She started, surprised and alarmed he knew her name. "You always seem to be in the wrong place at the wrong time."

"She's *mine*, devil," Azazel hissed, his voice low and menacing as he tried to stand on wobbly feet.

"Leave her alone!" shouted Sam through the door, which he was shaking forcefully.

"My, *oh*, my but you do stir up the passions, dear Rachel," the devil said. He gave her a slow once-over.

"I'll crush you," Azazel ground out, menace in his voice.

"You'll die before you even lay a finger on me, I'm afraid," Satan said. "And even if you weren't poisoned, you're no match for me without your army and you know it. Now, Rachel, let's see what all the fuss is about."

The devil flicked his wrist, and suddenly Casiphia's grip went slack and Rachel found herself being pulled across the courtroom and then up in the air. She was briefly relieved to be out of Casiphia's reach but alarmed that it was the devil who did the rescuing. She doubted she'd fare better with him.

"You *are* a pretty thing," Satan said, admiring her as he turned her from side to side. "Shapely."

At that moment Sam managed to get the courtroom doors open, and he climbed over the barricade, tossing chairs and benches out of his way.

"Rachel!" he shouted.

"Here!" she answered, reaching for him, even though it was no use. She kicked her feet, but met nothing but air.

"She's *mine*, I say!" Azazel coughed, weakly trying to walk to him. He fell to his knees, coughing and turning red. He let out a choking sound, and then he fell still. The devil flicked his other hand, and in a small poof of smoke, Azazel disappeared.

"What did you *do* with him?" Casiphia cried, running toward the spot where he'd been standing.

"Sent his soul to hell, where it belongs," the

devil said. "He'll be fine, as long as he can get used to the smell of brimstone."

"No!" Casiphia shrieked.

"Silence!" the devil commanded, and Casiphia found herself voiceless, her hands on her own throat. "Now, Sam," the devil continued. "Want to tell me just why you've been avoiding me lately?"

"I'm not going to be turned," Sam said, standing his ground. "Even if you send me to hell, I won't turn."

The devil eyed Sam and then nodded. "Casiphia was much easier to convince; I can see that. But then she goes and stages this little revolt with Azazel, and I have to say, Cass, I am *very* disappointed in you. After all the cool powers I gave you, too. I mean, I thought we really had something special." Satan sighed and looked a little forlorn. "I guess you just can't trust anyone nowadays."

Rachel glanced down at Sam, but his face showed no emotion.

"But, Sam, old friend," the devil said. "I have a little proposition for you. What say I give you a little challenge, and if you win the challenge, then you get to go free. If you lose, I get your soul?"

"No," Sam said, shaking his head.

"Oh, come on, Sam. A little wager." The devil shook Rachel with an invisible hand, and she let out a little squeak. Sam bristled, clenching his fists. "I'm afraid you don't have a choice, old sport. I could just end her life now."

"No!" Sam shouted, taking two steps forward.

"Okay, then. My proposition. You can have your powers restored—forever—with no strings attached, or you can sign your soul over to me for eternity, and this little mortal, Rachel, goes free."

Sam grimaced.

"So what will it be, Sam? Free Rachel and sell your soul? Or let her die and live forever?"

He flashed a malicious grin then, and Rachel's entire body went cold.

"I can't trust you to keep your word," Sam said.

"Oh, I'll give you the demon pinky swear if you want," the devil said. "But in the meantime you have thirty seconds to choose. Starting . . . now."

A giant stopwatch appeared in a puff of red smoke above Sam's head, the second hand ticking off seconds.

Sam glanced briefly at Casiphia, and Rachel seemed to know what he was thinking. Hadn't Father Daniels said he only looked after himself? Eternal life and power without strings had been what he always wanted. He would never give himself over to the devil for her. Not that she'd want him to. She couldn't bear the thought of him in the devil's army.

"Don't give in to the devil," Rachel pleaded. "It's what he wants—your soul. I'll be fine. Just promise me you'll take care of Cassidy. That's all I ask."

"Ack—nobility and self-sacrifice," the devil said, wrinkling his nose as if he smelled something bad. "Ms. Farnsworth, you disappoint me. I was hoping for some pleading or blubbering. Still, perhaps we might get some blubbering yet when I'm through with you . . ."

"Leave her alone," Sam growled. The second hand reached the thirty-second mark, and the floating stopwatch started beeping.

"Decision time," Satan said.

Sam's voice didn't falter. "I choose Rachel."

"Sam!" cried Rachel, shocked.

"You *sure* you're making the right choice?" the devil said. "You can't take it back once it's made. And you've got five more seconds to think about it . . ."

"Let her go. I choose Rachel. You have to let her live."

The devil waved his hand, and Rachel dropped from the ceiling. She landed with a thump on the courtroom floor. Sam rushed to her side.

"Are you all right?"

"Fine," Rachel said, still a little stunned. He'd picked her! She still couldn't quite believe it. "But you can't give yourself to the devil! You just can't . . ." Rachel's eyes brimmed with tears. The thought of Sam's spending eternity in hell because of her made her feel sick.

"I'm ready," Sam said, turning to face the devil. "Do what you want with me."

"Not so fast, devil," came a voice above Rachel's right shoulder. She glanced up and saw Gabriel Too floating there with his harp. "You can't take Sam's soul, not when he's given it in self-sacrifice. That's stipulation 12–092006 of the Holy Geneva Convention."

The devil frowned and then hissed, "I know my codes, thank you very much. You can't blame me for trying to sucker him into it, though."

Lightning flashed outside, and thunder rumbled, and suddenly three more angels were standing in the room, but these were wearing black instead of white. The Archangel Special Forces—Rachel recognized them from the Mega-Mart parking lot.

"Good," said the ASF leader. "Then you won't mind taking Casiphia and leaving now."

"No need to get pushy," the devil said, eyeing the ASF. "I was just leaving."

"No—wait—this is some kind of mistake," cried Casiphia, finding her voice again, as the devil walked over and unceremoniously picked her up and dumped her over his shoulder like a sack of potatoes.

"Let's go, my sweet," the devil said, and then he climbed back down into the hole in the ground that he'd come from. He grunted a little and shifted Casiphia on his shoulder. "What have you been eating on earth? Good grief, you are heavy."

"Shut up," she said, pounding her fists on his back. "And let me go!"

"What? No kisses? Tsk, tsk. Well, we'll just see what a few hundred years in a lake of fire does to that attitude."

The last thing Rachel heard before the ground closed up over them was Casiphia shouting Sam's name, along with about a dozen expletives not fit to print.

"You going to stay out of trouble if we leave you here?" Ethan, the ASF commander, asked Sam.

"If trouble doesn't find me first," Sam said.

"I guess that's good enough," Ethan said. "For now."

In a burst of light, the ASF angels moved into action, quickly setting the courtroom back to what it had been before. The float on the courthouse lawn disappeared, too, and was placed neatly back in the parking lot. In another burst of light, Rachel and Sam were zapped out of the courtroom and onto the street, where they were both set to watch the Dogwood Festival parade. In front of them, the real Dogwood Queen sat atop her float, wearing her royal tiara and waving to the crowd. In Rachel's arms, Cassidy wiggled, trying to get free.

It was as if the last few hours had never happened. Rachel squeezed Cassidy and twirled him around. He just giggled and wrapped his little arms around her neck.

"Wow—what happened?" Rachel asked, blinking hard against the sunlight.

"We got lucky," Sam said and gave her arm a little squeeze.

"I still can't believe you picked me," Rachel said, staring up at Sam. "I thought immortality was what you wanted."

"I've come to see that it's overrated," Sam said. "It's time I made a real life for myself. Here. With you." He looked at Rachel as he said this. Rachel's heart leapt.

"Does that mean you'll help me with Cassidy?"

"Only if you'll help me with being human," he said. "I might just be ready to settle down."

In a second Sam had swept her and Cassidy into his arms and given her a long, sweet kiss.

"Ewwww," Cassidy whined, wrinkling his nose as they separated, laughing.

Forty

Three months later

"Cassidy!" shouted Rachel. "What did I tell you about that fire business?" She was standing above the charred remains of a bag of Goldfish crackers in the kitchen of their new rented house.

"Oops!" said Cassidy, flashing a smile and looking contrite.

"Cassidy—can we fix it like I showed you?" Sam said, kneeling beside the toddler. Cassidy closed his eyes, concentrated, and then put his finger on the bag. Instantly the bag was restored to its former, pre-charred glory.

"How did you get him to do that?" Rachel asked, amazed.

"It's an angel trick," Sam said. "Demons and angels aren't that far apart in their powers. They overlap."

"I'm impressed," Rachel said, nodding. Then

again, things had changed since Sam had decided to move in with them. Cassidy idolized him and followed him everywhere, and keeping the fire-breathing under control had become a lot easier with Sam around. And Rachel had discovered that she could have happiness beyond Kevin. Even her mother approved. It felt like a new start on life.

Sam grabbed Cassidy and tickled him, and then put the still giggling boy on his shoulders and trotted him around the house. On his way through the living room he winked at Rachel, and she felt her heart swell. She'd never felt so happy.

"Oh, I just love happy endings, don't you?" Frank the New said, sniffling.

"Of course I do! I *am* an angel," Gabriel Too said, sighing.

"Hey—watch this," Frank the New said. He shook a little angel dust out of his sleeve and made a flower appear below them. This would have been a fine trick except for the minor point that the flower happened to be growing out of the stove top. "Okay, so I haven't perfected it yet, but give me a little time."

"You don't have much more time to practice before our earth duty is over, which is in about two seconds," Gabriel Too said.

"Do you think we'll be back soon?" Frank the New asked.

"There's no telling, although I bet we're not done with that Cassidy just yet." Gabriel Too nodded at the little boy, who was running in circles around Sam's legs. Sam dipped down and gave his mother a kiss, and while both were distracted, Cassidy got a devilish look on his face as he ran off to set fire to another package of Goldfish.

"That one certainly is a live wire," Frank the New agreed.

Cassidy looked up at the two angels, clapped his hands, and started giggling. Then he blinked twice and disappeared, teleporting out of the kitchen and into the backyard.

"Cassidy Farnsworth!" Rachel shouted, once she'd come to realize what had happened. "Get back here right now, young man!"

"I'm thinking we'll definitely be back," Gabriel Too said as he and Frank the New started their ascent into heaven.

"Most definitely," Frank the New agreed. "By the way, are you going to show me how to do that teleporting trick? Last time I tried it, I ended up in Paraguay."

Gabriel Too just shook his head and sighed. "Newbies," he muttered, rolling his eyes.

Discover love's magic with

a paranormal romance from Pocket Books!

Nice Girls Don't Live Forever
MOLLY HARPER

For this librarian-turned-vampire, surviving a broken heart is suddenly becoming a matter of life and undeath.

Gentlemen Prefer Succubi
The Succubus Diaries
JILL MYLES

Maybe bad girls *do* have more fun.

A Highlander's Destiny
MELISSA MAYHUE

When the worlds of Mortal and Fae collide, true love is put to the test.

**Available wherever books are sold or at
www.simonandschuster.com**